a fate worse than death.

bound
by vengeance

Cora Reilly

Copyright ©2017 Cora Reilly
All Rights Reserved. This book or any portion thereof may not be reproduced
or used in any manner whatsoever without the express written permission of the
author except for the use of brief quotations in a book review.

This is a work of fiction. All names, characters, businesses,
events and places are either the product of the author's imagination or used fictitiously.

Subscribe to Cora's newsletter to find out about her next books,
bonus content and giveaways: www.corareillyauthor.blogspot.de/p/newsletter.html

Cover design by Hang Le
Book design by Inkstain Design Studio

bound
by vengeance

prologue

—GROWL—

Wide eyes. Parted lips. Flushed cheeks. Pale skin. She looked like a porcelain doll: big blue eyes, chocolate hair and creamy white skin; breakable beautiful, something that I wasn't meant to touch with my scarred, brutal hands. My fingers found her wrist; her heartbeat was fluttering like a bird's. She'd tried to fight, tried to be brave, tried to hurt me, maybe even kill me. Had she truly hoped she could succeed?

Hope; it made people foolish, made them believe in something beyond reality. I'd gotten out of the habit of hoping a long time ago. I knew what I was capable of. She had hoped she could kill me. I *knew* I could kill her, no doubt about it.

My hand traced the soft skin of her throat, then my fingers wrapped lightly around it. Her pupils dilated but I put no pressure into my touch. Her pulse hammered against my rough palm. I was a hunter, and she was my prey. I'd come to claim my prize. That was why Falcone had given her to me.

I liked things that hurt. I *liked* hurting others. Maybe even loved it, if I were capable of that kind of emotion. I leaned down until my nose was inches from the skin below her ear and breathed in. She smelled flowery with a hint of sweat. Fear. I could smell that too. I couldn't resist and I didn't have to, not anymore, not ever again with her. Mine. She was mine.

I lowered my lips to her hot skin. Her pulse throbbed under my mouth where I kissed her throat. Panic and terror beat a frantic rhythm under her skin. And it made me fucking hard.

Her eyes sought out mine, hoping—still hoping, the foolish woman—and *pleading* me for mercy. She didn't know me, didn't know that the part of me that hadn't been born a monster had died a long time ago. Mercy was the furthest thing from my mind as my eyes claimed her body.

chapter I

—CARA—

The first time I met him, he was in disguise, dressed up in a stylish black suit, made to look like he was one of us. But while the layers of fine fabric covered his many tattoos, they couldn't hide his true nature. It shone through, dangerous and chilling. Back then, I didn't think that I'd get to know him and the monster within better than I knew anyone else—that it would turn my whole life upside down. That it would change my entire being to the very core.

"I can't believe they let you go with them," Talia muttered. I turned away from the mirror to look at her. She sat cross-legged on my desk chair, dressed in her shabbiest jogging pants, and her long brown hair was piled atop her head in a messy bun. Her T-shirt, a faded gray thing littered with holes and stains, would drive our mother into a meltdown. Talia smiled grimly when she followed my gaze. "It's not like I need to dress up for anyone, you know."

"There's a difference between not dressing up and what you're doing," I said with a hint of disapproval. I wasn't really annoyed at my sister for wearing her shabbiest clothes, but I knew their only purpose was to rile Mother up, and it was a likely scenario given our mother's tendency for perfectionism and overreacting. I really didn't want her mood to turn sour so shortly before the ball. I'd be the one to suffer, since Father was definitely out of the question when it came to becoming Mother's favorite target. Mother had a tendency to take it personally if Talia or I weren't perfect.

"I'm making a point," Talia said with a small shrug.

I sighed. "No, you're being petty and childish."

"I *am* a child, too young for a social gathering at the Falcones' mansion," Talia parroted in her best imitation of Mother's chiding tone.

"This is an event for adults. Most people will be over eighteen or far beyond. Mother's right. You'd have no one to talk to and someone would have to keep an eye on you all night."

"I'm fifteen, not six. And you are only four years older than me, so don't act all grown up," she said indignantly, pushing up from the desk chair, and staggered toward me. She eyed me squarely, the challenge unmistakable. "You probably told Mother not to take me with you because you knew you'd have to watch me. You *were worried* I'd embarrass you in front of your oh-so-perfect friends."

I glowered. "You're being ridiculous." But a flicker of guilt flashed through me at Talia's words. I hadn't talked Mother into making Talia stay home, but I hadn't fought very hard for my sister to join us either. Talia was right. I'd been worried that I'd be stuck with her all evening. My friends tolerated her when we met at home, but being seen with a girl four years younger at an official gathering wouldn't sit well with them. A party at the Falcones' always meant the best chance to meet eligible matches, and having to babysit your friend's sister didn't really help with that endeavor. I wanted this night to be special.

Something from my train of thoughts must have shown on my face because Talia scoffed. "I *knew* it." She turned on her heel and stalked out of the room, slamming the door shut so hard that I couldn't help but wince.

I let out a small breath then turned back to my reflection, checking my makeup and hairdo one last time. I'd watched countless tutorials of beauty bloggers to make sure I got the smokey-eyes-look right. Everything needed to be perfect. Mother was a harsh critic, but Trish and Anastasia were even worse. They'd notice if I matched the wrong tone of eyeshadow to my dress or if my hand had trembled while holding my eyeliner, but their scrutiny had made my preparations meticulous. They were the reason I was never slacking. And that was what friends were for.

My dress was dark green, and my eyeshadow just a few shades lighter. Perfect. I checked my nails one last time for chinks, but they, too, looked immaculate: a subtle dark green sheen. I smoothed down my dress a few times until I was satisfied with the way the hem brushed my knees, then smoothed my hair back again, too, for good measure, turning to see if the bobby pins were still all in place holding my light brown hair up.

"Cara, are you ready? We need to leave," Mother called from downstairs.

I checked my reflection and neatened my dress again, scanned my tights, then finally forced myself to hurry out of the room before Mother lost her patience. I could have spent hours checking my outfit for possible mistakes if I'd had the time.

Mother stood in the doorway when I came downstairs, letting the cool autumn air into the house. She was checking her golden watch but the moment she spotted me, she grabbed her favorite winter coat, a splendid thing that had cost many ermines their lives, and put it on over her long dress. Even with the temperatures being unusually cold for Las Vegas in November, a fur coat was completely over the top, but since Mother had bought it many years ago in Russia and loved it to pieces, she used every chance she got to wear it, no matter how inappropriate.

I walked toward her, ignoring Talia who leaned against the banister of the staircase, a sulk on her face. I felt sorry for her, but I didn't want anyone or anything to ruin this evening for me. Father and Mother hardly ever allowed me to attend parties, and tonight was the biggest event of the year in our social circles. Everyone who aspired to be someone in Las Vegas had tried to get an invitation to Falcones' Thanksgiving feast. This would be my first year attending. Trish and Anastasia had been lucky enough to attend last year, and if Father hadn't forbidden me from going, I'd have gone too. I'd felt small and left out whenever Trish and Anastasia had talked about the party in the weeks prior and after, and they'd done so nonstop, probably because that gave them the chance to gloat.

"Give Trish and Anastasia my best, and Cosimo a kiss from me," Talia said sweetly.

I flushed. Cosimo. He'd be there as well. I'd only met him twice before and our interactions had been more than a little awkward.

"Talia, put those horrendous rags into the trash. I don't want to find them anywhere in the house when we return," Mother ordered without glancing at my sister.

Talia jutted her chin out stubbornly, but even from across the room I could see the hint of tears in her eyes. Again guilt flooded me, but I stayed tethered next to the front door.

Mother hesitated, as if she, too, realized how hurt Talia was. "Maybe next year you'll be allowed to come along." She made it sound as if it hadn't been her decision to exclude Talia from the party. Though, to be honest, I wasn't sure if the Falcones would be too happy if people started bringing their younger children along, considering that Falcone wasn't known for his patience or family sense. Even his own children were sent to boarding school in England, so they didn't grate on his nerves. At least, if one believed the rumors. Falcone's children were somewhat of an off-limit topic.

"Put on a coat," Mother said. I grabbed one that wasn't fur, which wasn't an easy task in Mother's wardrobe, and followed Mother out of the house. I didn't look back at Talia as I closed the door. Father was already waiting in the driver's seat of the black Mercedes in our driveway. Behind it, another car with our bodyguards was parked. I wondered how it was for people who weren't always guarded.

Mother opened her coat a bit wider. This was Las Vegas, and not Russia, I wanted to tell her. But if she preferred to melt, so she could stride around dressed in her fur coat, then that was her problem. No pain, no gain. Years of ballet classes had taught me that.

Mother sank down on the passenger seat while I slipped into the back of the car. I did another quick scan of my tights for runs, but they were immaculate.

Always immaculate.

I thought companies should put a warning on their packing like "Only for standing, no moving allowed," considering how easy it was to get a run while doing nothing but walking. That was why I'd stuffed two new pairs of tights into my purse, just in case.

"Buckle up," Father said. Mother leaned over and patted his bald head with a tissue, soaking up the drops of sweat that had gathered there. I couldn't remember Father ever having hair.

"Cara," Father said, a sliver of annoyance entering his voice.

I quickly buckled up, and he slid the car out of our driveway.

"Cosimo and I have had a short talk this afternoon," he said matter-of-factly.

"Oh?" I said. A knot of worry formed in my stomach. What if Cosimo had changed his mind? What if he hadn't? I wasn't sure which option caused my stomach to constrict harder. I forced my face into a neutral expression when I noticed Mother watching me over her shoulder.

"What did he say?" I asked.

"He suggested you two marry next summer."

I swallowed. "So soon?"

A small frown appeared between Father's brows, but Mother spoke first. "You are nineteen, Cara. You'll be twenty next summer. That's a good age to become a wife, and mother."

My head spun. While I could somehow wrap my mind around being someone's wife, I felt way too young to become someone's mother. When would I get the chance to be myself? To find out who I really was and wanted to be?

"Cosimo is a decent man and that's not an easy thing to find," Father said. "He's responsible, and he's been Falcone's financial advisor for almost five years. He's very intelligent."

"I know," I said quietly. Cosimo wasn't a bad choice, not by any standards. He wasn't even bad looking. There just wasn't that flutter I'd hoped for when meeting the man I'd have to marry. Maybe tonight. Weren't occasions like a party the perfect place to fall head over heels for someone? I just needed to be open to the possibility.

We entered the premises of the Falcone mansion fifteen minutes later and drove for another two minutes until the driveway finally opened up to a majestic palace-like house and the huge fountain in front of it. The thing spewed water in blue and red and white out of its Roman statues. Apparently, a stonemason from Italy had created the thing for Falcone. It had cost more than Father's car. It was just one of the many reasons why I didn't like Falcone. From what Father had told me about the man, he was a sadistic show-off. I was glad that my family and I were on his good side. Nobody wanted to have Falcone as their enemy.

Everywhere you looked, expensive cars were parked. From the sheer number, I wondered how all the guests would fit into the house without stepping on each other's feet. Several bellboys rushed toward our car the moment it came to a stop and opened the doors for us. A red carpet led up the stairs and through the front door. This was so over the top ostentatious, it was ridiculous. I shook my head but quickly stopped at a look from Mother. She and Father made me walk between them as we headed toward the front door, our bodyguards trailing us. There, another servant was waiting for us with a professional smile on his face. Neither Falcone, nor his wife, was there to greet us. Why was I even surprised?

The entrance hall was bigger than anything I'd ever seen. A myriad of crystal figures in all sizes stood against the walls and on the sideboards, and several huge portraits of Falcone and his wife plastered the high walls.

"Be polite," Mother whispered under her breath as we were led toward the double doors that opened up to the ballroom with crystal chandeliers and high tables that fringed the dance floor. One wall was lined by a long table filled with canapés, piles of langoustines and lobsters, bowls filled with crushed ice that were topped with the biggest oysters I'd ever seen, tins with Ossetra caviar and every luxurious piece of food I could imagine. The bellboy excused himself the moment we arrived inside the ballroom and rushed off to the next guests.

Once inside, I let my gaze glide over the guests, looking for my friends. I was eager to join them and let my parents seek out their own preferred company, but Mother didn't give me a chance to search very long. She touched my forearm lightly and whispered in my ear. "Be on your best behavior. We'll have to thank Mr. Falcone for the invitation first."

I looked past her to where Father was already talking to a tall man with black hair. Father held his shoulders in a hunch as if he was trying to bow before his boss without actually doing so. The sight left a bitter taste in my mouth. With Mother's palm resting against the small of my back, I crept closer to my father and his boss. We stopped a couple of steps behind them, waiting for them to turn to us. Falcone's dark eyes found me first, before Father noticed our presence. The coldness in them sent a shiver down my back. His white shirt with the stand-up collar and black bowtie made him look even more intimidating, which was difficult to pull off, considering that bowties usually made their wearers appear comical to me.

After the exchange of a few meaningless pleasantries, I was finally dismissed and rushed toward one of the waiters balancing a tray full of champagne flutes on his palm. He was dressed in a white shimmery smoking jacket and white high-polished shoes. At least the outfit made it easy to spot them.

One of our bodyguards followed a few steps behind me as I strode away from my parents, while the other positioned himself at the edge of the gathered guests and kept an eye on my parents. I wondered why it was even necessary to have our bodyguards with us at a party of our supposed friends. I pushed the thought aside, wanting to enjoy this evening, and I took a glass of champagne with a quick thanks, then downed a long gulp of the prickling liquid, grimacing at the tart taste.

"How can you make such a face while drinking Dom Perignon? It's the best drink in the world," Trish said, appearing at my side out of nowhere and snatching a glass of champagne for herself.

"It's the water of kings," Anastasia intoned, and it was unnerving that I wasn't sure if she was joke or being dead serious.

"I'm trying to get used to it," I admitted, lowering the flute from my lips. The alcohol was starting to do its magic, and for that I was grateful after the short chat with Falcone. Both my friends were styled to perfection. Anastasia in a floor-length dream in silver, and Trish in a light green cocktail dress that brushed her knees. Not that I had expected anything less from them. They'd told me at length about their shopping trip for new dresses for the occasion. Of course, I hadn't been allowed to go with them, despite my best attempts to convince my parents. Instead my mother had made me wear a dress I'd bought for Christmas last year. My only consolation was that nobody but my family had seen me wear it, so I wouldn't embarrass myself in front of my friends.

"I hear it's an acquired taste," Trish added thoughtfully. She took a small sip from her glass, her expression turning into one of bliss. "I suppose I've always had a knack for Dom Perignon, and in the past year I've certainly had enough chances to get acquired to its taste. And I intend to drink even more of it in the future." She and Anastasia shared a laugh, and I cursed my parents again for sheltering me as much as they did. If Trish and Anastasia could brave the supposed dangers of our world, then so could I.

Trish gave me a teasing smile, then hugged me with one arm, careful not to ruin either of our hairdos or makeup. Anastasia only smiled. Her bodice was a masterpiece of pearls and embroidery. "I'm worried I'll pull a thread if we hug," she said only half-apologetically.

"That's reasonable," I said, taking another sip from my drink and forcing my expression into one of delight instead of revulsion at the taste. I knew for most people champagne was the height of their drink fantasies, but I just couldn't enjoy it. I'd have to try harder if I didn't want to see Anastasia's pitying expression again.

"One of your hairpins is loose," she said.

My free hand flew up to the spot she was looking at, and I tried to find the offending pin before it could ruin my hairdo. Other guests were throwing glances my way anyway, as this was my debut at a party. I couldn't risk appearing anything less than perfect.

"Let me," Trish said and simply pushed the pin a few inches back. "There. All done." Her smile was kind.

That was all? From Anastasia's reaction, one could have thought I'd committed an inexcusable fashion sin.

"There's a nice selection tonight," Anastasia said, her eyes lingering on a group of men across from us. So she wasn't talking about the buffet.

The men in her focus were all at least ten years older than us, and as I surveyed the rest of the room, I realized that we were among the youngest guests. Most of the attendees worked for Falcone. This was a party for his subjects; I doubted he had any friends. Men like him couldn't afford that luxury.

"But of course, you don't have eyes for other men anymore, now that you're engaged to Cosimo," Anastasia continued, dragging me back to reality.

I wasn't sure what to say to that. Her voice had been odd. Was she jealous? Her father was probably already looking for a suitable match for her, so she'd soon be engaged as well.

"We'll all be married soon enough," I said in a placating tone.

"You got your hands on the highest-ranking bachelor, that's for sure," she said with a tight smile. Then she let out a laugh and clinked her glass against mine. "I'm joking, don't look so shocked."

I laughed, relieved. I really didn't want to fight with Anastasia over Cosimo. We'd all marry good matches.

The music picked up and I took another sip of my drink. I was starting to relax thanks to the alcohol spreading in my blood and barely minded the occasional curious glances from other guests. At the next party, I'd already be one of them, and someone else would be the center of attention. Trish tapped her foot on the hardwood floor in rhythm with the song and hummed a few lines before Anastasia shot her a look. I had to stifle a laugh. The dynamic between them was ridiculous at times.

To my surprise, I realized that even my bodyguard had disappeared from view to give me privacy with my friends. Slowly, this evening was getting good.

I knew Talia would give me an earful when I returned tonight, but our parents had been right when they'd insisted she was too young for a social event at Falcone's house. Of course I wouldn't tell her that. It would be hard enough to make her forgive me as it was, though a few juicy rumors would probably placate her. Not that I was an experienced socialite. I'd have to rely on Trish and Anastasia for that.

Annoyance toward Father rose up in me. Maybe he'd refused to take me to a social function until now because he thought I'd embarrass him in front of his boss. I'd overheard him tell Mother several times how terrifying and brutal Falcone was, so it wasn't too far-fetched that Father thought I might cower in fear in front of that man, which was ridiculous. He was still human, not the monster Father always made him out to be, and even if he were, I doubted very much that he'd hate to see me cower in fear. It would probably excite him, if he were truly the man Father had described.

"They are a bit too old for my taste," Trish said, returning to our previous topic before she took another sip from her champagne.

"I don't mind. I want to be treated like a princess by my husband, and older men are more likely to appreciate me than a young guy," Anastasia said. She gave me a knowing smile. For some reason it felt false. "From what I hear the deal between your family and Cosimo is almost done, so your engagement party will be soon."

I frowned at the use of the word "deal" when it came to me marrying Cosimo. But in all honesty, it was probably the term that fit the whole arrangement best. I gave a small shrug, trying to act nonchalant. I didn't want to talk about him tonight, especially since the topic seemed to rile Anastasia up.

"Oh my God, Falcone invited his monster," Trish whispered, clutching at my arm and almost making me spill my champagne over her dress. I followed her shock-widened brown eyes toward a corner of the room where a tall, muscled man leaned against a wall. He was dressed in a white shirt that strained against his massive chest, a black suit and black dress shoes. In fact, he didn't look that different from the other men in the room except for the missing tie—*if you took only his outfit into consideration*. But the rest of him, *God have mercy*.

He looked way too tame for someone like him. Or at least he tried to appear that way. There was no fooling anyone: his nature seemed to radiate off him like a dark cloud of danger. It was almost palpable even from afar.

Father had mentioned him once or twice in hushed tones but I'd never seen him, and he definitely wasn't the type to appear in the gossip section of the newspaper. I doubted any journalist was crazy enough to risk the wrath of a man like him.

"The Bastard, that's what most people call him," Anastasia added. She looked like a cat that had spotted a bird. I knew why she was so excited. So far nothing interesting had happened, but Anastasia probably hoped this had the potential for some decent gossip.

"What's his real name?" I asked. I'd tried to get it out of Mother once, but the look she'd given me had stopped me from asking again.

"I don't know his real name. Nobody does. People call him 'Growl' to his face, and the Bastard behind his back."

I gave them a look. Really? Both were names he couldn't possible have chosen for himself. Someone had to know his name. At least, Falcone. He knew everything about his subjects. "Why would people call him that?"

Anastasia shrugged but didn't glance my way. "There's something wrong with his vocal cords since a horrible accident. That's why he's got that big scar."

I couldn't make out a scar from our vantage point. We were too far away. I assumed Anastasia had gotten that piece of information from the gossip mill as well. "What kind of accident?"

"I don't know. Some people say the Russian mob did it, others say he tried to kill himself because he isn't right in the head, but nobody knows," Anastasia replied under her breath.

Who would try to kill themselves like that? And Growl didn't seem the guy for suicide. He didn't look it, that was for sure, but who knew what went on in his twisted brain? The first story with the Bratva sounded far more likely. "So they call him Growl because that's what it sounds like when he talks?" I asked.

Anastasia barely seemed to register my words, but Trish nodded in confirmation.

I didn't ask why they called him the Bastard. That much I could figure out. People in our world didn't look kindly upon children who were born out of wedlock. It was old-fashioned and ridiculous, but some things never changed. I didn't know who his parents were. They couldn't be high-ranking members of society.

I directed my eyes back to the man. He seemed completely indifferent to what was happening around him, as if this party was just another of his duties. But something told me that despite his displayed boredom, he was alert. I doubted that much escaped his attention. He was holding a glass of champagne in his hands, but it was still full. The elegant crystal looked tiny compared to him, and I marveled that he hadn't crushed it between his palms yet. As if he could read my mind, he turned his head and stared straight at us. Trish let out a gasp and jerked beside me, spilling a few drops of her drink on the expensive-looking wooden floor. She really couldn't have acted more suspicious if she'd tried. After a moment, both Trish and Anastasia jerked their heads down, breaking eye contact. Maybe to make him believe they hadn't been watching him, or maybe they simply couldn't bear the power of his gaze.

Now, I understood why my parents and even my friends had sounded so terrified when they'd talked about him. Even from a distance his eyes almost made my knees buckle.

It wasn't only fear that made my heart speed up, though; there was something close to excitement too. It was like watching a tiger through the glass of its enclosure and marveling at its power. Only here the only thing keeping him from attack was the social rules even someone like him was bound to. The leash Falcone had him on wasn't a physical or visible one, but it was there.

I wondered what was going on in his head. How did he feel surrounded by people he had hardly anything in common with? He was one of them, and yet not really; a man of the shadows, because nobody wanted him in the light. When I realized how long I'd been staring, I averted my eyes, but my pulse kept up its erratic pace afterward. I wasn't sure when I'd last felt this…alive. My life always meandered in its predetermined pathways, but tonight felt like an adventure.

"Oh my God, that was creepy," Anastasia whispered. "He should have stayed in the hole that he crawled out of."

I couldn't say anything. My tongue seemed to be stuck to the roof of my mouth.

"Is he still watching?" I asked eventually, my eyes firmly plastered on the bubbles still rising in my glass.

"No, he's gone," Anastasia said with no small relief. "I can't believe he came here. People like him should stay among themselves and not pretend they belong with us."

I peered toward the corner he'd previously occupied but like Anastasia had said, he was gone. For some reason, it made me nervous that I didn't know where he'd gone. He was one of those people you'd like to keep track of because you feared they could sneak up on you. And I could have sworn that I could still sense his eyes on my skin. I shivered. Paranoia usually wasn't my style.

I searched my surroundings but he was nowhere to be seen. I tried to shake off the ridiculous feeling of being watched. It wouldn't do me any favors if I acted paranoid. If I embarrassed myself here, it would be a while before I'd be invited to anything again. Or worse, Cosimo would decide I wasn't fit to become his wife. Mother and Father would never forgive me if that happened.

"Look who's coming," Trish said under her breath, and for a ridiculous, heart-stopping moment, I actually thought it was Growl.

I turned to see who she was talking about and felt heat rush into my cheeks. Cosimo was heading our way. He was dressed in a gray double-breasted suit, dark-blond hair slicked back and thin-rimmed glasses on his nose.

"He looks like a broker," commented Trish in a low voice.

He managed Falcone's money, so that wasn't very far off. The suit was his second skin. I'd never seen him in anything else. It was a stark contrast to the man I'd been spying on mere seconds ago.

Trish and Anastasia took a step to the side, huddling together and pretending to give Cosimo and me some privacy, which was only pretense since I knew they'd be hanging on our lips, memorizing our words.

I doubted they'd be using them against me. They were my friends after all, but I didn't want to risk it.

Cosimo came to a stop a little too close, took my hand and brought it to his lips. I almost rolled my eyes at the gesture, though a small part of me relished in the appreciative glances Trish and Anastasia exchanged.

"Care for a dance?" he asked, voice smooth and even. That, like the suit, was always the same. Trish had compared him to a well-oiled machine once. The term fit too well. His eyes darted to my friends but he didn't say anything. I didn't follow his gaze, worried Anastasia would look pissed off. Sometimes I wasn't sure what the hell was going on with her.

I let him guide me toward the dance floor, aware of my friends' curious gazes following us, and they weren't the only ones watching. My parents, too, had turned their eyes toward us. I almost cringed at the force of their attention.

Don't trip, I told myself over and over again as we started moving to the music.

As we danced close together, I waited for a flutter, for something, the smallest hitch in my pulse, but nothing happened. Not that Cosimo looked as if he was madly in love with me. Not that love was required for a marriage, but it would have been nice.

Cosimo tried to make conversation. The weather, how lovely my dress was, this and that he thought I might be interested in. He couldn't have been farther off.

My friends were still watching Cosimo and me. Though "watching" wasn't the right term for the look Anastasia was giving me. I really hoped she'd find a man for herself soon. Knowing her, she was probably just pissed that for once I was in the lead, though I wouldn't have minded if my father had taken more time to find someone for me. I tore my gaze away from my friend's scowl and let my eyes settle in the corner where Growl had stood. He still hadn't returned.

"My friends and I noticed a man earlier," I said, not even sure what Cosimo had been rambling on about before I interrupted him. "My friends told me his name was Growl. He looked…"

I didn't get further.

Cosimo's grip on my back tightened. "He should have stayed where he belongs," he said with a sharpness that surprised me, then he gave me an encouraging look. "Don't worry. You're safe. He knows he's not allowed near women like you."

I opened my mouth for more questions, but Cosimo shook his head. "Let's talk about something else."

There was nothing else I wanted to talk about right then, but I let Cosimo's small talk lure me in. It didn't stop my gaze from searching the room for Growl, though.

Cosimo led me back to my friends and a look passed between Anastasia and him. Her scowl obviously hadn't slipped past his attention either. If I were braver, I'd have confronted her and asked what her problem was, but I definitely didn't want any trouble at my first party.

Cosimo excused himself and headed toward a group of men, including Falcone. Trish handed me a fresh glass of champagne. "How was it?"

"Good," I said automatically, unwilling to admit to them that I couldn't care less about my soon-to-be fiancé.

"You looked cute together," Anastasia said sweetly. Surprise surged through me, and I felt myself relax at once. Apparently, Anastasia had realized there was no reason for her to be jealous of Cosimo and me. It was finally time to enjoy the party.

chapter 2

—CARA—

I'd lost my way; the three glasses of champagne that I'd downed didn't really help my sense of direction. This house was a maze, obviously built to impress and intimidate, and not so much as a place to feel comfortable and actually live in. At least, I could not imagine ever feeling comfortable in a place like this, but maybe the almost life-sized paintings of Falcone had something to do with it as well. His cold eyes seemed to follow me wherever I went.

I fumbled for my mobile in my purse and pulled it out, but hesitated. How embarrassing would it be if I called Anastasia or Trish to tell them I'd actually managed to lose my way while looking for the ladies' room? They wouldn't let me hear the end of it. The atmosphere between us had been strained since my dance with Cosimo anyway. No need to give them any more ammunition against me.

Not for the first time I wished Talia were here. We'd laugh about this together, and she'd tease me about it for a long time, but never out of malice or schadenfreude. She wouldn't use it against me when talking to other people.

I paused, realizing with sudden horror that I didn't even trust my two best friends. I shook my head. This was the world I lived in. "You can't walk around trusting people, not even your so-called friends"—that's what Father always said. I'd never wanted to believe him. I put my phone back into my purse. There was no way I was going to call anyone.

Mother was out of the question anyway.

And Cosimo. No, I didn't need another reason for it to be awkward between us. And he was as good as a stranger to me. I had an inkling that wouldn't change until our wedding day and perhaps a long time after.

With a quiet sigh, I kept going. At some point, I'd have to see something I recognized and find my way back to the party.

I turned another unfamiliar corner—they really looked all the same— when I spotted someone in the corridor only a few steps in front of me. *Finally,* someone might be able to point me in the right direction!

My elation turned to shock, then fear when I realized whom I'd walked into.

Growl.

He didn't move. Just stood there. Tall and imposing. It seemed as if he'd been in this corridor for a while.

Waiting for a victim, and here I was all alone. *Don't be ridiculous.*

But as much as I wanted to scoff at the idea, I had a feeling it wasn't that far off. Fear and fascination battled in me, and I reminded myself that he wouldn't touch me. My father was too important to Falcone, and that meant I was too. Maybe Growl was merciless, barely more than a killing machine and monster, but he was definitely a clever monster or he wouldn't have made it this far. And yet I hoped my bodyguards would come to find me soon. But had they even seen me leaving the party? They'd tried to give my friends and me room. Now I wished they hadn't.

Growl's eyes showed nothing as he watched me. The suit was too tight around his broad shoulders, and the hint of black peeked out under his too white shirt. One of his many tattoos. I'd never seen them, but you couldn't be part of society and not hear the stories. Even dressed up in a suit, masked like one of us, he couldn't hide who he was. His tattoos showed, a small hint of the monster beneath the expensive attire. I wondered how he looked without the suit. Heat shot into my cheeks at the ridiculous thought. I'd definitely drunk too much alcohol.

The hint of a scowl crossed his face before it disappeared and I realized how long I'd been staring at him again, judging him. I probably hadn't managed to hide my thoughts about him very well. A mistake that could ruin everything in our world. My parents had taught me better.

The door behind him, however, looked faintly familiar. It led to the main lobby. I didn't move. Making my way back to the party meant going closer to him.

It was ridiculous. I wasn't just anyone. And we weren't just anywhere. He wouldn't do anything. Even he had rules he was bound to and one of them was that I was off limits, just like all the girls from families like mine. No matter how much nonsense Anastasia talked, that statement of hers held true.

I squared my shoulders and took a few determined steps toward Growl. *Closer to the party*, I reminded myself as my pulse quickened. For some reason this felt like a prowl to me. Growl was the hunter and I was the prey, which didn't even make sense since he had hardly moved since my arrival in the corridor.

"I'm Cara," I said in a rushed voice. Maybe if I could get him to talk, he wouldn't seem so dangerous anymore, but he didn't react, only watched me with an unreadable expression—and then the door behind him swung open, and my mother appeared.

Her eyes settled on me then moved on to Growl, and her expression grew rigid.

"Cara, your father and I are looking for you. Come back to the party," she said, completely ignoring the man in the corridor with us.

I nodded and rushed past Growl. His eyes—amber, not dark as they'd seemed from afar—followed me but he remained silent. When I had my back to him, a thrill shot through my body, and I had to stop myself from looking over my shoulder.

The moment Mother and I were out of the corridor and in the deserted hall, she grabbed my arm in a crushing grip. "What were you thinking being alone with that...that man," she practically spat the last word. Her eyes were wide and frantic. "I can't believe they let him in. He belongs in a cage in shackles, far away from anyone decent."

Her nails dug into my arm.

"Mom, you're hurting me."

She released me and I finally recognized the emotion on her face. Not anger, but worry.

"I'm fine," I said firmly. "I lost my way and came across..." I searched my mind for a name to call him other than Growl, which seemed like too much of a nickname to use around my mother, but came up empty-handed.

"Cara, you can't go running around like that, without thinking about the consequences of your actions."

"I was on my way to the ladies' room. I wasn't running around," I said indignantly.

"Cosimo is a good match. Don't go ruin it now."

I blinked, unable to believe my ears. "That's what you're worried about."

Mother took a deep breath and pressed her hand against my cheek. "I'm worried about you. But that includes your reputation. In this world, a woman is nothing without a good reputation. A man, that's a different matter. They can do as they please and it'll even help their reputation, but we are bound to different standards. We need to be everything they're not. We need to make up for their failures. That's what we're meant for. We, *you*, need to be gentle and docile and virtuous. Men want everything they see. We should keep our desires firmly locked away, even if men can't."

It wasn't the first time she'd said something like that to me, but the way she accentuated the word "desire" in her speech made me worry that she knew of my body's reaction to Growl's closeness.

She needn't have worried though. My fear of that man, of everything he stood for and what he was capable of, trumped whatever small thrill of excitement my body might have felt around him.

—GROWL—

I watched them leave the corridor. The door fell shut and I was alone again. Her vanilla scent still lingered in the air like an insistent flutter in my nose. Sweet. Girls like that always chose sweet scents. I didn't understand why they'd want to appear even more fragile by smelling like a delicate flower.

I pulled at my collar. Too tight. And wrong. All wrong. The fabric against my scar, I hated it. The pressure, the crispness. Like a collar for a dog. This suit, this shirt, that wasn't me. People never let me forget it.

The look on her mother's face had reminded me why I hated events like this. People didn't want me around. They wanted me to do their dirty work, and they enjoyed talking shit about me, but they didn't want me near.

I didn't give a fuck.

They were nothing to me.

I knew they watched me like a circus animal. I was the scandal of the evening. The sweet-smelling girl, too, had been watching me. *Staring*. I'd seen her and her friends observe me from across the ballroom.

But the sweet-smelling girl had surprised me. I knew her name. Of course. Falcone had talked about her father and her family too often in the last few weeks. Cara. She would soon learn how it felt to be fallen from grace.

She hadn't run away screaming, even though we'd been alone in the corridor. She hadn't even looked very scared. Yes, there had been fear; there always was, but there had also been curiosity—because I was a monster that they feared, and that fascinated them.

I didn't care. She was just a girl. A society girl with a pretty dress and an even prettier face. I didn't give a fuck about pretty. It meant nothing. It was fleeting, could be taken away in a heartbeat. Still, my eyes had sought her out several times that evening. I'd imagined ripping that pretty dress off her body, imagined running my not-worthy hands over her curves. But I'd forced my gaze away and left the ballroom before I could do something very stupid. She was someone I wasn't meant to have. Someone I shouldn't even imagine having. She was someone to admire from afar. And it was for the best.

—CARA—

That night, shortly after we returned home, Talia snuck into my room. I could make out her slender form in the dim light streaming in through the curtains. She perched on the edge of my bed. "Are you awake?"

I smiled. Perhaps she was still angry at me, but her curiosity won as usual. "No," I whispered.

"Tell me everything," she said as she stretched out beside me, her face so close I could smell her peppermint breath.

"It wasn't half as exciting as you think, trust me. But you'd have loved the pretty dresses."

"Something exciting must have happened. How was Falcone? Was he scary?"

"He was scary and creepy, but you know who was even scarier?"

She shook her head, holding her breath.

"Growl. I met him in the hallway."

"Growl," she repeated doubtfully. "Who's that?"

"Falcone's Enforcer. He's tattooed all over and he can't talk properly. He growls."

"Really?" I could tell that she thought I was trying to pull her leg.

"Really."

"Did you talk to him?"

"No," I said, wishing I'd heard his voice. "He only stared at me. It was strange."

"I wish I could have been there. Instead I got to watch TV all evening."

"I'm sorry," I said quietly, and touched her shoulder. "Perhaps next time you'll be allowed to come."

"I doubt it," she muttered, then sat up. "I'd better go before Mother catches me." She hopped out of bed and tiptoed toward the door. Before she left, she said, "By the way, your breath smells of alcohol."

I threw a pillow at her, but she slipped out and it bounced off the door.

The excitement of the night still filled my body. There was no way I could fall asleep yet. Hesitantly, I slipped a hand under the covers and into my pajama bottoms. My fingers found the sweet spot between my legs, answering to the need that had called to me ever since I'd seen Growl. The cloak of darkness washed away my resistance and my worry of being caught. Even my mother's words that echoed in my head weren't able to stop me. *Be proper, be virtuous. This is sin.*

The image of that fearsome man had caused a sweet tingle in my core, and I was unable to resist. *Wrong*, my mind screamed, but I banished the thought until finally my body shuddered with release. It felt thrilling to imagine this dangerous man.

But seconds after, a familiar sense of being dirty washed over me. This was sin. Mother hadn't stopped saying those words to me since the day she'd caught me touching myself two months ago. I'd not given in to my sinful needs since then, until tonight.

I took a deep breath, wishing my heart would stop racing. Wishing my body would stop reminding me of what I'd done.

Ever since Mother had caught me, there was a tension between us I could hardly stand. She avoided my eyes as I avoided hers. I was almost glad for my quickly approaching wedding so I'd finally escape Mother's judgment. I still felt a wave of blatant shame wash over me when I remembered that day and the look of shock on my mother's face. It hadn't been the first time I'd touched myself, but it was the first time I'd really understood the wrongness of it. I'd sworn to myself back then to never let my body overrule my brain again, and now I'd broken that promise. In the protection of the night, I'd dared to let my fingers roam again, all because of a man whom I shouldn't even think of, let alone fantasize about. *Wrong.*

I was weak and a sinner, but in the brief moments of pleasure, I'd felt more alive than at any other point in my life.

chapter 3

—CARA—

I knew something was horribly wrong as I watched Father during dinner. He had the nervous energy of a trapped animal. Talia's eyes flitted toward me, her dark eyebrows shooting up in a silent question. She tried to act like she was all grown up, and yet she still seemed to think I knew more than her. But there were always more questions than answers in our house.

I gave a small shrug and cast my eyes toward Mother, but her attention was focused on Father, the same inquisitive expression on her face that Talia was giving me. None of us seemed to get answers; Father stared intently down at his iPhone, but the screen remained black. Whatever he was waiting and hoping for, it wasn't happening. His fingers were tapping an erratic rhythm on the mahogany of our dining-room table, a quiet click-click of nails on wood. Father usually wore his nails meticulously short, but whatever was turning him into the nervous wreck before us had made him forget his personal hygiene.

"Brando, you've barely touched your dinner. Don't you like the roasted beef?"

Mother asked. She'd spent two hours in the kitchen to prepare our Sunday feast. On every other day of the week our cook was responsible for the cooking.

Father jumped in his chair. His widened, bloodshot eyes found Mother, then they registered Talia and me. Unease settled in the pit of my stomach. I'd never seen him like this. Father was calm and analytical. Little could get a rise out of him. But since the party at the Falcones', he'd seemed somewhat stressed.

"I'm not hungry," Father said before his gaze returned to his cell phone.

I glanced at the pouch straining over his belt. Father loved to eat, and he never let Mother's roasted beef go to waste.

The screen of his phone flashed with a message and Father's face drained of color. I set down my fork, no longer hungry. But I didn't get the chance for another questioning look at Mother, because Father shot to his feet. His chair toppled over and crashed to the hardwood floor. Mother rose as well, but Talia and I were frozen to our seats. What was going on?

"Brando, what—"

Father rushed off before Mother could finish her sentence. After a brief moment of hesitation, Mother followed after him. I stared at the closed door, listening for any sounds of conversation. Finally I got to my feet. Talia was still glued to her chair. She blinked up at me. "What's gotten into Father?"

"I don't know," I admitted. My eyes darted to the door, torn between running after our parents to find out what was going on and following the rules. We weren't supposed to get up from the dining table without permission. I didn't like that rule, but I'd always followed it. Dinners were the only time our family got the chance to spend quality time together, after all.

The door to the dining room flew open again and Father was back, two guns in his hands. He set one down, only to pull out his phone and press it against his ear. I stared at the weapon on our table. I knew what Father was doing for a living, what he was. I'd known for as long as I could remember, even if Mother, Talia and I lived a fairly normal life. Even if you tried to remain blind to the truth, it sometimes smacked you in the face without invitation. But so far Father had tried to keep up the illusion of normalcy around us. It hadn't exactly been difficult for him because until a few months ago, Talia and I had both attended an all-girls boarding school and only been home on the weekends and during the holidays. And soon I'd be busy organizing my wedding and eventually I'd move in with Cosimo, and Talia would return to school. I'd never seen him openly display a gun. I'd never seen a gun this close at all. Father was involved in organized crime, but many people who dealt with gambling were in Las Vegas; I wasn't even sure what exactly he was doing, except that he managed most of the Camorra's casinos.

Mother came into the dining room, looking completely out of it, but Father didn't glance her way. "When will you be here?" Father hissed into the phone. He nodded after a moment. "We'll be ready then. Hurry."

Finally he turned to us. He was trying to look calm, but failing miserably. His left eye was twitching and it was driving me crazy. "Talia, Cara, please pack a bag. Only things you'll absolutely need to get by for a few days."

Mother had become stiff like a salt pillar. "Brando?"

"We're going on vacation?" Talia asked with the hope and naiveté I wished for myself.

Father always humored us if we said something silly. Not today. "Don't be ridiculous, Talia," he barked. She jumped in her chair, obviously taken aback by the harsh tone.

"Are we in trouble?" I asked carefully.

"I don't have time to discuss the details with you. All you need to know right now is that we don't have much time, so please grab a few things."

The phone flashed with a message. Father's shoulders sagged with relief. "They are here." He rushed out of the dining room without an explanation.

This time all three of us followed him into the entrance hall of our house. Father opened the front door and several men I'd never seen before entered. They looked rugged: ill-fitting jeans, leather jackets, sneakers, strange tattoos of Kalashnikovs.

They looked like the kind of guys I wouldn't want to meet in the dark—or at all. Their calculating eyes slid over me. They were the kind of men who made you cross the street to avoid them.

I had to stop myself from wrapping my arms protectively around my chest. If Father had invited them in, they couldn't be dangerous.

Father pulled an envelope from the pocket in his jacket and held it out to one of the men. Talia's arm brushed mine as she moved a bit closer. I wished I could give her the comfort she was obviously looking for, but my own nerves were wrecked.

The man looked inside. "Where's the rest?" he said in a heavy accent. Were those Russians? They looked slightly Slavic, but I hadn't considered the option of them actually being Russians. Father worked for the Camorra, and it was no secret that the Russians were the enemy. Weren't we all committing treason by having these men inside our house? My head was spinning but I kept the questions to myself, from fear of making things worse.

"You'll get it once my family and I are safe in New York. That was the deal, Wladimir," Father said.

Talia slanted me a confused look, but I didn't dare take my eyes off what was going on. Why were we going to New York? And what had Father done that he needed Russians to protect him? He'd rarely spoken about business in our presence, but whenever I'd overheard the occasional snippet about New York or Russians, it hadn't been positive.

Wladimir exchanged a look with his companions, then gave a quick nod. "That won't be a problem. Tomorrow you'll be in New York."

Father turned to us. "What are you still doing here? I told you to pack your bags. Hurry."

I hesitated, but Mother grabbed Talia's hand and led her toward the staircase. After a moment, I followed, but not without glancing over my shoulder again. The Russians were talking amongst each other. Father seemed to trust them, or at least trusted that they wanted the rest of the money badly enough to get us to New York. That reminded me. I caught up with Mother and Talia, then whispered, "Why New York? I thought we couldn't go there because the ruling family doesn't get along with Father's boss."

Mother halted. "Where did you hear that?"

"I don't know. Sometimes I overhear things. It's the truth, though, right?"

"New York is a difficult topic. I haven't been there in a very long time."

There was longing in her voice. I opened my mouth to ask her about it when a bang sounded downstairs, then men were screaming.

"We need to hide," Mother whispered as she dragged Talia toward the master bedroom. I was about to go after them when steps thundered up the staircase. I quickly pushed into the closest room, Talia's, and hid in her overcrowded closet. There was a pile of discarded clothes on the floor, and I used it to conceal myself even more. I could still see most of the room through the slits in the door, but with only the dim light from the corridor spilling in, it was difficult to make out much. I'd barely had time to crouch down and become still before the door was flung open. My heart pounded wildly in my chest. Someone staggered in. For a moment, light hit the man's face and I recognized him as one of the Russians. He was bleeding from a wound in his arm. He moved toward the window. Was he going to jump? He tried to push the window up, but it got stuck because of his frantic movements.

I held my breath and buried myself deeper into the heap of clothes. Another man, much taller and more muscled than the first, stalked in and grabbed the

Russian. Everything happened too fast to see much, but something seemed familiar about the second man. There was a short struggle. The Russian pulled a knife, but he never got to use it. The other man grabbed him by the neck and twisted. I stifled a gasp as the Russian toppled over, collided with the door so it was pushed open all the way, and eventually dropped to the ground in a lifeless heap. Light now filled the entire center of the room. Empty, dead blue eyes stared unseeingly in my direction. Dead. Killed.

My gaze moved back up to the murderer. His back was turned to me. But I knew him. I had dreamt about him several times in the last couple of weeks since the party.

Growl, of course.

chapter 4

—CARA—

His black T-shirt stuck to his skin from sweat, and his muscled arms were covered in tattoos and scars. Without the suit and cool demeanor, this man was pure danger. There was nothing controlled about him now. Everything about him screamed death. My heart pounded in my chest as I waited for him to turn around and discover me. I didn't dare move or breathe from fear of making a sound. Would he kill me as well?

He wouldn't. He couldn't. My family's status still had to count for something, right? No. There were Russians in our house. Russians that were supposed to take us to New York. Whatever power my family—*my father* had held, it was surely gone.

Growl walked out of the room without another glance at the man he killed—or at the wardrobe I was hiding in.

Only when he was gone and I didn't hear his steps anymore did I dare to breathe. And then a new fear set in. Where was Father, and what was happening to him? And what about Mother and Talia? I had to go looking for them, even if every fiber of my body screamed at me to stay where I was. We needed to stay together, but leaving my hiding place was a huge risk. I glanced toward the dead body in the middle of the room again. Was that our fate too? Sickness crawled up my throat, but I swallowed it back. No time for weakness.

Then a more hopeful thought crossed my mind. Maybe we'd be spared. It wasn't a surprise that soldiers of the Camorra, like Growl, killed members of the Bratva, their archenemies. Maybe there was a way we could convince everyone that the Russians hadn't been here for our protection, but instead to kill us.

Screams and shots rang out below. I stiffened as I listened for a familiar voice, Father's voice, but it wasn't among the screams, and neither were Talia's or Mother's. They were probably still hiding in the master bedroom.

I closed my eyes. I wasn't used to this world, even though I'd grown up around people who were part of it. I'd always only brushed the edges of the nastiness my father was involved in. Now that I was thrown in headfirst, I wasn't sure how to act. Waiting like a mouse in a trap wasn't the solution, though. At some point, they'd search the rooms properly, and I didn't want to make it easy for them. I pushed to my feet and slowly opened the door, then stepped outside. Although I knew better, I crouched beside the Russian and pressed my fingers against his throat. He was still warm but there was no pulse. I considered doing CPR, but then I noticed the way his neck was twisted and shoved away.

A violent shudder overwhelmed my body and for a moment I was sure I was going to have a panic attack, but the sound of voices brought me back to reality. I stood, my gaze falling on the knife the Russian had dropped during his struggle. I was about to take it when the words of the self-defense instructor who had given a weekend seminar at our school popped into my mind: "A weapon you can't control is another advantage for your enemy."

I had no doubt that I'd be disarmed in no time. I'd never learned how to fight with weapons, or to fight at all. My friends and I hadn't taken the self-defense seminar very seriously. Now I wished I had. But we'd been so busy ogling our instructor that we hadn't had time for anything else. Indecisiveness kept me rooted.

A high-pitched scream echoed through the house. *Talia.*

I started moving without thinking and stormed out of the room. I wasn't sure how to help her, but I knew I needed to get to her. I didn't get very far though. I crashed into someone, my temple colliding with a hard shoulder. My vision turned black and I staggered back, gasping. I dropped to my knees. Pain shot through my legs from the impact. After a moment, I peered up and found myself staring at the man who'd killed right in front of my eyes, the man who'd scared and fascinated me since our first encounter. He was even taller this close up, and there was a long faded scar that reached around his throat. Growl. Always Growl.

My fascination gave way to pure fear when his amber eyes met mine. He didn't look human in that moment.

A killer, a monster; there was nothing human about his expression, or eyes, or *him*.

His face didn't register recognition. It didn't show any kind of emotion. Nothing. He grabbed my arm and pulled me roughly to my feet. My vision swam again. "Take her to the others," he rasped. That voice, so deep and rough, sent a shiver down my back.

Another man took me by the arm and led me away. I threw another glance over my shoulder, but Growl, the man with the scar and no mercy, was gone. I hardly paid attention to my surroundings and almost fell down the stairs when my captor dragged me down them until we arrived in the living room where Father, Mother and Talia were already gathered.

Father knelt on the floor in front of Falcone, who was dressed in a pinstriped suit and a high-collared stark white shirt. Talia and Mother stood a few steps back, looking as terrified as I felt. I was pushed toward them, and Mother immediately wrapped an arm around me. The other was already holding on to Talia. I gave Mother an inquiring look, but she was watching Falcone with terrified eyes. Finally, I turned toward him as well. He'd been creepy at his party, but today he looked truly frightening.

Benedetto Falcone, Father's boss and the head of the mafia in Las Vegas, was in our house, and the look in his eyes turned my stomach to ice. That he was in our living room was a horrible sign. It could only mean one thing: Father had messed up badly. And the way Father was sweating profusely only confirmed my worries.

Somewhere in the house, I could still hear the telltale sounds of a brutal fight. Grunts, screams, shots. I shivered. The men gathered in this room all looked like they'd come for blood. The dead man I'd just noticed in the corner and upstairs in Talia's bedroom didn't seem to be enough.

Heavy steps thundered down the staircase, and a few seconds later Growl stalked in. His hands and forearms were covered in blood. I wasn't sure if it was his own, but I doubted it.

Falcone looked his way. "All clear, Growl?" he asked with mild curiosity, as if he knew the answer already, and I supposed he did. All the stories I'd heard in whispered voices flashed through my mind.

Growl was invincible.

The man in front of me tonight had little to do with the man I'd seen at Falcone's party. Back then Growl had been in disguise. While other people had to put on masks, the elegant suit and cleaned-up appearance had been his, but beneath it, the same monster had been lying in wake.

Now there was no mistaking who or what he truly was: the best soldier in the ranks of the Las Vegas Camorra, and a monster. That was what people always said behind his back, and now I saw it too. He was a fighting machine without emotions, a brutal hand of Benedetto Falcone.

"All clear," Growl said in that deep rumble.

My eyes darted to the long scar around his throat. His vocal cords must have been badly injured for him to lose his normal voice. Growl shouldn't have survived a wound like that, but somehow he had, and perhaps it had turned him into the monster he was now. Or perhaps he'd only survived because he was a monster.

Falcone turned away from his soldier and Growl backed away, fading into the background. I wasn't sure how he managed to do it; a man with his size and aura shouldn't have been able to blend into his surroundings that easily, to make you forget he was even there. It probably was one of the skills that made him such a feared fighter.

Falcone stepped closer to Father, forcing him to tilt his head back.

"I hear you've been busy these last few months," Falcone began in a pleasant drawl that made the hairs at the back of my neck rise. His grin was nasty and malicious. It promised punishment.

Father swallowed, but he didn't say anything. Why wasn't he saying anything?

"How much of my money have you kept for yourself, Brando?" Falcone asked, still in that horribly pleasant voice.

My stomach constricted. I couldn't believe Father had stolen from his boss. He wouldn't have been that stupid. Everybody knew what happened to people who messed with Falcone.

Falcone's smile widened and he gave a small nod toward one of his men, who immediately went outside and returned a few moments later with Cosimo at his heels, as usual impeccably dressed. What was he doing here?

Perhaps he would vouch for Father. I tried to catch Cosimo's gaze, but his was firmly focused on Falcone.

Father blanched at the sight of my future husband, and I knew my hope was in vain. Father opened his mouth as if to say something, but then he closed it and remained silent.

I shifted forward, trying to catch Cosimo's eyes again, but his gaze didn't once seek me out. Why was he ignoring me? We were practically engaged; our engagement party was set for New Year's. Shouldn't he take care of me?

He was looking at Father with an expression that made my stomach turn. This was going to end badly.

"Why don't you tell me again what you told me a few days ago?" Falcone said to Cosimo, never taking his eyes off Father.

"After we'd come to an agreement about the engagement to his daughter, Brando came to me and asked me if I wanted to earn some extra money. He told me about the deal he had with the Bratva, and that he was taking money from you."

Mother's arm around my shoulders jerked, her eyes shock-wide. Talia must have felt it, too, because she raised her eyebrows at me. Scared as she was, she looked much younger, and I wanted to protect her, but I didn't know how.

Father didn't say anything. I wanted to shake him, wanted to make him deny Cosimo's outrageous claims. With every second that he didn't, my hopes for a merciful ending to this evening disappeared.

I tried to catch Cosimo's gaze one last time, still hoping, and when he finally looked my way, my heart sank. There was no emotion in his eyes. He would not be my knight in shining armor today. He'd made his decision. He'd chosen his career, and not me.

Falcone turned toward my mother with a shark-like expression. Mother stiffened but she kept her head high. She was a proud woman; it was one of the things I admired most about her. I worried Falcone might enjoy breaking her. He was that type.

He advanced on Mother, and finally Father sprang into action. "She doesn't know anything. My family wasn't involved in any of this. They are innocent." His voice rang with fear and alarm. Seeing his terror, hearing it, petrified me to no end. This wasn't a game.

Talia looked at me for help again. God, how I wished I knew how to help her, how to help my family, but I was useless.

Falcone stopped right in front of my mother, closer than was socially acceptable. Mother didn't flinch back, though most people would have under his stare. I hoped for the same strength if Falcone confronted me. He reached for her throat, and for a crazy moment I thought he was going to strangle her. Father made a move to get up, but Falcone's man pushed him back down.

Falcone curled his fingers around Mother's golden necklace. "But they're reaping the rewards of your betrayal, aren't they?"

Father shook his head. "I didn't buy the necklace with that money…" He trailed off, a pained expression on his face. That was a guilty plea if I'd ever heard one. I wanted to cry. Father had really stolen from the mob. That meant his death, and maybe ours as well. Falcone wasn't known for his kindness. Tears of fear prickled my eyes as I considered what lay ahead. These could be our last minutes in this life.

"No?" Falcone said with fake curiosity. He ripped the necklace off Mother's throat. She gasped and flinched, releasing me as one hand flew up to touch her skin. When she pulled her fingers away, they were bloody. The gold chain had cut her.

Then he pointed at Talia's earrings. Talia took a step back. "And those?" He reached for one earring.

"Leave her alone," I said before I could stop myself. Father and Mother stared at me as if I'd lost my mind. Falcone slowly turned to me, eyes narrowing. He stepped back from Talia and stalked toward me. It took every ounce of my courage to stand my ground when all I wanted to do was to run as fast as my feet could carry me.

I wasn't wearing any flashy jewelry he could hold against me, or my father, but I knew that wouldn't protect me.

His cruel eyes seemed to pierce me to the very core. I tried not to show my revulsion and fear. I wasn't sure I was succeeding. I had no experience in facing true evil.

"You are a brave one, aren't you?" Falcone said. I had a feeling it wasn't meant as a compliment. I waited for him to do something to me, to punish me for my insolence, but he merely eyed me before he turned on his heel and walked back to Father. For some reason his leniency worried me. It made me think that maybe he had something worse in mind for me later. This wasn't over.

"I wonder if you actually believed you'd get away with this, Brando?" Falcone asked. He touched Father's shoulder in a mock friendly gesture.

"I always made more money than any of your other managers. I'll work for free for as long as you want me to. I'll make it up to you, I swear."

"You'll make it up to me?" Falcone repeated. "You betrayed me. You stole from me and gave my money to the filthy Russians. My enemies. How are you going to make it up to me?"

"I'll do anything," Father said.

Falcone touched his chin in contemplation. It looked as if he'd practiced the move countless times in front of the mirror. "There is something you can do for me."

Father nodded eagerly, but I wasn't as optimistic. The look in Falcone's eyes promised nothing good. Falcone pulled a gun out of a holster under his jacket and held it against Father's head. "You can die."

He pulled the trigger.

I cried out, taking a step forward to help my father, and so did Mother, but two men stepped in our way. Talia screamed, a high-pitched sound that made the hairs at the back of my neck stand up. I peered toward Father, expecting the worst, but he didn't topple over. He was unharmed. I shook, horror being replaced by relief.

Father closed his eyes, his lips moving in silent prayer before he glanced up at Falcone. There was definitely relief in his gaze, but also trepidation.

Falcone smirked. "But first we need to know everything you know about the Russians and everything else that might harm my business, don't you agree?"

Falcone didn't wait for Father's reply. Instead, he pointed at Growl. "Talk to him. And make it quick. I have better things to do." Growl didn't hesitate. He grabbed Father by the arm, hoisted him up and dragged him into the adjoining dining room.

Mother, Talia and I were ushered into a corner and had to wait while listening to Father's muffled cries and moans. Talia pressed her palms against her ears and squeezed her eyes shut. Mother tightened her hold on both of us. I wanted to close my ears off to the sounds of Father's torture, but if he had to bear the pain, I could at least bear this. I kneaded my hands nervously, wondering if Father would give up secrets that would make things even worse. Did it even matter?

It grew quiet in the adjoining room. I stared at the closed door, willing it to open and Father to step through. What if the silence meant that Father had lost his consciousness? Or worse.

The door creaked open. Mother stiffened. Father was led inside by Growl. Without the other man's steely grip, Father would have toppled over.

Falcone rose from his chair. "All done?"

Growl gave a nod. He led Father into the center of the room, then let go of him. Father dropped to his knees. Growl blended back into the background as Falcone stepped in front of Father. "You disappointed me greatly, Brando. It's a pity, really. You should have considered your family before you decided to screw me over."

Father coughed, then rasped, "Don't...don't punish them for my..."

Falcone didn't give him the chance to finish the sentence. He turned his back to my father. "Growl," he said.

Growl came forward, waiting for orders. He was going to kill my father; there was no other option.

"You did good, Growl." Falcone's lips pulled wide, revealing too many teeth. "That's why I have a gift for you."

Growl stood still, dripping with blood and sweat, eyes cold and empty, as if there was nothing behind them, a dark emptiness that consumed anything around. I shivered. I didn't remember his gaze being this horrific at the party. Killing and maiming must have brought the monster to the surface.

Father shook his head. "You can't!"

I startled.

Growl barely glanced his way, but then his eyes found me, and they didn't move on. God in Heaven, have mercy.

chapter 5

—CARA—

"I can and I will." Falcone nodded toward one of his men, a silent order. The man stepped forward and punched Father in the stomach, making him sputter and cough. Blood dripped down Father's chin as he raised his eyes to me.

I didn't understand what this meant.

Falcone opened his arms. "You've been a good soldier, and you deserve a reward." He pointed a single finger at me, and my world came crashing down. I could see my life crumbling right before my eyes, and then everything turned so much worse. Falcone's finger moved on from me to my sister. Growl's eyes darted toward her. "One of them. It's your choice."

"No," I cried out, tearing away from my mother and past the man barring my way. My newfound freedom was short-lived, however, as the man grabbed me by the arms, bruising me. I winced from the pain shooting through my body.

Talia was frozen in fear and shock beside our mother.

"Please," Father said, his hands linked in a begging gesture. "They are innocent. Punish me but don't hurt them."

Falcone barely glanced his way. "Oh, I will punish you, don't worry. But it won't be that easy." It was obvious he was enjoying himself tremendously. This room was filled with plenty of monsters, but I had a feeling he was the worst of them.

"It's your choice, Growl. Take whoever you want. I'm sure you'll enjoy either of them," Falcone said with a nasty smile. I wanted nothing more than to wipe it off him, to take the heavy marble sculpture of a naked Greek god my mother loved so much and smash it against Falcone's ugly face. I didn't know where those brutal notions came from. I'd never been the violent type, but I supposed that anyone could be driven to the worst in a situation like this.

Growl's eyes rested on my face. I'd have thought he would check out my body, but his gaze never strayed away from my face. I almost wished it were different. His eyes were like amber lakes of nothingness. I didn't want to find out the horrible secrets they harbored in their depths.

"Oh, I think the choice is made," Falcone said with a laugh.

Growl gave a small nod. "Her," he rumbled, eyes still glued to me.

Horror, fear, despair crashed down on me. There should have been relief as well. Relief because Talia had been spared. I didn't want my sister in my stead, but I couldn't feel relief when my own life was falling apart.

"Very well then," Falcone said in a patronizing manner, waving a hand. "She's yours."

She's yours.

He was talking about me.

I was Growl's.

"You can't do that," Father roared. I hadn't expected that much power left in him. I was empty, no fight, nothing. All gone.

"Take me. She's just a child," Mother pleaded.

Falcone laughed again, a menacing sound. "Who'd want an old prune when they can have a juicy peach?"

"Now watch your mouth," Father hissed. Maybe I would have admired his sudden bravery more if he wasn't the reason for our demise. "I won't stand by while you insult my wife and give my daughter to that…" He glared at Growl with disgust. "That monster."

Falcone nodded. "You're right. You shouldn't have to watch this." He pointed his gun at Father, and my mouth opened for a scream, but before a sound escaped, Falcone pulled the trigger. This time it wasn't for show. The bullet tore through Father's temple. His head whipped back violently, eyes widened in shock. His body toppled backwards, his legs getting stuck under his back in an awkward angle.

A scream ripped from my throat. Finally. Too late.

What had happened? How was this happening? It seemed too surreal, like something from a movie, something that couldn't possibly take place right in front of my eyes. A dream. A nightmare.

"No," Mother screeched. She stormed toward Father and fell to her knees. She patted his chest helplessly, as if that would wake him. It almost appeared like she was looking for his wallet, and for a horrible moment, something like a laugh wanted to bubble out of me, but at the same time my throat felt too tight. It was hard to breathe, and perhaps that wouldn't have been the worst thing right now, to stop breathing until everything faded to black. Mother cradled Father's head in her lap but when she pulled back her hands, they came away covered in blood and something white. Blood. Brain.

Oh God.

My vision blurred and bile traveled up my throat. I swallowed hard, forcing myself to keep face among the horrible creatures surrounding my family and me. For some reason, I looked down at my own hands as if they, too, would be covered in blood. They weren't. I couldn't help but wonder how it would feel if Falcone's blood covered my hands, how it would feel to end his life like he'd done with Father's. I suspected it would feel marvelous, and it scared me that I even entertained those thoughts.

"Your job here is done, Growl. Mike and Mimo will take care of the rest. Take your reward home and enjoy her. I'm sure she'll keep you entertained for a while."

It took a moment before I realized he was talking about me. Before I could react, Growl appeared in front of me, massive and tall, smelling like gunpowder and blood. My gaze flitted up to his face, but the look in his eyes made me recoil and I stared at his chest instead, at the muscles straining against his shirt.

He clutched my arm. His grip was tight, on the verge of painful, but I didn't pull away. Behind him, my mother was still kneeling beside Father, a horribly empty expression on her face. Growl nudged me in the direction of the door and when I didn't react, he started pulling me along.

Talia's tear-filled eyes met mine. I tried to rip away from Growl's grip, but it was like he wasn't even human. He hardly seemed to notice my resistance. I was a bothersome fly attacking a lion.

"Wait!" I screamed and to my surprise Growl actually halted, an uncomprehending expression on his face. I twisted until I could see Falcone again. "What about my sister and mother? What happens to them?"

"That's none of your business," he said with that malicious grin. Then he glanced at Growl. "Take her out of my sight. I'm growing tired of her."

Growl tightened his hold and dragged me away despite my protests. Talia tried to run toward me but was stopped by another of Falcone's men. Mother was beyond our reach, trapped in her sadness.

"Cara!" Talia cried, her eyes pleading with me to do something, to help her.

But how?

Growl opened the door, and then we were outside. Talia screamed again but her words weren't intelligible.

The door closed between us, and Talia's terrified cries died away. I walked on autopilot. Not that it would have changed a thing if my legs had given way. Growl would just have dragged me along. I finally drew my eyes away from my home. I couldn't bear looking back at it a moment longer, knowing that I might never see it again.

As my gaze settled on the tall man pulling me toward an enormous black Hummer, the fear for my sister and mother took a backseat as my own fate registered. Falcone had given me to his cruelest fighter. If I survived today, would I even want to live any longer?

Maybe death would seem like the sweetest mercy after Growl was done with me.

chapter 6

—GROWL—

My mind was racing as I pulled Cara toward my car. I'd often thought about the first time I'd seen her at Falcone's party. I'd regretted ever attending that fucking party, especially because her image had haunted my sleep in the weeks after.

I'd felt like a monkey in a suit, and I knew I looked that way too. Something, a *monster*, they wanted to keep in a cage until they needed to unleash it. I knew Falcone only invited me so people would have something to talk about. Even after all these years, they still regarded me as the monster to fear.

I was a monster, no question. But I wasn't the only monster in that room. I wasn't even sure I was the worst.

I'd killed the most people with my own hands; I couldn't deny it, and I didn't want to. I was fucking proud of what I'd done. Most of it, at least. It was the only thing I was good at, killing. I was the best. And maybe my talent for kill and maim rolled off the tongues of many men gathered at that ball, how they relished in their power to do so.

I wasn't sure if that didn't make them just as bad. But it wasn't my place to decide anyway. Maybe one day all of them, me included, would have to face a higher power. That day wouldn't end well for these men.

I wasn't too worried, however. I'd lived through hell, still lived it. There was nothing to fear for me. Nothing waiting for me beyond death could possibly do worse damage than had already been done. There was nothing of me that hadn't been broken, nothing left to destroy, except for my body perhaps, but I wasn't worried about that either. I knew pain, agony even. It was the only constant in my life. I'd almost come to see it as a friend. Something I could count on, something predictable.

No, I didn't fear pain, or death for that matter. Falcone always said that made me such a valuable asset. And that was something I was proud of, even if the words coming from Falcone's mouth left a bitter aftertaste.

They took me for dim-witted, thought of me as nothing but a stupid lapdog to do their bidding without the barest inkling of what they were up to. Like one of the many fight dogs that Falcone and so many of the other men kept for entertainment.

But many people had made the same mistake—confused silence for stupidity, equated lack of words with lack of understanding and knowledge. It was an error they might pay for one day. I knew most of their deepest and darkest secrets, simply because they didn't keep their fucking mouths shut when I was around. They thought I wasn't listening, and even if I were, how could I ever grasp what they were saying?

I despised them, but they paid well and respected me for my strength and brutality; that was enough for me. I had no intention of using my knowledge. I didn't need much: money to buy food for my dogs and myself, and for women and a drink now and then. I liked my simple life. I didn't want complications.

I cast my eyes over to the cowering girl in the passenger seat. I hoped she wouldn't turn out to be a complication. I could hardly give her back. Falcone wouldn't like that.

Not that I had any intention of ever giving her back. She was my most valuable possession to this date. She was looking out of the window, ignoring me. Like she'd done at the party. Like they all did until they couldn't ignore me anymore. Did she still think she was above me? I turned my gaze back to the road. It didn't matter. She was mine now. The idea sent a stab of pride through me, and my groin tightened in anticipation.

Mine.

—CARA—

I could barely breathe. From fear, and because of the stench. God, the stench was worse than anything I'd ever smelled before. Blood. Metallic and sweet, oppressing. I could still see the pool of blood spreading beneath Father's lifeless body, could see Mother kneeling amidst the red liquid, and Talia's horror-widened eyes. Every moment of tonight seemed to be burned into my mind.

My eyes flitted to the man beside me.

Growl. He steered the car with one hand, looking relaxed, almost at peace.

How could anyone look at peace after what had happened? After what he'd done?

His clothes were covered in blood, and so were his hands. So much blood. Revulsion crippled me.

A few weeks ago my bodyguards, who'd betrayed my family, would have quickly ushered me away from a man like him. My mother had practically dragged me away from him at Falcone's party.

And now I was at his mercy.

He was a brutal, violent hand of Falcone's will.

My whirring thoughts halted when he turned to me.

His eyes were empty, a mirror to throw my own fear back at me. His arms were covered with martial tattoos, knives and thorns and guns.

I couldn't stop looking at him, even though I wanted to. I *needed* to, but I was frozen. Eventually he returned his attention back to the street. I shivered, and let my head fall forward until my forehead came to rest against the cool window. There was a low buzz in my head. I couldn't think straight. *Get a grip.*

I needed to figure out a way out of this.

But we were already slowing down as we turned into a shabby residential area. The paint had peeled off of most of the house fronts, and garbage littered the front yards. Cars missing tires and with broken windows were parked in a few driveways. They wouldn't be driving anywhere. This was the end for them, and for me.

Growl stopped the car in front of a garage which was freshly painted, and then he climbed out. Before I could come up with a plan, he was at my side and opened the door. He grabbed my upper arm and pulled me out. My legs could hardly support my weight, but he didn't seem to care. He led me around the car, over cracked pavement and an overgrown front lawn. A group of teenagers were clustered together two houses down, listening to music and smoking, and across the street a woman with a tattered tank top and tattoos snaking up her arms took out the garbage, looking like she would be giving birth any second.

I opened my mouth to call for help.

Growl released a harsh breath. "Do it. Scream. They won't help you. They have their own problems."

I hesitated. The teenagers and the woman were actually looking at us, watching how Growl was dragging me toward his house, and they didn't even blink. Even the blood on Growl didn't seem to shock them. There was resignation in their expressions; it seemed to seep from their pores. They didn't have the energy to take care of themselves, to take control of their own lives, to fight for their futures, much less for mine.

I pleaded with my eyes anyway, hoping. Still hoping after everything. The woman was the first to look away and walk back into her own house, and moments later the teenagers returned to whatever they'd been doing.

Those people didn't care what was happening to me. They wouldn't help me.

We arrived in front of a door. The paint had peeled off, revealing sun-bleached wood. Growl opened it. It hadn't been locked. My eyes darted toward the group of teenage boys again. They didn't look like they'd pass up an opportunity to break into a house that wasn't even locked.

I peered up at my captor, at the scar running the length of his throat, the blood on his shirt and hands, the hard lines of his face.

Growl met my gaze head-on, and my legs almost buckled under the darkness in his amber eyes. He didn't say anything.

"Even in this area nobody dares to cross you," I whispered.

"That's true. But that's not why I don't have to lock my door. Most of the people in the area are junkies and have nothing to lose." Growl pulled me into his home and closed the door. The inside of the house was even worse than its exterior. The AC was running at the maximum, turning the small corridor where we stood into a freezer.

I shivered violently but Growl seemed immune to the cold. There were no pictures on the walls, no decoration at all. This house was a lonely, dark place. All the doors were closed, but behind one of them I heard sounds I couldn't place. Like tapping. Did he have another woman locked in one of them?

Tears pressed against my eyes. This was it. Everything was over.

Had the fight already drained out of me?

He dragged me into a room. His bedroom? The only pieces of furniture were a bed and a wardrobe, but what the room lacked in furniture, it made up for with wall decorations. Daggers and knives mocked me from every direction. Growl released me and I stumbled forward. I dropped to my knees. The only other option would have been to fall onto the bed, and I wasn't going anywhere near that thing. I quickly turned, throat tight with fear as Growl watched me from the doorway. He looked like he'd risen from hell: a man wrapped in darkness, death and blood. A monster.

Oh God, oh God, oh God.

"I'll be back," he murmured before he turned and closed the door.

chapter 7

—CARA—

I*'ll be back.*

I didn't hear a lock. Was he so sure of himself that he didn't think he needed it? His steps moved away until I couldn't hear them anymore. What was he doing?

I'll be back.

That had sounded like a threat. My eyes found the bed and I quickly got up. I wasn't stupid. I knew what he was going to do once he returned. How was I going to get out of this?

I tried to stifle my panic, but my heart didn't stop racing and my hands were damp with sweat. The blades flashed in the corner of my eye. I knew I wasn't a fighter, and I didn't know how to handle a knife or any other weapon. I'd never had to hurt somebody. I wasn't sure if I was capable of it.

I approached one of the daggers. It was the least flashy one, no curved or zig-zagged blade. It was the one that scared me the least. I reached out and curled my fingers around the handle. It didn't feel wrong like I'd expected, but I didn't kid myself into thinking I could do more with it than hold it. I took it off the wall. It weighed more than I'd expected, and somehow I was relieved to have something substantial to hold on to.

My eyes flitted around the room. Adrenaline had mostly banished my terror for now. I hurried toward the window but there were bars in front of it. A bubble of hysteric laughter bubbled up my throat, but I swallowed it. No sense in going crazy—yet. The windows were covered in a layer of dust, giving the illusion that the outside world was even farther away. Not that the outside of the house was any more enticing than the inside. This was a hopeless place altogether.

I backed away from the window and clutched the knife tighter. This was my only chance. It might as well have not been one at all. Steps rang out, and for a moment I was frozen with indecision and fear. Maybe things would only get worse if I attacked Growl, but I wasn't sure how that was possible. There was no light in his eyes, no mercy or kindness, nothing I could cling to and hope for an acceptable fate. Maybe there was little hope of me succeeding, but...

My eyes darted to the bed, only queen-sized, which was strange for a man of Growl's size. The blankets were dark red, probably to hide bloodstains. I shuddered as images bloomed in my mind, one more horrible than the next.

I sprang into motion, fear now greater than indecision, and hid behind the door. I needed to catch Growl by surprise if I wanted any chance at injuring him. But would that be enough? I had a feeling that Growl was like a bull in the corrida. A few wounds wouldn't bring him down. An image of Growl with several knives buried in his chest, still coming after me, flitted through my mind. I needed to aim to kill.

A new wave of panic washed over me. This wasn't who I was. This wasn't who I wanted to be. For the first time in my life, I hated my father. He'd brought this upon us, had forced us into a life neither of us had chosen. God, what was happening to Talia? Was she all right? She was too young for this. What if she was given to another mobster? She was only fifteen. I should have been there for her, should have protected her; instead I wasn't even sure if I could protect myself.

Growl's steps stopped right in front of the room. I quickly shook off my high heels, then held my breath to hear better and lifted the knife. I'd have to aim for his throat. Even I knew that was the most vulnerable spot on a human's body. But he had survived an injury like that once before. How could I hope to succeed in killing him when others had obviously failed?

He was much taller than me, so I'd have to drive the knife upwards. Would I be able to put enough force behind the stab? The door started to open and then Growl's tall form came into view. Adrenaline pumped in my veins as I lunged at him.

Growl brought his bare arm up to fend off my attack. The blade sliced along his inked forearm and blood welled up at once. But his face didn't show pain. He made a grab for my arm but I dodged him, using my smaller form to evade him. I slammed the knife upwards again, almost blindly. With a low sound deep in his throat, Growl gripped my wrist. I cried out in pain from the force of it and dropped the knife.

Cold fear slammed through me as I watched my only weapon land on the floor with a resounding clang. My eyes shot back up.

Growl's face was a mask of nothing, but I didn't kid myself into thinking that he wasn't furious. This man had killed people for lesser transgressions. I jerked back, but his fingers around my wrist were relentless. That didn't stop me though. I only had this one chance. He could very well decide I wasn't worth the trouble and kill me.

I kicked at him but missed due to his quick reflexes. He thrust me toward the bed like I weighed nothing. I had no chance of stopping my fall and landed on my stomach on top of the mattress. The air rushed out of my lungs, and for a moment I was certain I'd die from lack of oxygen, but then I sucked in a deep breath.

I tried to push myself up but Growl's muscled body pressed up against my back, trapping me between him and the bed. Panic shot through me. I bucked my hips in an attempt to free myself. When that didn't work, I lashed out with my arms, trying to hit Growl. With an impatient sound, he flipped me around so he straddled my hips and grasped both of my wrists in one palm. Now I had no choice but to look into his face, to look at every inch of his frightening body. He'd changed out of his blood-covered clothes and now wore a tight white shirt that was stained with his own blood from the wound in his arm.

His hands were rough and scarred; they looked almost alien-like against my pale skin. A horrible terrified sound pressed out between my lips. Growl's strange, emotionless eyes found mine. His cheekbones and chin were sharp lines in his face. There was nothing soft about this man, least of all his heart.

His grip on my wrists didn't loosen. He did nothing except stare. I knew I should look away. Wasn't that what you were supposed to do if you were faced with a dangerous dog? But I was not just trapped by Growl's powerful body, but also by the terrifying look in his eyes. His breathing was calm, with no sign of our fight. For him this was nothing. One of his hands moved lower toward my stomach. My shirt had ridden up during our struggle and revealed the skin beneath. I tensed when Growl put his hand against my stomach. What was he doing? He stared intently at his hand resting against my paler skin. His fingertips and palm barely touched me. Slowly his gaze rose again to meet mine.

Growl was watching me like I was an unknown species, something he couldn't possibly understand. And perhaps that was true.

I made another half-hearted attempt to free myself, but it was almost laughable. Perhaps if he'd been capable of that kind of emotion Growl might have actually laughed at me.

"Stop," he ordered calmly.

And for some reason, I did stop.

—GROWL—

I did have a reputation, and I was fucking proud of it. My reputation was feared, respected, and that was a great deal more than anyone expected from someone like me. The worthless son of a whore. The bastard. The boy who never spoke.

I was meant for the gutter.

I'd never had something to myself, never even dared to dream about owning something so precious. I was the unwanted bastard son who'd always had to content myself with the leftovers of others. And now Falcone had given me what only a few weeks ago had been out of my reach, someone I wasn't even allowed to admire from afar, one of society's most prized possessions.

Thrown at my feet because I was who I was, because they were certain I would break her. I was her punishment, a fate worse than death, a way to deliver the ultimate punishment to her father who had displeased them so greatly.

And a warning. Nobody would dare to oppose Falcone if that meant their precious daughters might end up in the hands of a man like me.

Cara, a name fit for someone like her, someone too beautiful for a place like this, too beautiful for someone like me. A princess and a monster, that's what we were.

Wide eyes. Parted lips. Flushed cheeks. Pale skin. She looked like a porcelain doll: big blue eyes, chocolate hair and creamy white skin; breakable beautiful, something that I wasn't meant to touch with my scarred, brutal hands. My fingers found her wrist; her heartbeat was fluttering like a bird's. She'd tried to fight, tried to be brave, tried to hurt me, maybe even kill me. Had she truly hoped she could succeed?

Hope—it made people foolish, made them believe in something beyond reality. I'd gotten out of the habit of hoping a long time ago. I knew what I was capable of. She had hoped she could kill me. I *knew* I could kill her, no doubt about it.

My hand traced the soft skin of her throat, then my fingers wrapped around it. Her pupils dilated but I put no pressure into my touch. Her pulse hammered against my rough palm. I was a hunter, and she was my prey. The end was inevitable. I'd come to claim my prize. That was why Falcone had given her to me.

I liked things that hurt. I *liked* hurting. Maybe even loved it, if I were capable of that kind of emotion. I leaned down until my nose was inches from the skin below her ear and breathed in. She smelled flowery sweet with a hint of sweat. Fear. I imagined I could smell that too. I couldn't resist and I didn't have to, not anymore, not ever again with her. Mine. She was mine.

I'd never liked sweet things, but perhaps she would change that.

I lowered my lips to her hot skin. Her pulse throbbed under my mouth where I kissed her throat. Panic and terror beat a frantic rhythm under her skin. And it made me fucking hard.

Her eyes sought out mine, hoping—still hoping, the foolish woman—and *pleading* me for mercy. She didn't know me, didn't know that the part of me that hadn't been born a monster had died a long time ago. Mercy was the furthest thing from my mind as my eyes claimed her body.

I tore at her shirt, revealing inch after inch of immaculate skin. There wasn't a single scar or blemish. She couldn't possibly be mine. She was too perfect, simply too much.

I curled my fingers around her shoulder. Soft. Softer than any woman I'd touched. None of them had been like her, not even close, not even the same species if you asked me.

The bones of her shoulder were sharp against my palm. So fragile. She looked like a doll. Breakable but beautiful. Nothing I was meant to own. My skin looked dirty compared to hers and I raised my hand a few inches, half expecting her skin to come away smudged from my touch.

She was nothing I had ever thought was in my reach. She wasn't meant to be. Nothing I was meant to touch with my scarred, brutal hands.

I wasn't worthy.

Not worth it.

Not worth it.

Not worth it.

Something hot and sharp clawed at my chest. I didn't like it, not one bit. I pushed off the bed, staggering to my feet. She stayed on her back, eyes full of confusion and questions, and again that flicker of fucking hope.

"You'd better stop it," I growled.

"What?" she whispered.

"Hoping. It's a waste of time." I picked her up. To me she weighed nothing. I needed her gone, out of my view. I carried her out of my room and into the small guest room, which I'd never had to use before. She trembled against me and for some reason it made me even angrier. I dropped her on the bed and she let out a shocked breath. I turned on my heel, tired of looking at her, of wondering, of doubting myself.

It shouldn't...it *didn't* matter why Falcone had given her to me. She was mine to do with as I pleased. I headed toward the door and slammed it closed behind me. Tomorrow I'd claim her. Worth it or not. I fucking deserved something good in my life.

chapter 8

—CARA—

I winced as the door slammed shut. Surprised the sound had managed to penetrate the fog of fear and the hammering of my heart. I felt dazed. Slowly I sat up. My body ached, and I wasn't sure if it was from my fight with Growl or if it was terror manifesting in a more physical way. I knew nothing anymore. My world had been shattered, and soon I'd share the same fate. Growl had left, had spared me for now, but he'd return.

He'd return.

I turned my head very slowly and peered down at my torn shirt, at my naked shoulder. I remembered his touch there. My fingertips brushed the skin, and I shivered, then traced my throat and the spot beneath my ear. His touch was still there, like an imprint. I closed my eyes, released a harsh breath. My heartbeat didn't slow. My heart raced, as if it was eager to beat its way out of my chest, away, far away from my body.

I wished it were that easy, leaving your body, drifting off to better places and times. But this was foolish thinking. There would be no miracle that would take me away from this place, from Growl's reach. Most of my life I'd lived in a bubble, removed from the harsh reality that so many people faced. I couldn't allow myself that luxury anymore. If I wanted to flee my fate, I'd have to save myself. No one would come to my rescue, not my bodyguards who now served Falcone, probably always had. Not my traitorous fiancé. Not my father, who had probably already been dumped somewhere no one could find him, or been given to Falcone's fight dogs as a snack. My chest clenched, but I fought the emotion. There was no sense in pitying the dead. They had nothing to lose anymore. But I had, my mother had, Talia had.

I let out a shuddering sob and quickly clamped my palm over my lips. I didn't want Growl to overhear me, lest it excited him and he changed his mind about sparing me for tonight. I crawled toward the edge of the bed and put one foot on the hardwood floor, then waited for my muscles to stop shaking before I dared to get on my feet. My legs felt unsteady. Everything did.

I looked around. This room was even sparser than the last. The walls were empty. The wooden floorboards completely scratched.

Bloodstains marred my shirt. It was ruined. I couldn't bear wearing it a second longer. I ripped it off my body and wrapped my arms around myself. There were no clothes in the one shabby cupboard I found. Everything I owned was still at my house. There wasn't another door except the one Growl had left through, so I didn't have a bathroom to myself. There was nothing, except the shabby furniture. I sank back down onto the mattress. Maybe I could try to sneak out of the house after nightfall. I draped the blanket over my shoulders, covering myself up. If Growl returned, I didn't want to be wearing nothing except for a bra. *As if clothes would stop him.*

I heard sniffing and then scratching at the door. My body tightened with fear as I crept toward the door. It sounded like dogs. When I arrived in front of the door, a deep bark sounded and I jumped back. The dog sounded big, dangerous. Hadn't Father once mentioned that Falcone bred fight dogs for entertainment?

My head swam. This was all too much. I backed away and dropped back down on the bed. What if the dogs found a way inside? They would probably tear me into tiny shreds. That was what they had been bred and trained for. Rumors said that Falcone made millions with bets on dog fights.

My heart sank. I would never be able to leave the house without the dogs noticing. Even if I managed to creep past Growl—and that seemed unlikely considering his vigilance—the dogs were an insurmountable obstacle.

I curled myself into a tight ball on the bed and buried my face in the pillow. It smelled stale, unused. Growl probably didn't have many overnight guests. The idea almost made me laugh. I wrapped my arms around my legs and closed my eyes. Outside a couple was screaming obscenities at each other, cars were driving by with screeching tires, and doors were slammed.

I wasn't sure how long I lay like that, but night fell around me and with it came a bone-chilling silence. I wanted the screaming and banging and screeching wheels back. This utter silence made me feel as if I were already dead.

I listened harder for sounds and then wished I hadn't, because suddenly there was scratching and creaking and rustling. I wasn't sure what part of it my mind had conjured and what was reality. I was tired and thirsty and hungry. Maybe I'd die from thirst or hunger. Maybe Growl would just forget about me. Starving couldn't be that bad compared to what might lie in my future if I stayed alive, could it?

Stop it.

I had to stop these crazy thoughts. Going crazy wouldn't get me out of here. I needed to keep my wits about me, needed to figure out a plan. An image of my mother and Talia flashed behind my closed eyelids, so vivid it was as if they were right before me. Happiness and deep sadness overcame me at the image. Would this memory be the only thing left of them? Would I ever see them again?

Tears welled in my eyes and I didn't stop them, let them squeeze past my lids and trail down my cheeks. It felt good, a relief after pretending to be strong. I wasn't, not really, but maybe I could learn. I could be strong for my family, or what was left of it. If not for me, at least for them, I could gather what little courage I possessed and fight against Growl. Again. And again, until one day, perhaps I'd escape my prison.

—GROWL—

I hated feeling. Hated the sharpness and intensity of it. Hated being reminded that I was still human in that regard. I needed to be the monster everyone expected of me; I wanted to be that monster.

I'd fought so hard to be something, anything, more than the bastard and the scar around my throat, more than the son of a whore—I wanted to be more. Always more.

I pushed the gas pedal hard. Perhaps I should have run. I needed to get rid of that excess energy, of that dangerous tightness encompassing my chest. But where I needed to go was too far. I couldn't wait that long. I needed to release some tension now. Needed to get rid of that sensation in my body. I needed to become myself again. Needed to remind myself of who I was, of *what* I was.

In the past I'd had to do so almost daily. Convince myself of my worth, of who I was. But recently I had felt like I'd arrived, and now that girl so out of my league was ruining everything.

I pulled up in front of the Baton Rouge in the non-parking zone, ignoring the car behind me that honked. I threw open the door and got out of the car. The bouncer didn't say a word about the hazardous way I had parked, only took a step back as I stalked past him without a word of greeting. I was almost sad the asshole hadn't told me off. I wanted to break bones, wanted to maim and kill.

The inside of the brothel was stuffed with whores and their johns. There was false laughter and too sweet perfume. There was sweat and sex and smoke in the air. There was a tension so thick, you could cut it with a knife. I hated the red leather couches and red lacquer tables, but I wasn't here for the design.

Some of the tightness in my chest loosened. This was familiar. This was what I needed. A few whores glanced my way then quickly away, hoping I'd choose someone else. Their refusal didn't matter. I'd never cared for their opinion. I'd had them all and most of them were not worth my time. They couldn't give me what I wanted, what I needed.

But there was someone who could, who liked to scratch and bite, who liked it hard and merciless.

Lola had turned away from her potential suitor, a fat asshole in a dark suit. I didn't know the man, so he didn't matter. I knew everyone who mattered in this town, everyone you shouldn't cross, and most of them were clever enough not to get in my way anyway.

Fatguy clamped a meaty hand down on Lola's thigh but she shook him off, and opened her legs wide for me. Her dress moved up, revealing a clean-shaven pussy, a piercing glittering in the dim overhead light. Fatguy glowered, then followed Lola's gaze toward me. His expression fell. He quickly slid off his stool and disappeared from view, looking for another whore.

I didn't give a fuck. I walked past the bar toward the back before I stepped into the second room on the right. It was vacant, but the smell of sex, disinfectant, and rubber lay heavy in the air. I stalked toward the bed and seconds later the door closed behind me.

"Hard day," Lola said in a raspy voice. No question—a statement. She knew better than to ask questions. I knew she was close when the smell of stale and fresh smoke closed around me. When she didn't have a drink or a dick in her mouth, she was smoking.

I turned. Her lips were coated in red lipstick, looking glossy and false. Everything about her did. Her black hair, dyed too many times, fell straight down her back, held down with hairspray and whatever else women used to make their hair do things it wasn't meant to do. Her lips twisted into a flirty smile, while her eyes, rimmed with too much makeup, flickered with eagerness. Oh yes, she liked it.

She wasn't out of my reach.

I grabbed her arms and twisted her around, then threw her down on the bed. My hand tangled in her hair, pulling hard as my other hand opened my zipper, pulled down my pants, then shoved up her skirt and drove into her in one sharp merciless thrust. She cried out, in pain or lust, I didn't know, didn't care. She twisted her arms back, raked her long nails over my thighs, drawing blood. I hissed and fucked her harder, and harder until the image of porcelain skin left my mind, until I was back to being who I was meant to be.

A monster, nothing else.

chapter 9

—CARA—

I was woken by a sound I couldn't place. Like claws on wood. My eyes flew open, staring up at a white ceiling, not my canopy bed. A few dark stains dotted the white that was actually more gray, as if someone had swatted flies or mosquitos and not bothered to clean up afterward. Confusion slithered through my sleepy mind, and then everything that had happened came crashing down on me. I jerked into a sitting position. It took a moment before I figured out the noise I'd heard. The dogs. They were in front of my door again. Sniffing, scratching.

I really needed to go to the toilet, but with the dogs waiting for me that was out of the question. Not that I even knew where the bathroom was.

I stood slowly, legs shaky, and peered out of the small window. It looked out into a small garden. The lawn hadn't been mowed in a while and like the house, the garden, too, was devoid of any decoration. Someone was screaming in the neighboring house. A woman, followed by a man. The same couple I had overheard last night.

I leaned against the windowsill, analyzing my surroundings. I'd always been good at math. I liked things neat and predictable. And where had all my well-laid-out plans gotten me?

The fence caging in the garden was topped with barbed wire. Could I get over it? Probably not without hurting myself badly, and then Growl would just have to send the dogs after me and they'd follow the trail. And what about the neighbors? Would they help me hide, or would they just call Growl in hope of a reward? Probably the latter considering the people I had encountered so far.

The door screeched. I whirled around, body tensing with fear. Growl stepped inside, his eyes landing on me. I quickly covered my bra with my arms.

He seemed less unhinged than last night, and though his gaze slid over my half-naked upper body, his expression didn't show any reaction. His right forearm was bandaged where I'd cut him. Above it there were more marks. Scratches that I didn't remember inflicting, but I'd been in a panic so I wasn't sure what exactly I'd done. He followed my gaze briefly but didn't react. He didn't seem to resent me for injuring him. I hoped that was a good sign.

"You are awake," he said in a low voice. He'd never raised his voice the few times I'd heard him speak, but his words carried enough power anyway.

I huffed at his statement but didn't say any more. The pressure on my bladder was growing close to unbearable. Behind Growl, two massive dogs appeared. They only reached his knees but considering Growl's stature, that was more than a little intimidating. What was worse: they were panting and giving me a good look at their sharp teeth. They were definitely some kind of fight dogs. And judging by the scars on their faces and the rip in the ear of the black one, they'd fought a few battles. Growl put a backpack I hadn't noticed down on the ground between us. "I got a few things for you from your house."

My house. I tried to conjure up an image of my cozy, beautiful home but images from last night were all I could come up with, and I'd rather not remember my house at all than like that. I stepped forward. "Did you see my mother and sister? How are they?"

Growl frowned. "No. They aren't my concern."

"But you must know something, anything. What did Falcone tell you before you came to our house?"

"I didn't ask Falcone what his plans were. You shouldn't ask so many questions. I don't have the answers," he said tersely and was about to turn around.

"I need to go to the bathroom," I babbled. I felt ashamed that I had to ask someone if I was allowed to go to the bathroom.

Growl paused, frown deepening. "Then why didn't you go?"

I almost laughed. "Because I don't know where it is and I thought I was supposed to stay in the room."

"You can walk around the house whenever you want. I won't lock you into your room. You aren't a child."

"Only a prisoner."

One of his dark brown brows twitched, but I couldn't link the reaction with an emotion. I didn't know him well enough. And I doubted anyone knew him like that. To be honest, I wasn't sure if he was capable of emotions at all, or if his facial expressions were just his body's natural reaction to outward influences or something he'd learned to imitate from being around other people.

When the silence became unbearable, I asked, "So I can leave if I want to?"

Growl's amber eyes pierced me to the core. "You can try," he rumbled. "But I will find you no matter where you go. I will follow you to the end of the world."

"How romantic," I whispered with false bravado.

"You are mine."

"I'm not," I snapped. I wasn't a trophy Falcone could hand out to his soldiers.

He tilted his head, appraising me. "Come on." He turned without waiting for my reaction. I couldn't believe him. I grabbed the backpack from the ground and was about to follow when I saw the dogs standing in the hallway in front of the room. I jerked to a stop. They both watched me calmly but with definite interest. My pulse picked up again. And I'd thought I was too tired to be afraid anymore. Definitely not.

"They won't hurt you. They are good dogs," Growl said, waiting for me down the narrow corridor. I wasn't sure, but I thought I heard a hint of amusement in his voice.

"They don't look like good dogs," I said hesitantly as I crept closer to them.

"Don't judge things by their looks. Looks are deceiving."

My back against the wall, I walked past the dogs. They followed me slowly, their keen eyes never straying from me.

My gaze wandered over Growl. His tattoos and scars. "Sometimes the outside and the inside match," I said quietly.

His expression shifted, but again I had no chance of knowing what was going on in his head. At least he'd caught my hint, so he wasn't as ignorant as some people considered him to be.

He pointed at a door. "That's the bathroom."

"There's only one?" I asked, and then almost cringed at how that made me sound.

"This is your life now, better get used to it," he said.

I rushed into the bathroom and locked the door, feeling a flood of satisfaction at having that sliver of control, if only for a moment. I ignored the worry that Growl might be lingering in front of the door and listening to whatever I did, and went to the toilet. He'd heard and seen worse, no doubt. But I made sure to hurry and was glad when I was done.

I caught a glimpse of myself in the mirror over the washbasin when I washed my hands and almost recoiled from my own reflection. My hair was a wild mess and mascara smudged the skin around my eyes from crying, but worst of all was how pale my face was and how hollow my eyes looked. Only one day and not only my life had changed, but my body too.

I didn't want to imagine how much worse off I'd be in a few weeks or months. I didn't want to imagine having to live through that many days with Growl as my captor. I took a deep breath and turned the water to cold, then splashed my face with it until I felt more like myself. I tried to forget where I was for the moment, tried to let familiar motions take over my body. When I peered into Growl's bathroom cabinets for a toothbrush, I was greeted by the same emptiness that I'd encountered elsewhere in the house. There was a toothbrush and toothpaste, a razor, and deodorant. No cologne or other body care products. I put some toothpaste on my forefinger and used it to brush my teeth.

After that I turned to the shower, but hesitated in front of it, debating if I should risk getting naked. But the stench of blood still lingered on my skin, mingled with sweat and Growl's musky scent. I got out of my clothes. I wasn't safe anymore. I needed to take a shower, even if that meant lowering my guard. Sooner or later Growl would do whatever he wanted to do, and there was nothing I could do to stop him.

The shower stall was old but clean, the faucet creaky, and it took a long time for the water to turn moderately warm. I scrubbed my skin until it felt raw and hot, and would probably have continued to do so if a knock hadn't interrupted me.

"You've got two more minutes."

I turned the water off. Despite my first instinct to provoke Growl, I didn't want to risk him coming in. I quickly dried myself off and then opened the backpack. My breath hitched when I caught sight of my clothes. It was strange how little things suddenly meant so much.

I carefully took out a crème-colored cotton dress that hugged my body. I'd wanted to donate it because it wasn't in vogue anymore. Now it felt like the most precious thing I owned. I slid the soft fabric over my body and put on tights. Being dressed in my old clothes felt wrong in this place, like a relic from better times.

When I left the bathroom, Growl wasn't there, nor were his dogs.

I lingered in the hallway, unsure of what to do or where to go. The walls were grayish white like in my room, and the dark wood floor had seen better days.

The scent of coffee drifted over to me and eventually lured me into a big kitchen. Growl leaned against the kitchen counter, a cup of coffee in his hand and his dogs lying on blankets in a corner of the room. His gaze was directed at a message on his mobile. There weren't any chairs or a table. Apparently, Growl preferred to take his meals while standing.

He looked up and his eyes traveled the length of my body, lingering on my legs and hips and breasts.

I forced myself to remain calm, to hide the nerves the heat of his gaze created.

He wore a tight white shirt that didn't manage to hide his muscles, nor the outlines of too many tattoos. My eyes drifted to the scar around his neck.

"Here," he said, pushing a cup of coffee over to me. "Drink."

"I prefer my coffee with milk," I said.

"No milk in the house. Black or nothing."

I took the cup, relishing the heat of it, and downed a few gulps of the hot liquid. His attention had returned to the cell on the kitchen counter again. "There are eggs in the fridge if you're hungry."

I stared at him. "Are you serious?" I asked, setting the cup down hard on the counter. "Yesterday Falcone gave me to you like a present and now you pretend like this is normal, like we can act normal around each other. Why don't you do us both a favor and let me go."

He was in front of me before I could react. I craned my neck to peer at his face. I was trapped between him and the kitchen. He grabbed me by the waist and hoisted me up on the counter, then pressed between my legs, bringing our faces close together. I held my breath, stunned by his sudden movement.

My heart was beating frantically against my ribcage, but I tried to hide my fear of him behind my hatred. His hand cradled the back of my head, keeping me in place and then his mouth came down on mine, his tongue sliding past my lips. I made a sound of protest but it was swallowed by Growl's mouth. He tasted of coffee, and the hint of toothpaste. His lips were soft, but not his kiss. His tongue claimed my mouth. The kiss was dominant, overwhelming.

I jerked my head back, panting, and glared at him. I hated him. Hated him for who he was, but worse, for what he'd made me feel. For the barest moment I'd allowed myself to drown in the kiss because it managed to make me forget everything, helped me drown out the sadness and fear and worry. And in that short instant, it had felt wondrous and good. So good that my body had tingled and I'd felt it in my fingertips and toes. Everywhere. It was wrong. God, so wrong. Like the man in front of me.

I wiped my mouth, and then just like that the tingling was gone and what was left was revulsion. "Don't touch me," I hissed. "Ever again."

He smiled humorlessly. "Why?"

"Because you repulse me. You are a monster and I don't want your hands on me, not when they're covered in blood."

—GROWL—

Emotions. I'd never quite understood them. Most people had too many, and showed them too willingly. Women especially seemed too unconcerned about showing that part of themselves. Cara was no different. Hate—it had been plain on her face.

She hated me.

Everyone did.

She feared me.

Everyone did.

I was used to that kind of reaction. I didn't care.

I wasn't a smart man, not even close to being as smart as her. I knew it, and maybe that made me smarter than most of Falcone's men. I knew my limitations, felt them every day and accepted them, but never let them stop me. But despite my lack of smarts, I knew that Cara wasn't really a reward for me. That wasn't why she'd been given to me. Of course, she was a reward, was the greatest gift someone like me could hope for, was more than someone as dark and dirty as me deserved, but that wasn't why Falcone had made her my gift.

This wasn't a reward *for me*, it was a punishment *for her* and her father. And of course, I was a true punishment. I knew that, and maybe I should have felt insulted, should have felt guilty, should have refused a gift like that, but I wasn't that kind of man, and that was why Falcone had chosen wisely.

I was the punishment no one deserved, least of all her. But now that I had her, Cara, my gift, I would never let her go. The kiss, it had given me a taste of what was to come, of Cara, and damn, she'd tasted sweet with a hint of bitterness from the coffee. Sweeter than any woman I'd kissed, but there hadn't been many and my last kiss was a long time ago. I didn't like to kiss the whores. Not because they took other men's cocks into their mouths, though that bothered me, too, if I was perfectly honest with myself, but mostly because it was too intimate. I'd never understood the value of kissing, when sex and a blow job brought quicker satisfaction, but since the first time I'd seen Cara's pink lips, I'd wondered how it would be to kiss her. In the beginning it had been a ridiculous fantasy, one that would never come true, but then it had become a possibility.

I stared down at her furious face, and the hard set of her lips. I wanted to kiss her again, taste her again, but I had learned to control my desires. The way she looked at me now reminded me of the first time we'd met, of the looks every woman in society gave me. I stepped back before my anger could get the better of me like it had last time. I didn't have time for another visit with Lola. And if I was being honest, it hadn't been as satisfying with her as usual.

I could take Cara. I wanted her. She was mine.

She was *mine*.

But I couldn't imagine treating her like I treated Lola. Not just because Cara wouldn't react the way I wanted, but also because I didn't like the idea of doing that to her. She was too precious. She was a present I was reluctant to unwrap.

I backed away from her and took up my phone again. Falcone wanted to see me in the afternoon. I doubted the man had a real job for me. He wanted to hear gruesome details of what I had done to Cara.

I glanced her way. She still sat on the counter where I'd put her, but she'd crossed her legs protectively and was watching me cautiously. Even like that, she managed to look graceful and ladylike, and absolutely out of place in my house.

Perhaps Falcone hadn't just meant to use me as a punishment for Cara. Perhaps he'd also hoped to put me in my place, to show me that despite my years of service, I still wasn't worthy.

chapter 10

—CARA—

My lips were still tingling from his kiss despite my disgust and anger toward Growl. He backed away slowly, with an expression I could not decipher. I hopped off the counter, wanting to get out of this compromising situation, and froze with fear when both dogs jumped up from where they'd been resting in the corner of the kitchen.

The only dog I'd had close contact with over the years had been Anastasia's Chihuahua that she'd bought after it became an essential fashion item according to the magazines she perused. But that dog had been the size of a guinea pig with teeth barely strong enough to scratch one's skin. These dogs, on the other hand, were monstrous in size and most likely character—like their master. I sucked in my breath and backed up against the counter again. There was nowhere else I could go, and the way they were watching me, they would probably follow me anyway. My heartbeat quickened and I seized up completely.

The dogs didn't move either but they looked tense, as if they were ready to lunge at me if I moved the wrong way. Growl gave me a look that made it clear he thought I'd lost my mind, but I didn't trust him when it came to judging the danger and monstrosity of his dogs.

"If you act scared, you'll make them suspicious," he said like I was a child.

I glared at him. His words only worsened my fear and made me tense up even more. Growl set down his coffee again and watched me like he was trying to figure something out. My own eyes darted between him and his dogs.

Growl stalked toward me, his arm coming my way. I flinched away, expecting a punch.

He looked frustrated as he froze with his arm in midair, and the lack of understanding on his face grew even stronger.

"What are you doing?" he rumbled, slowly lowering his muscled arm. There were more scratches on his upper arm, I noticed now. I was pretty sure they couldn't all have come from me. A red dot began spreading on his bandages slowly, and I grimaced. Growl lowered his gaze to his injured forearm and blew out a breath. "You are a lot of trouble," was all he said. He raised his eyes to mine. I couldn't read his expression.

"Maybe you should go see a doctor," I said instead of the nasty comeback I had in mind. So far Growl had been more civil than I'd thought possible, and I couldn't risk provoking him into a change of mood.

"I don't need doctors. I stitched the wound up myself. I've done it before. But you cut me pretty deep and I shouldn't move the arm so much."

I'd thought I'd barely left a mark on him with the knife from his reaction yesterday, but he was probably too careful to show the extent of his injury during a fight. Although, to call the short struggle between us a fight was laughable.

"Why did you shy back?" he asked. I'd hoped he'd forgotten about my reaction to his approach.

I shrugged and turned my attention back to the dogs watching us. They still hadn't moved from their spots at the end of the kitchen, except that the black one had sat down. "I thought you were going to hit me," I said eventually.

Silence followed, until I couldn't stand it anymore and lifted my gaze to find Growl staring at me with blatant confusion.

"Oh come on," I muttered, growing angry despite my best intentions not to provoke him, but his shock was ridiculous. "Don't act like that's impossible. I saw you yesterday. I saw you kill a man with your bare hands by twisting his neck."

"Where were you? I didn't see you anywhere."

"In the closet."

Growl nodded. "He was the enemy."

"And I'm not?"

For some reason he seemed closer than before, and his scent finally registered. Not of sweat and blood and death like last night, but fresh and musky. It seemed too normal for someone like him.

"No. Enemies need eliminating because they mean danger, and often death. You don't."

"I tried to kill you last night," I said indignantly.

He didn't say anything, and that was worse than an insult.

I crossed my arms. I was starting to tire of this conversation, of the situation, of everything. I closed my eyes but the moment I did, images from last night came back up, and I quickly opened them again.

I really wished Growl would stop watching me with that intent expression. He looked like an explorer who'd discovered a new species. "What's going to happen now?" I asked quietly.

"I have work to do, and you'll stay here and watch TV."

I laughed. Had he misunderstood me on purpose? "That's not what I meant. Will you keep me locked up here until I die or you grow tired of me?"

"I haven't given it much thought yet. I didn't know Falcone would give you to me or I would have made plans," he said.

Plans for my captivity, *how considerate*. "So what now?" Everything seemed so meaningless. My life had never been free. There had been rules and expectations, but now I had no choices at all.

"I will go to work and you will stay here."

I gave up. Either he couldn't or he didn't want to understand me. "Will you take them with you?" I nodded toward the dogs.

Growl shook his head. "They will stay here with you."

Their white teeth drew my attention toward them. "Are you sure they won't tear me apart?"

Growl turned to his dogs. "Coco, Bandit."

They didn't hesitate. They waggled toward him, then sat down and looked up at him in adoration. "They are well-trained," he explained. "You can come closer."

I nodded, but didn't move from my spot against the kitchen counter. The way they were panting, I got a good look at the size of their teeth.

He frowned. "You'll have to get used to them. You'll spend a lot of time with them in the future, and I won't always be around to help you."

The idea of him being helpful to me was ludicrous. I certainly wasn't eager for his presence.

"If you want to touch them, you should always give them the chance to smell you first. At least until they know you better. They are distrustful dogs. Most people haven't given them much reason to be trustful." He held his hand in front of Coco's, then Bandit's nose before he patted their heads. "If they move back, let them. Don't try to pet them if they don't want you to."

How was I supposed to know when they wanted to be petted? Not that I had any intention of touching them without good reason, or without Growl close by. They scared me. I couldn't help it. They looked like they knew how to tear things into shreds. Their many scars spoke of their hard past.

"They are fighting dogs, right?"

Growl nodded. "They both fought in many fights. They won most of them."

"I bet you won a lot of money with them then," I muttered, hoping he could hear my disgust. Why would people enjoy watching dogs tear each other apart? But I'd never understood the appeal of boxing matches either; the boxers, at least, chose to fight of their own free will.

He patted Coco and Bandit once more before he turned his full attention to me. "I never sent them into fights. I bought them when they were getting too old to win." His voice was gentler when he talked about his dogs, even though it still held the hard edge of a growl due to his injured vocal cords.

"Why?"

"Because they would have been killed and after what they went through, they deserve to live in peace for the rest of their lives."

Was there actually a flicker of kindness in this man? It seemed unlikely, but the way he took care of his dogs, I couldn't deny the possibility. Maybe he felt a connection with the dogs because they'd been forced into a life of violence. There wasn't much known about Growl's past, but nobody was born like that, nobody was born evil. Perhaps he, too, had been forced into this existence. Perhaps he'd never experienced a normal life.

It didn't justify his actions, but it was an explanation that helped me understand him better, and understanding was always the first step to a solution. If I wanted to get out of my horrible situation, I'd first have to find out more about my captor, even if that meant actually spending time with him.

"So you never bet in dog fights? I hear some people made millions with it." Looking at his shabby home, I was certain that he could use the money.

He shook his head. "I don't care about money and even if I did, I wouldn't want to win it by letting dogs tear each other apart."

This man was an enigma.

He gestured for me to come closer again. "Come. You need to get to know each other, and I don't have much time left."

I took a few hesitant steps closer and when neither dog stirred, I bridged the remaining distance between us.

"Get down on your knees," Growl ordered, and the words brought another image into my head that unsettled me even more than the dogs with their big teeth. I quickly shoved the memory away and crouched down.

Growl took my hand, startling me. I barely stopped myself from pulling away. His palm was callused and warm, not unpleasant. I held my breath when he positioned my hand in front of the light brown dog's muzzle. It sniffed, then wagged its tail mildly. Next Growl put my hand down on its back. "This is Coco. She's eight years old, and I've had her for two years." Coco seemed like too tame a name for a dog like that.

I ran my hand down the length of Coco's back. Her fur was soft and I marveled at the feel of the dog's muscles. She felt strong, even stronger than she looked. I could only imagine what a sight the dog had been in the fighting arena, and pity for her rose up in me again. Her brown eyes were curious and kind. I couldn't see a hint of aggression.

Growl took my hand again and held it out for the other dog, Bandit, to inspect. He too sniffed a few times, but he didn't wag his tail or react in any other way. He didn't seem to care much about my presence.

Growl shrugged. "He needs to get to know you better. Give him time." He let go of my hand, and I withdrew it quickly and rose back to my feet. This was too strange. Growl was acting like we were going to be some kind of family.

Growl stood as well, towering over me. "I need to go now." He grabbed his mobile from the kitchen counter and headed into the corridor.

"Are you meeting with Falcone?" I blurted, following him. The name stung like acid on my tongue.

Growl frowned over his shoulder at me. He didn't say anything.

"Can you ask him about my sister and mother?" I said, then added, "Please? I'm going crazy not knowing if they're okay."

"Falcone will either tell me or he won't. If I ask him, he will be more likely to keep it to himself because it's an additional piece of power."

"I need to know if they're okay," I repeated.

Growl nodded. "I took the dogs on a long walk this morning, so it's enough if you let them out into the yard around noon. I'll take them for a walk when I'm back," he said, then added, "Don't try anything. It won't do you or anyone else any good." He gave me an expectant look until I finally nodded, before he walked out and closed the door. A moment later I heard the sound of the lock and I was alone.

I approached the door, listening for the sound of his car driving away. Then I hesitated again. Perhaps this was a trick? Perhaps he just wanted to see if I'd try to run if given the chance. Perhaps he was even eager for a chance to punish me?

I blew out a breath and walked back into the kitchen, trying to ignore the dogs; they had returned to their blankets. There were no curtains in the house, so I had a clear view toward the driveway. Growl's car was gone, but I still couldn't believe that he'd actually left me to myself. My eyes began scanning the neighborhood for something out of the ordinary, but for me everything was. This area was born out of misery.

An old man sat on his porch across the street. He was watching me, or at least Growl's house. Had Growl paid him to keep an eye on the front door?

I backed away from the window and hurried to the back door that led out into the garden. When I put the handle down, it opened. Growl hadn't locked it. Since that man was too vigilant to leave his door unlocked by accident, this was either a trap or he knew I couldn't escape even if I tried. Both dogs appeared at my side, startling me. But they weren't interested in me. Instead they stormed into the garden and started chasing each other. I stepped outside and took a close look around. The only way to get over the high fence was if I used a chair or table to climb over it.

Since the kitchen was devoid of any such luxury as chairs, the garden furniture was my only option. Though the table didn't look stable enough to hold my weight, and the chairs were too low to give me a sufficient height advantage. When I tried to move the chairs, however, they wouldn't budge. I glanced at the ground and found them bolted to the concrete porch. Had Growl done that? But when? Last night while I was sleeping? I let out a sharp laugh, and sank down on one of the chairs. I couldn't stop laughing. The dogs stopped their game of chase and watched me, obviously unsettled by my laughter. I even scared myself with the sound. Every piece of furniture, even a weight bench, was bolted to the ground.

I fell silent and closed my eyes, then slowly let my head fall forward until it rested on my legs. I let the images from last night assault me, hoped that reliving them again would stop them from haunting me. It would take time, I knew that. Perhaps the horror would never go away.

Talia. Mother. What were they doing now?

I had no way to reach them, no way to tell them I was okay and to be strong. Maybe this was the worst, worse even than being Growl's prisoner. Something nudged my neck and I raised my head to find Coco standing very close to me, her warm dog breath ghosting over my face. At first I was afraid, but then I realized the dog was trying to console me. I didn't move, worried I'd startle her if I did. "Thank you," I whispered, though I felt silly talking to a dog. Coco trotted off to where Bandit was scratching at a spot near the fence.

I rose from the chair and glanced around once more, then moved closer to the fence for another check, but with the barbwire at the top, there was no way I could get over it. And what would I even do if I got over it? Where would I go?

I had no money, no ID, no mobile. Nothing. I had nothing. And there wasn't even someone I could run to. Father's parents had died when I was little and he didn't have any siblings, and Mother… Mother had never talked about her family. I supposed she'd run off to marry Father. Trish and Anastasia were out of the question as well. Their parents were loyal to Falcone. The moment they saw me, I'd be handed back to Growl.

I was completely alone until I found my mother and sister, and there was no way I could do it without Growl's help. I had no choice but to figure out a way to turn Growl to my side.

The couple started screaming at each other again. This area was so depressing, I wasn't sure how anyone could live here by choice. But most people probably didn't have a choice.

I headed back into the house before my mood could go on a further downward spiral. The dogs were still busy near the fence.

"Bandit, Coco, come here!" I called, and surprisingly they both obeyed my command without hesitation and ran inside. I closed the door and with a deep breath, turned around to face the house. It was bleak and almost felt like an enemy in itself. No decorations, no cozy furniture. This place was only meant for the barest needs. I took a look into the fridge but except for a carton of eggs and a few cans of Coke, that too was empty. I considered preparing an omelet, though I'd only done that once before. I wasn't really hungry anyway.

I returned to the living room and sank down on the sofa. A spring dug into my butt and the old thing squeaked under my weight. I'd never had to watch TV all day. I'd always been busy with school, friends and hobbies. I leaned back slowly. The only other items in the room were a TV, a TV board, which looked like Growl had found it on the side of the street, and a small table. There weren't any cabinets, pictures or anything else. Growl couldn't possibly spend a lot of time here.

I needed to figure out a way to get out of here as fast as possible.

I grabbed the remote from the table and turned the TV on. I zapped through the many channels, but there was nothing even remotely interesting on. I put the remote back down, letting the nature channel run in the background as I got back up to discover the remaining rooms, but I'd pretty much seen them all already. There was the bathroom, my room and Growl's. He hadn't locked it despite the weapons decorating his walls.

There wasn't even a single book in the house. Nor did I see a computer anywhere.

Frustrated, I settled back on the sofa and left with nothing else to do, I eventually fell asleep again.

The sound of the lock woke me and I jerked upright. Goose bumps covered my skin. The AC was simply turned too cold. I searched the room for a clock, but even that was missing.

It was still light outside, so I knew, at least, that it wasn't night.

The dogs yapped happily, and then Growl's steps sounded. He appeared in the doorway, scanning the room quickly before giving me a once-over.

"Everything okay?" he asked suspiciously.

"No," I said. What a stupid question.

Growl held up a milk carton. "For your coffee."

My lips parted. "Uh, thanks?"

We stared at each other. He seemed as unsure about the situation as I was. I began rubbing some warmth into my arms. "Cold?"

I nodded. He went away and the AC stopped blowing cold air into the room. Why was he being this way? It made me suspicious of his motives.

"Any news?" I asked when he came back.

His expression tightened. He turned around and headed down the corridor toward the kitchen. I pushed off the sofa to rush after him. He stood in front of the open fridge. "You haven't eaten anything."

Was he daft? "I'm not hungry." That was a lie. "What about my question? You met with Falcone—did he say something about my mother or sister?"

"You need to eat," Growl said. "Starving yourself won't change a thing."

"I don't care! Answer my question, goddammit!"

Bandit let out a low rumble, but Growl silenced him with a movement of his hand.

I stiffened. "Not dangerous, hm?"

"What do you expect when you're screaming at their owner?"

"Come on, it's not like I'm a danger to you," I said mockingly.

He glanced down at his bandaged arm, then shrugged. "You're not, but you're being disrespectful."

"You don't deserve my respect."

Growl closed the fridge, tilting his head to watch me. Again I could tell that he didn't know what to do with me. "I'm going to order pizza. I haven't had anything for lunch. What kind of pizza do you want?"

I crossed my arms and leaned against the doorframe. "I'm not going to eat anything until you answer my question."

"And I'm not going to answer until you eat something."

"Does that mean you know more?"

"I do," he said simply.

chapter 11

—CARA—

My fingers shook at the prospect of news about my mother and sister. "Okay. I'll eat the pizza. Just tell me what you know."

"What kind?"

I blew out a breath in exasperation, but I couldn't lose it again or he might decide to tell me nothing. "Tuna and onions, I suppose."

Growl picked up the phone and ordered pizza for six p.m. That left more than one hour.

He must have seen the dismay in my expression because he said, "Coco and Bandit need walking. If you come along, I'll tell you everything I know."

I nodded eagerly, and since the only pair of shoes Growl had brought in my backpack were my running shoes, I was equipped perfectly. The moment we stepped out, I realized how trapped I'd felt inside that house. Growl didn't bother putting his dogs on a leash. They began sniffing the local shrubs as Growl and I walked side by side. It felt strange. I'd been with him for almost twenty-four hours, and so far he'd been far more decent to me than I'd have expected. But I had a feeling that had more to do with the fact that I confused him than with mercy or pity. "So?" I began, when it became obvious that Growl enjoyed the quiet of the walk.

"Falcone seems to be content with the punishment he's inflicted on your family so far. With your father dead, and you with me, he sees no necessity to punish your mother and sister at the moment."

"So my mother and sister are all right?" I asked in relief, pushing aside the memories of my father's death.

"For now," Growl said matter-of-factly.

"Where are they?"

"Your mother is in your old house. I'm not sure where your sister is."

"What do you mean, you're not sure? What happened to her? How can you be sure Falcone didn't hurt her if you don't know any details? What if he gave her to someone as a gift?"

Like he did with me, I added in my mind. I wanted to be there to protect her. It was my job to do so.

"Falcone hasn't been very forthcoming with information today. After your father's betrayal he's even more cautious. But he has some kind of plan, and it seems to require that your sister and mother are well."

"But—"

"No," Growl said firmly. "That's enough. I told you what I know." His brows drew together and he shook his head, more to himself than to me. I still marveled at how tall he was, towering a head over me. My eyes traced his muscled arms, inked from his wrists up to the edge of his T-shirt and beyond. Especially the skull and the snake baring its teeth gave me the creeps. I wondered how much more of his body was covered like that.

"We should keep going or we'll miss the pizza," Growl said.

My eyes shot up to his face. How long had I been staring at him again? His jaw was tight, his eyes filled with a fire that made me nervous.

I quickly walked ahead, and he fell into step beside me shortly after. We didn't talk again.

—GROWL—

I staggered into the yard toward my fitness area. I needed to let off some steam and my workout was due anyway.

Something was fucking wrong with me. I had Cara in my house. I was allowed to do with her whatever I wanted, and what had I done so far? Nothing. Something about her made me incapable of just grabbing her and having my fucking way with her.

I'd never forced a woman to sleep with me. Perhaps that was it. I liked it when they fought me, when they bit and scratched and sometimes even screamed, but not because they didn't want it—because they did. I had no trouble hurting people, hurting women, but that was different. That was my job. And I enjoyed it. There was no denying it. But sex was something else. I didn't want to force a woman. I wanted the woman to want me.

Of course, many of the whores I'd had in the past probably hadn't really wanted me either, but they'd done it by choice because they wanted the money. I could live with that. And Lola, she definitely liked me more than her other johns.

I sighed and put more weight on the barbell. With a grunt, I pressed it up.

The worst was the way I'd caught Cara looking at me today. She liked the sight of my muscles. I was fairly sure she was attracted to me on some base level. Yet she hated me, too, and that was stronger than any desire she might feel for me.

Fuck, I wanted her. The door creaked and Cara stepped out onto the porch.

When she noticed me doing my workout, her eyes widened a tad, then they traveled the length of me before she caught herself and looked somewhere else.

I groaned inwardly.

I wasn't one for games. Or for analyzing the subtleties of a woman's behavior. This was giving me a fucking headache.

Her gaze settled on the porch table. "Did you bolt it to the ground so I couldn't use it to get over the fence?"

How did she come up with that kind of logic? "No," I said, putting the barbell into the holder. "I didn't know you'd live with me. Did you want to use it to get over the fence?" I'd suspected she might try to escape. I'd also known that she wouldn't succeed.

"Why are there no tables or chairs in your kitchen?" she asked. "And why are there no books?"

Why, why, why. Why did she always have to ask questions?

I got up from the bench and stretched my arms. Again. That look. Fuck it. I crossed the distance between us and pressed her against the wall. Her squeak of surprise was silenced by my mouth. I plunged my tongue into her mouth, relishing in the fucking sweet taste of her. She shivered against me. That wasn't only fear. Fuck. She was attracted to me. I knew it. I kissed her harder, fucking tasting every corner of that pure mouth. Her nipples rubbed against my chest through our clothing. I wanted to pinch and suck them. I wanted to eat her pussy, have her juices on my face. I wanted all of her. Her kiss was unpracticed, hesitant, but mine wasn't. I didn't give her time to consider, to doubt. I slid my hand below her skirt and pressed my palm against her crotch. Even through her panties and her tights I could feel the heat radiating off her pussy.

She tensed but didn't push me away. I pressed a finger between her folds, rubbing her clit through the fabric, and she moaned into my mouth, then stiffened again. Her wetness was starting to soak her tights, and my cock sprang to life. Fuck. I wanted to take her right here on the porch until she screamed my name.

Her palms started pushing against my chest and she tore her mouth away from my lips. "Stop it!" she gasped, then firmer, "Stop it!" She shoved me hard, and I yielded, taking a step back and dropping my hand from her pussy. Her eyes were dazed. She glanced at my cock straining against my pants, then at the neighboring houses, and flushed an even darker shade of red. She whirled around and stumbled into the house.

I let her, even though it was one of the hardest things I'd ever done. I stared down at my bulge, then I lifted my finger to my mouth and licked her taste off. Fucking sweet and salty. Cara's body responded; only her fucking mind was still messing things up. I knew now that she'd been wet for me, there was no way I would be able to keep my hands to myself. I wanted to taste her, wanted to make her body overrule her mind. I would give her a good lick, make her come hard, until she was soaking, and then I'd have her.

—CARA—

I didn't stop running until I'd closed the door to my room behind me. What had I done? What had I let Growl do? God. My heart was pulsating wildly in my chest. I could feel the thud, thud even between my legs. I covered my eyes with my hand and took a deep, shuddering breath. I'd never felt this unhinged before. But being driven by instincts, my mind had been blissfully silent.

I'd wanted to feel his fingers so desperately, even through the fabric the touch had ignited me. Why did my body do that to me? I hated Growl and yet my body responded to him. He wasn't poster boy pretty. He was edgy and dark and scarred.

And my body wanted him because of it.

I shuddered, dropped my hand and staggered to my bed, where I let myself fall. Being near Growl felt like falling, too.

Part of me wanted to return to the yard and let Growl finish what he'd started. I could regret my actions later, could perhaps even convince myself to blame Growl for everything. Maybe this was some kind of Stockholm syndrome?

Did that work for sexual attraction as well? I gasped out a laugh. I was losing my mind.

The throbbing between my legs still hadn't stopped. If possible, it had gotten even worse. I put my hand on my lower belly, then stopped. This wasn't right. Even just fantasizing about someone like Growl was wrong, and touching myself while doing it? Surely that was a sin.

My mother would never forgive me.

I curled my hand into a fist on my stomach. I'd be strong. I wouldn't let my body dictate my actions. I was better than that.

The next two mornings I didn't want to face Growl and waited until I heard him leave the house before I walked out of my room. I couldn't hide forever, but my embarrassment was still too fresh. At least he didn't seek out my company.

As usual, I first checked the front door and windows to find them locked. The dogs lay in their beds, wagging their tails half-heartedly as I passed them. I considered patting them, but I didn't dare without Growl close by. Which was kind of amusing, considering that not too long ago I'd considered him the most dangerous thing in my life. And he probably still was. I headed to my usual spot on the sofa and startled at the sight of six books neatly stacked on top of the living-room table. I didn't know any of the authors, but it was a mix of romances and thrillers. I lowered myself to the sofa, stunned by Growl's consideration. I was more confused than ever. Why was he treating me with respect? I picked up the book at the top and began reading, trying to immerse myself in another world and silence my thoughts.

When he returned in the evening, he brought pizza again and put it down on the living-room table next to my new books. My face burnt with shame when his gaze finally settled on me. He looked completely unaffected by my obvious embarrassment over our last encounter. "Thanks for the books," I said.

He nodded and settled on the sofa before he opened the pizza carton and grabbed a piece. The spicy scent wafted over to me and reminded me that I hadn't eaten since the morning. Growl had stocked the kitchen with a few more essentials since I'd moved in.

"Have you found out more about my sister?" I asked.

A few times as we ate I caught myself staring at his long fingers, remembering how it had felt to have them on my body.

I needed to stop this madness. Focus on something else, I told myself, and finally I settled for his scar. My eyes traced the angry red line around his throat. It was jagged, as if they had used a saw-toothed knife. How could someone survive something like that? It seemed impossible. I couldn't imagine how it must have felt to have the blood drain out of you. I shivered. There were so many rumors about how it had happened, and even more about how he'd survived.

I suspected that many of them were the foundation for Growl's notorious reputation. Why was he alive? A wound like that, a cut throat, always meant death. Why had someone like him, someone who didn't deserve to live, survived, while others died from less? It seemed unfair and cruel. Maybe it was stupid of me to expect life to be fair, to give everyone what they deserved.

I tore my gaze away, afraid he'd notice it and get angry. But he was probably used to the staring by now. Wherever he went people watched in awe and fear. I doubted he enjoyed the attention—so different from his boss. I'd seen the pride and delight on Falcone's face whenever people shied away from his most feared assassin.

"Eat," Growl rasped.

I jumped and again my eyes found his throat. This was my chance to get answers, to find out if there was a sliver of truth to the rumors my friends and I had whispered to each other in hushed voices. My chance to figure out the man in front of me, and how to influence him. Yet I wasn't sure if I wanted to find out more about him. People fear what they don't know—that was a quote I knew to be true, but I had a feeling that not knowing was a blessing when it came to the man in front of me. With every layer that I peeled off, more horrors would be exposed.

"Ask or stop looking," he said. He didn't sound angry.

I glared. I wanted to ask and at the same time didn't. Not when he had almost ordered me to, but then my curiosity won. "What happened to you?"

Growl pushed another piece of pizza into his mouth and chewed slowly. He swallowed then looked at me. His amber eyes held no emotions, but his strong jaw was set tight. "Someone wanted me dead, cut my throat," he replied in a monotone rasp. "But I survived."

I stared. That wasn't an answer, at least not one that allowed me to find out more about Growl. It was generic and emotionless, but it showed me something. That I'd found a topic Growl was uncomfortable with.

He nodded toward my untouched pizza. "Either you eat or I'll feed it to the dogs."

I was too hungry to give the pizza to the dogs out of spite, and so I started eating.

Afterward, Growl went outside again to work out, and I decided to hide in my room. I didn't want to risk something like last time, but I couldn't restrain myself very long and peeked out of the window into the yard. Growl was covered in sweat as he pushed two massive dumbbells over his head, face scrunched up with strain. His upper arms bulged, his chest tensed.

I let out a breath and quickly slipped into bed.

chapter 12

—GROWL—

I knew she'd been watching me from her room. I'd seen her at the window. This was eating away at my control. I couldn't think about anything but her body anymore, about her taste—mouth and pussy.

I returned into the house after an hour-long intense workout, but I still didn't feel like I'd calmed down. I went to the bathroom and grabbed a towel to wipe my sweat off.

A sound caught my attention, so I walked closer to Cara's room. The noise was coming from inside. It sounded like she was moaning.

I lowered the towel slowly, my groin tightening. I moved closer and put my ear to the door. Again, a moan, low and drawn out. I closed my eyes. She was touching herself because of me. I had no doubt about it.

Fuck. I could feel myself hardening at the mere idea of what was going on behind that closed door.

Why was I even still standing here? I grabbed the handle and pushed the door open. I made sure to be as quiet as possible. I didn't want her to notice me right away I peered inside, and couldn't believe my eyes. She wasn't even awake. Her eyes were closed and her breathing too low. I stepped inside as I watched one of her hands move between her legs.

Her lips were slightly parted and another moan slipped out. I dropped the towel and approached the bed. Fuck, I wasn't a good man, not even a decent one, and she was making this damn hard for me. I could practically smell her arousal, or my mind was already starting to trick me.

I perched on the bed, careful not to wake her. But I needn't have worried. She was lost in her dream. She writhed then parted her legs under the blanket. I stifled a groan at the sight. I took the edge of the blanket and slowly pulled it down to her knees. She was wearing a nightgown that had slipped up to her hips, laying her pussy bare to me. I drew in a deep breath as I watched one of her slender fingers slowly slide over her lower lips.

It was the first time I'd seen her pussy. She wasn't clean-shaven like the whores I'd had in the past. She trimmed herself, but soft brown hair covered her mound. My cock was so hard, I was surprised I hadn't exploded yet. Perhaps this would be the first time I would come in my pants. She mewled again, needy, but her own touch didn't seem to get her where she wanted to go. I could tell that her touch wasn't practiced. Damn it. I was tired of resisting when it was so obvious that she wanted me as much as I wanted her.

I leaned over her, letting her heady scent flood my nose. I took a long lick over her swollen pussy lips, and her taste was so sweet, it drove me completely crazy. She shuddered and moaned loudly. I couldn't take anymore. I pushed her hand away and slipped my tongue between her folds. I licked her tight hole, lapping up her juices, and slowly traveled up to the small nub at the top. She moaned and then tensed. She was awake, but I was determined not to let her mind get the better of her. I drew her clit into my mouth, and sucked in a gentle rhythm. My tongue nudged her clit as I suckled, and she quivered.

She inhaled sharply. The tension in her body remained, but she didn't push me away or say anything. She was conflicted—I could tell. I used all my skills to convince her. I let her clit slide out from between my lips and drew soft circles with my tongue before I licked my way back down to her tight channel again. I dipped in. She was slick with arousal. Hot and willing.

"We can't do this," she said shakily, but there was hardly any conviction in her voice, and that was all I needed. I licked her harder, dipped my tongue into her, then suckled her clit again. She cried out, and like that she came already, flooding my mouth with her sweetness. I didn't stop. This had only been the first battle. I kept licking then fucked her with my tongue again. I didn't give her time to recover. I slipped a finger into her. She was so wet, I was met with barely any resistance.

My cock was almost raw from rubbing against my pants, but I needed more time for her. I needed to prepare her for what was to come. This time there was no stopping.

—CARA—

I could hardly breathe. My body was burning up, my pulse speeding. Everything felt so incredibly intense. Growl was practically buried in my lap, licking and kissing and sucking. I was so close to my second orgasm. His hand snaked under my nightgown and up to my breast. His fingers closed around my nipple and twisted, and just like that another wave crashed over me, even harder than before. What was happening? I couldn't grasp a clear thought.

I hardly noticed him getting out of his clothes and only realized what was going to happen when he crouched over me. I wasn't ready for this, would never be. I needed to stop him, needed to end this before everything was too late.

He climbed between my legs, parting them. His eyes held mine. I couldn't move, couldn't say or do anything. I'd feared this moment when Falcone had gifted me to Growl and now it was happening, but so different from how I'd imagined it.

And then he started pushing into me, and I clung to him tightly, my fingers gouging the inked skin of his upper arms. He was tearing me apart. He didn't slow, didn't stop. But he watched my face. Laid me bare with his gaze in so many ways. Wasn't it enough that I was lying naked beneath him? Did he have to strip away the wards over my soul, did he have to make me feel even more vulnerable than I already was? I gasped. It hurt. In so many ways. Was this how losing yourself felt?

My body yielded, and yet I was tearing apart. Not physically, though I wished my inner tumult would manifest in a physical way. Pain wasn't enough. Not this pain, not when it mingled with hints of pleasure. I wanted to lower my eyelids, wanted to black out the world around and the man above me but I kept my eyes open, kept looking up into that striking face of my captor, my owner, and now lover. Hatred should have been at the forefront of my mind, but it wasn't. It was still there, still strong, but it was battling with other emotions. Emotions I didn't want to feel. Compassion and understanding. Gratefulness for his almost kindness and even hints of pity.

With every thrust, Growl seemed to rip a piece of me away. I wasn't just losing my innocence; I seemed to be losing parts of myself.

Then stop him. Do it, as long as there's still something left of you. My nails buried deeper into Growl's arms and he grunted, eyes flashing with pleasure. He was enjoying it. And in turn my own body hummed with delight. He never slowed, never took his eyes off me. His muscled chest glistened with sweat. Pain gave way to something warmer, something that thrilled through my body stronger than any sting could. I drew my fingers up to Growl's shoulders, scratching, leaving a red path along my way, and relishing in it, and in the droplets of blood that dotted the spot where I'd clung to him.

Growl began shaking, head falling forward, and he let out a groan before he dropped to the mattress beside me.

Red half-moon-shaped marks littered his arms, proof of what had happened. Not proof of a struggle, of resistance, of a fight. Not proof of what should have been. I couldn't draw consolation from those marks. They weren't signs of my unwillingness, of a brave struggle against Growl's taking of me. No, I'd let him conquer me, had relished it even. What was wrong with me? How could I have let it happen?

I could only imagine what Trish and Anastasia would say if they saw me now. They'd be shocked and disgusted, and they would talk about it for days. But they didn't matter, not anymore.

Mother and Talia did, and they *would* judge me just as well if they knew. How could they not? How could anyone not condemn me for what I'd allowed Growl to do?

Is this how losing myself feels? That question still ghosted around my brain, but now another question had been added to the mix, one that scared me even more. *How could you lose yourself if you never had the chance to find yourself?* I pushed the thought away, banished the myriad of thoughts crowding my brain. I couldn't take them anymore. Growl lay panting next to me. His face looked relaxed, blank, more so than ever before, as if through the carnal act of sex he'd managed to free himself, managed to banish whatever demons haunted him.

This wouldn't be the last time. And I wasn't horrified by the idea. Despite the soreness, and even pain that throbbed between my legs, I wanted it again. I allowed myself that moment of realization. The damage was done. I had nothing more to lose.

Growl sat up and swung his legs over the edge of the bed. I jerked into a sitting position as well. Was he already leaving after what we'd done?

Growl peered at me over his shoulder, and now his gaze on my naked skin didn't make my body hum with delight and triumph. I drew the blankets up over my chest, clinging to the crisp fabric like I'd clung to Growl's strong arms mere minutes before. I didn't voice my questions, didn't want to sound desperate and needy, especially when he was the last person I should need.

For a moment, we both seemed to be frozen, but then I averted my eyes under the power of my own shame, and Growl rose to his feet. From the corner of my eye, I watched him gather his clothes from the ground, but he didn't bother getting dressed. Instead he walked out and began to close the door but stopped. "There's something for the pain in the bathroom." He paused and I wondered if he'd say something else, but he just closed the door. I waited for his steps to fade away before I freed myself of the blankets and quickly slid out of bed. I couldn't bear being in it now. It was clammy with our sweat, and it smelled of sex. I stared down at the white of the sheets. At the sight of the small pink spot I let out a shaky breath. Betrayal came in so many shapes and forms. Sometimes it was a purposeful act, and sometimes it was something you let happen.

—GROWL—

I took several long swigs of cold water. Even now my body seemed to boil with lust. My orgasm hadn't diminished my desire for Cara one bit. Not because the sex hadn't been satisfying, though that was true, too. I'd had stronger orgasms, had had better sex, but whatever had happened between me and Cara had been the most intense thing I'd ever experienced. It didn't even make sense.

She wasn't someone who could sate my hunger, and she wasn't someone I'd have usually chosen to satisfy my desire, and yet right in this fucking second I couldn't imagine being with any other woman. I wanted Cara, wanted to see if I could draw her out of her shell, make her more forward and demanding. I wanted to release her hunger. She tried to hide it but tonight I'd caught glimpses of it, and I wanted more.

Before Cara, I'd been satisfied with what I had, with the cards I'd been dealt, but she made me want more and that wasn't exactly safe in this world.

What was she doing to me?

Cara's door opened and closed. Quietly. She didn't want me to hear, like so often when she crept through the house. But if my life had taught me anything, it was vigilance. There wasn't a sound that got past my hearing. Her steps were careful, and then they stopped and another door opened and closed. I took another gulp of water and was about to put it back into the fridge and go to bed, but then the shower sprang to life. She was taking a shower. I never showered right after sex. I liked the smell of it, and the sticky feeling. I liked being reminded of what I'd done. But women always liked things clean, at least women like Cara. The whores I usually dealt with, they showered too, of course, but that was for practical reasons. They couldn't go walking around stinking of their last john when their next client came along.

I tensed. Another sound disturbed the monotone sloshing of water. Sobbing. I pushed away from the kitchen counter and stalked into the corridor and stopped in front of the bathroom door. The sobbing was a low sound, meant to be drowned out by the shower. It wasn't meant for me. Cara was crying.

I reached for the door handle, my fingers clutching the cold metal until my bones ached from the pressure. I let go and stepped back. Why was she crying?

Anger surged through me, burning hotter than lust. I turned on my heel and stalked away from the sound of her tears, and I didn't stop until I was outside on the porch. Both dogs had followed after me and now watched me with curious eyes.

I curled my hands into fists and stared up at the night sky. I'd never found the sight calming or even inspiring. For me it had always looked too vast, too uncertain. Something I couldn't control or comprehend, not even begin to.

Cara, she, too, was like the night sky. As beautiful, there was no doubt about it.

I could *control* her, at least physically, but what went on behind that perfect face…that was completely out of my grasp. Her brain worked in ways mine would never be able to. I liked things simple. Uncomplicated. She was anything but. Comprehending her? That was something I would never manage.

My eyes found the door. If I went inside now, would she still be crying? "Fuck," I growled and kicked the ground. Both Coco and Bandit jumped back and eyed me warily. Anger was something I was familiar with, something I even found consoling. But tonight it didn't make me feel better. I was angry at her but I couldn't unleash my fury on her. No, I *could*, but I didn't want to. And that made things worse.

She'd enjoyed herself. I'd seen her enjoy herself. Her body had responded to me. She'd moaned, had given herself over to pleasure. And now she was crying.

I was angry at myself, too. I shouldn't give a shit about her feelings. I'd heard people cry before, had heard them beg and scream in terror. What was one woman crying? Nothing. But it didn't lessen my anger. I kicked the ground again. Coco hid behind the chairs and Bandit backed even farther away from me.

I got down to my knees and made a soothing noise. My dogs had never been afraid of me. After a moment of hesitation, first Coco and then Bandit came toward me and pressed up to my body. I patted them for a long time, and finally some of the fire beneath my skin faded. That's why I preferred the company of dogs. They weren't complicated. They showed you what they were feeling.

I stood and returned into the house. I wouldn't let anything or anyone drive me out of my own home. Coco and Bandit followed me closely. I closed the terrace door, then listened. The shower wasn't running anymore. I waited another moment, but it was silent. No sobbing, no nothing. Coco left my side and trotted toward Cara's door, sniffing before she sat down. I sighed. Coco especially had taken to Cara, but even Bandit, who never liked anyone, seemed to enjoy the woman's presence.

I strode toward Coco and listened even more closely, but silence reigned behind the door. I grabbed the handle, and before I could stop myself, I pushed it down and opened the door. My eyes found the bed where Cara lay curled up, her legs pressed against her chest. Her face was turned away from me, and if I was being honest with myself, I was thankful for that fact. I didn't want to see her tearstained face. Her breathing was even, and she hadn't tensed when light had spilled in. She was truly asleep.

That didn't make me feel better. The sight shouldn't have made me feel anything at all.

chapter 13

—CARA—

I considered staying in my room, but it would have been stupid to do so. I hated myself for what had happened last night, but perhaps I could use it to my advantage. I wanted to get on Growl's good side, so he would help me and my family. Sleeping with him was perhaps the first step in the right direction, no matter how crazy it sounded.

When I walked into the kitchen, Growl wasn't there but the door to the yard was ajar. I stepped outside to find Growl sitting on one of the chairs, staring off into space. The dogs were at his feet, sprawled out on their sides, but they briefly glanced my way, their ears twitching. Growl's eyes turned to me, and my cheeks heated, but I returned his gaze.

There was a flicker of surprise on his face when I approached him. I sank down on the chair across from him, wincing slightly. Goose bumps erupted on my skin from the cold morning air.

"You all right?" he rumbled, brows drawing together

I nodded. "I'm fine," I said. I didn't want to discuss my soreness with Growl.

"There's coffee for you inside," Growl said. Then he rose and I thought he wanted to avoid me, but he returned a few minutes later with a cup of coffee. He'd put way too much milk in it, but I was glad for his consideration. I took a sip, then asked a question that had been bothering me for a while.

"What's your real name? Growl was given to you after that thing with your vocal cords."

"Was it?" he asked calmly.

I frowned. Suddenly unsure, but nobody was called Growl at birth. "Yes, because of how you sound."

"Growl," he repeated and hearing him say the name, it fit him even better.

"So what was your real name?"

"What does it matter?"

"I just want to know," I said quietly.

He stared off again, as if lost in the past. "I've been Growl for a long time. That other name, it doesn't matter anymore."

"Why do you say that? It's the name your mother chose for you."

"But the boy given that name doesn't exist anymore. He was erased forever."

"So you don't mind people calling you Growl? Isn't it frustrating to be reduced to that small part of you?"

"Growl is a name that scares people. It's the name that fits me now. It's a name that holds power and meaning because I worked hard."

"But isn't your old name better than a name that reminds you every day of what happened to you?" I wanted to ask him about the events, but he was already tense, and I had a feeling he wouldn't be very forthcoming with more information if I asked him now.

"I don't need a reminder. I won't ever forget. It's here." He pointed at the scar on his throat. "And here," he added, indicating his temple.

I could only imagine what kind of images haunted him at night. Perhaps that was why he could handle his own actions so easily, because the horrors of his past overshadowed anything else. We sat in silence for a while, each lost in our own thoughts until Growl had to leave to do Falcone's biding.

He appeared eager when he returned home that night. I put down my book on the coffee table. It was the third I'd finished so far. Growl immediately joined me in the living room, but he didn't sit down and stayed in the doorway instead. Always cautious not to get too close except when we were being intimate.

"I have news," he said calmly. "Falcone had a few drinks today, and that always gets him talking. He told me more about your sister. She's hidden away in one of his properties."

I sucked in a breath. "He didn't say where? And why is he hiding her? What does he want with her? What if they are hurting her?" I clutched my knees. The mere idea of my sister being hurt in any way tore at me.

Growl drew nearer, obviously uncomfortable with my distress. "I doubt it very much. Your sister is too valuable as leverage to hurt her. That's not to say that Falcone won't do it if he sees it as beneficial for his goal."

"I don't understand. What goals? What does it mean?"

"Falcone needs to control your mother. And he's threatening her with the possibility of doing to Talia what he did to you. Giving her to someone who would hurt her. Your mother isn't in a good state of mind right now. Apparently she feels guilty because of what happened to you and would do anything to protect your sister when she couldn't protect you."

"It's not her fault."

Growl smirked in a twisted way. Perhaps because we talked about him like he was a curse, but to be honest, that was exactly why Falcone had given me to him—because everybody feared Growl.

"What I don't get is how my mother could be useful to Falcone in any way. She's never been involved in Father's business. She's always just been a housewife. The only thing she knows is how to organize a dinner party and where to buy the best shoes."

I cringed at how horrible that sounded but it was the truth. I couldn't see how Falcone could use either of those things.

"Your mother doesn't have to know anything about business. Her blood is what matters."

I froze. "What do you mean?"

Growl searched my face as if he couldn't believe I didn't know. "Your mother isn't from Vegas. She was born in New York, but ran off with your father."

I'd suspected that Mother had run off with Father. She'd hinted at something like that. But New York? I thought back to the few times I'd talked about New York with my mother. She had always avoided the topic. I had never given it much thought, but it all made sense now. And yet it still didn't explain why that made her an asset for Falcone.

I peered up at Growl, more confused than ever.

"Do you know who Salvatore Vitiello was?" he asked as he perched on the armrest of the sofa. The thing creaked under his weight.

Salvatore Vitiello? Everybody knew that man. Even people who had nothing to do with the mob knew who he was. His death had been all over the newspapers. "Of course. He was the head of the New York Famiglia. But he's dead now."

Growl nodded. "He is. And your mother is his sister."

My eyes grew wide in surprise. "My mother is related to the head of the New York Famiglia?"

"She is. I suppose she and her brother never got along very well, that was another reason why she left New York."

"Okay, but why would Falcone care if my mother was related to Salvatore Vitiello?"

"Because that means she's the aunt of the current head of the Famiglia, and that makes her the perfect contact person."

"I thought Las Vegas wants nothing to do with New York. They hate each other. That's what my father always said."

"That's true," Growl agreed. "Falcone wants the Famiglia dead, and the Chicago Outfit as well. But his power is waning. The Russians have grown too strong in Las Vegas. And now that Chicago and New York are working together, Falcone worries that the Russians will lose interest in those cities and focus all their energy on taking control over Las Vegas. If Falcone wants to hold his city, he needs the support of the other families. And that won't be easy. He's made a lot of enemies over the years."

I snorted. "I'm not surprised. He's a sadistic bastard, and never really cared about working together with anyone. Why should the Vitiellos even consider coming to the Camorra's aid?"

"Because of your mother. Apparently, Luca Vitiello is very family oriented. Or at least he's been since he married Aria. If your mother, as his aunt, contacts him and asks for help, Falcone's chances are much better than without her."

"Why hasn't Falcone asked my mother before? Why now?"

"Falcone has been trying to solve things on his own as he did in the past, but now that your father has betrayed him with the help of the Bratva, even Falcone realizes that he needs to do something soon or Las Vegas is lost."

"I say let the Bratva have the city. They can't possibly be any worse than Falcone. The city will be better off without the bastard."

"Perhaps," Growl said with a shrug. "But that's your answer. And as long as

Falcone hopes for New York's support and as long as your mother does as he says, she and your sister will be safe."

"But what if New York refuses to help Falcone?"

"Then Falcone will probably threaten to kill your mother and sister. That could change Luca Vitiello's mind. Though I doubt that he'll risk New York for an aunt he doesn't know only because Falcone threatens to kill her. Luca has almost as much blood on his hands as I do. He can make hard decisions."

"But if that happens, my mother and sister will die!"

"It's a possibility."

"And even if Luca agrees to help, Falcone will keep my mother as a prisoner and my sister as leverage. They won't be better off than me."

Growl's face tightened, but he nodded in agreement. "Their only chance is to escape from Las Vegas. If they go to New York, Luca will probably take them in. His wife will certainly convince him."

New York. That was the solution to everything.

"When can I see my mother? I want to talk to her to make sure she's doing okay."

Growl raised his eyebrows. "Do you think I lied to you? She's doing as well as possible considering everything, believe me."

"I do," I said. "But I need to see her. Please."

Growl sighed. "It's not that easy. Falcone keeps a close eye on her. He won't be happy if you go to her."

"There has to be a way," I said imploringly.

Growl shook his head. "I don't know why I'm even telling you all this. This could be treason. I'm working for Falcone."

"Or perhaps he figured you'd tell me and he hopes it'll make me easier to control. He can't truly believe you won't mention anything to me," I said. Growl looked doubtful. He was slipping away again. I wasn't sure how to bind him to me. The only time he'd let down his guard at all was when we'd had sex.

I scooted a bit closer to him, but I'd never had to use my body to get what I wanted. I could tell Growl hadn't stopped admiring my body from the moment he'd come in. He still wanted me, so last night hadn't been enough. If only I knew how to seduce him. I wasn't sure what to do at all. My body was definitely already imagining how it would be to feel his touch again. I tried not to let thoughts of appropriateness ruin this for me. But I'd always been taught to act reserved and like a lady. Seducing someone wasn't something my mother would have ever condoned. I faltered, my eyes tracing Growl's muscles straining against his thin T-shirt, then lower to his strong thighs bulging against his jeans. My belly filled with warmth at the sight. I had already slept with him. This was easy now, I tried to tell myself.

Growl must have seen something in my expression because he let out a low groan and pulled me toward him, claiming my mouth for a kiss. When he pulled away, he rasped, "Do you even know what you're doing?"

chapter 14

—CARA—

Did I know what I was doing? God, no, I didn't. The only thing I was sure of was that my body wanted him, had wanted him from the first moment we'd seen each other, and now I could justify my desire with something else. He was my only chance to get what I wanted, and if that required using my body to get it, I was willing to do so. He kissed me again, harder this time, and began tearing at my shirt. I wanted to protest but before I could he'd ripped it apart, leaving me in nothing but my bra. And then that was gone too, and he sucked my nipple into his mouth. I cried out in surprise, and barely had time to catch my breath when Growl staggered to his feet. Confusion shot through me. Was he leaving? Had I done something wrong? I'd thought he wanted me even more than I wanted him.

I peered up at him, feeling shame rise up in me, but then I saw him remove his shirt, revealing inch over inch of muscles and tattoos. My gaze dipped as his hands fumbled with his belt and shoved his pants down. His cock sprang free, already big and glistening at the tip. Warmth spread between my legs at the sight despite the soreness I was still feeling.

With his cock standing at attention, he moved closer. It was on eye level and I finally had an idea what he had in mind. Nerves fluttered in my stomach. I wasn't sure if I could do it and if I'd like it at all. Growl didn't give me much time for uncertainty though. He stopped right in front of me, his cock only a few inches from my face. He smelled clean, and part of me wondered how he would taste. Growl had seemingly enjoyed what he'd done to me yesterday, especially my taste. I peeked up at him again.

His hand raked through my hair and came to rest on the back of my head. He pushed me forward lightly until my lips brushed his tip. This was wrong, wasn't it? Growl saw nothing in me but a thing to give him pleasure. For a moment my instincts told me to lock my jaw, but then I let him slide into my mouth. He tasted slightly salty but not in a bad way.

Lust flashed in his eyes.

My own body flushed with elation, and a new wave of heat gathered between my legs. I shouldn't want, shouldn't enjoy this. This was wrong on so many levels but as Growl's movements became harder, as his length slid in and out of my mouth faster, my hands grabbed his butt on their own accord. His muscles flexed under my fingers, hard and unrelenting.

His thrusts became jerky, and then he released into me with a low groan. I had trouble swallowing around him, but he didn't stop pushing into me. He slowed gradually, still shuddering. His eyes met mine and I shivered at the possessiveness in them. I tried to pull back but his hands kept me in place. After a moment, he slid his length out of my mouth inch by inch. It was still hard but smaller than before. He took a step back, and my face became unbearably hot as shame washed over me at what he'd made me do, at what I'd done, even enjoyed doing. God. If my mother knew. If anyone knew. I knew what Trish and Anastasia would say about me. They'd call me a dirty slut. My conflicted emotions made me feel like I had a split personality.

Suddenly the taste of him made me feel dirty. I could hardly stop myself from spitting on the ground. Rough hands pulled me to my feet and flush against his body. Before I had a chance to react, he thrust his tongue into my mouth, tasting me, tasting himself.

My knees became weak as he explored my mouth. Didn't he mind tasting himself? I thought men would find it disgusting. He sucked my lower lip into his mouth, then released it. "Your mouth tastes fucking perfect with my cum in it," he growled.

Embarrassment washed over me again, but Growl knew no mercy. He unzipped my jeans, and shoved them and my panties down before he thrust a finger into me. I gasped first from discomfort, then something else, something incredible. He curled his finger deep in me, and I could feel nerve endings inside of me I'd never felt before. Growl added a second finger, then began sliding them in and out slowly, and I was ashamed at how easy his path was, wet and hot and eager. Giving him pleasure had turned me on. Was it normal to be that turned on by something so dirty? My forehead fell against his strong chest. I couldn't hold it up anymore, couldn't even stand on my own legs. The sensations held me in their stronghold. Growl's thumb flicked over my nub of nerves, again on the edge of almost being painful, and my whole body reverberated with desire.

A cry sat on the tip of my tongue but I bit it back, pressing my lips against Growl's chest, his skin hot and soft. I could control the sounds I made, but my body shook with the wave of sensations crashing over it. Everything was quiet except for Growl's and my rapid breathing. I swallowed, trying to make sense of what had just happened. But again Growl didn't give me time to ponder. He released me and I almost lost my balance.

"I'll order pizza. What do you want?" came his matter-of-fact question as he grabbed the phone.

I felt like someone had plunged me into cold water. Now that the pleasure was fading, guilt and shame and loneliness reared their ugly heads again. The brief moments of passion had made me forget what kind of arrangement this was, what kind of man Growl was. I was nothing more than his whore, cheaper than the ones Made Men usually used in Falcone's whorehouses, and unlike them I hadn't even pretended to enjoy what he was doing. *Stop it. You're doing what's necessary.*

I sank back down on the sofa. My legs were shaky and I felt drained, emotionally and physically. I needed to make a decision. Either I was going through with this and trying to make Growl trust me that way, or I'd have to figure out a way to get out of this situation without him. There was no other option.

"Cara?" Growl repeated. Hearing my name from his mouth always sent a shiver down my back. That voice, so deep and rough. "What do you want?"

I shrugged. I didn't care. Pizza was the last thing on my mind right now. It was obvious that Growl enjoyed being with me physically, but on an emotional level I wasn't getting anywhere. It seemed like he always withdrew after sex. As if he couldn't bear physical closeness after the actual act. I wasn't sure how to change that. The worst was that I actually wanted to be close to him. The physical intimacy of sex made me long for more afterward.

Growl sighed. "I'll get you tuna," he said. "You need to eat enough or you'll get sick."

At least he was concerned about my physical well-being in a way. Though he was probably only looking after his possession. "I don't think food will be the reason I'll get sick," I muttered.

Growl didn't say anything, but I thought perhaps he'd caught the hint. It was difficult to say since his eyes were always blank or guarded, and his expression just the same. He picked up his phone and ordered two pizzas, still stark naked. I couldn't stop myself from admiring his muscled butt. When he turned around, I could read the inked text over his breast for the first time. So far I'd always been too busy with other things. The huge black letters read "I shall bathe in the blood of my enemies and feast on their fear."

Martial words that crossed Growl's entire broad chest. Why had he chosen them? To remind himself of who he was? Perhaps it had something to do with how he'd gotten his scar, but I still wasn't sure how to breach the subject without making him close up completely. It was obvious that he didn't like to talk about the topic. Growl grabbed his pants from the floor and put them on. My own shirt was ripped, and I wasn't really in the mood to put on my tight-fitting jeans. "Do you have a shirt for me?"

For a moment Growl seemed stunned by the request, but then he went to his room and returned with a black T-shirt. He held it out to me with an almost hesitant expression. I took the shirt from him, then pulled it over my head. It reached my knees but it was very comfortable. I could feel Growl's eyes on me the entire time. If I wasn't mistaken, there was wistfulness on his face. Why? What was he thinking?

His expression turned blank again. I stifled a sigh and sank down on the sofa. Growl sat down beside me. Close enough that I could smell his musky scent mixed with sex, but without touching me.

"Why don't you buy kitchen furniture so we can eat there?" I asked when it became clear that he didn't mind sitting in absolute silence. His head had to be an incredibly exciting place considering how much time he spent there.

"I never needed it. I don't eat breakfast and I can drink coffee while standing. And we can sit in the living room," Growl said, pointing at the table in front of us.

"I know, but it would be more cozy to sit in the kitchen than in front of a TV with a table that's barely reaching our knees."

Growl shrugged. "I don't need much."

That was true.

"Don't you ever have guests?"

"I don't have guests."

"What about family?" I was treading dangerous ground, but it was time to find out more about the man who controlled my body in a scary way.

"I don't have a family."

But I did, and I needed to return to them. I couldn't imagine being without my family forever. The mere thought stung in my chest. I would do anything to save the family I had left. I moved a bit closer to Growl and pressed my hand against his chest.

Growl peered into my eyes, brows pulling together, then he glanced down at my hand. He seemed unsure how to react. I could see that he was uncomfortable from the way his shoulders tensed, but he didn't push me away.

"You never had a family?" I asked to distract myself from my worry over my own family, and the way my own body was springing back to life just from touching Growl's chest.

My fingers traced the many ridges on Growl's chest, scars of all shapes and textures, always finding new paths across his body. Tracing his muscles and scars was a good way to quiet my nervous mind. As long as my fingers remained in motion, my brain seemed to slow down.

"I had a mother," he said in a low voice.

My fingers froze over his collarbone, surprised by his words. I would have thought he'd avoid the topic. Did that mean he was beginning to trust me?

My gaze rose to his face, but he was looking up at the ceiling with an unreadable expression. He didn't want me to see his eyes, and that only made me more curious. "What happened to her?"

Silence reigned between us for a very long time and I began to worry I'd messed up my chance to gain Growl's trust, when he finally said, "She's dead."

"How?" I asked. Growl's hand went up to his throat but he didn't touch himself there. He seemed to avoid touching his throat altogether, not just the scar.

"The person who slit your throat killed her?" I risked a guess.

For a moment, Growl was silent, and he even seemed to have stopped breathing. "He did. He killed her right in front of me. Made me watch her bleed out. He cut her throat too. But first mine to punish her. He thought I'd die quickly, but my mother was dead within a minute and I kept living." He sounded almost sorry, as if he wished he'd died that day.

My mouth became dry. "What about your father? Where was he?"

"He's not dead." Why wasn't he answering my second question?

"I can't believe anyone would do this to an innocent boy." I traced the letters on his chest. These words, all the scary tattoos, everything began to make sense.

"I wasn't innocent, not even back then." His words rumbled in his chest—I could feel them against my palm.

"Why would you say that? How old were you back then?"

"Five."

God, how could anyone hurt a five-year-old like that? People called Growl a monster, even I thought of him like that, but whoever had almost killed Growl as a small boy was so much worse. "Everyone's innocent at that age. Nobody's born bad. You were so small. Why didn't you try to hunt down the person who did this to you? You're not the small boy of the past—you have connections and power now. I'm sure Falcone wouldn't have cared if you'd gone and avenged your mother."

A short laugh vibrated in his chest. It made the little hairs on my arms stand on end. "Falcone would care."

"Why? Is it someone he does business with?"

Growl met my gaze square on, and the look in his eyes made a horrid suspicion settle in my mind. But I couldn't be right...

"Falcone was the man who did all this," Growl said, motioning toward his throat.

I pulled my hand away from his chest. "So," I said slowly. It was difficult finding the right words, or any words, really. "Falcone killed your own mother and wanted to kill you too, and you decide to work for him?" I wanted to understand him, but how could I possibly understand something like that? This was so far from normal, it blew my mind.

Growl gave an almost imperceptible nod. His face was unmoved, but there was a flicker of something in his eyes I wouldn't have noticed a few days ago. I was becoming more perceptive and growing used to the small changes in his facial expressions.

"Why?" I whispered. Why would anyone want to work for such a man? Maybe something had been irrevocably damaged when Growl had to watch all that at such a young age. Part of me wanted to reach out to that damaged little boy and squeeze him into a tight hug and tell him everything would be okay. But for one, I wasn't sure if that boy was still hidden away somewhere inside of Growl, or if he'd shriveled with time and with the horrors he'd witnessed. And second, I knew I would be lying to that boy. Few things would be okay in Growl's life. That boy would be molded into a monster through abuse and cruelty. Perhaps it would have been better if he hadn't survived in the first place. Not only to spare him the horrors of his life, but also to save the many he'd tortured and killed for Falcone.

I'd given up on an answer from Growl when he said, "Because he's my father."

I sucked in a deep breath. "Falcone?" I asked because it seemed impossible. I didn't doubt Falcone had many mistresses beside his wife. A man like him couldn't be faithful. But it simply seemed impossible that word hadn't gotten out. That people didn't mention Falcone's name in one breath with Growl, the bastard. My eyes searched Growl's face, but if there was something of Falcone in his features, it remained hidden to me.

He nodded again. "That was one of the reasons why he wanted to get rid of me. And why he killed my mother. She threatened to tell people. Falcone doesn't let anyone threaten him."

"He killed your mother. The woman he had a child with," I said slowly.

Growl didn't react.

"How could he do that? What kind of monster would do something like that?" I winced, suddenly worried I'd gone too far. For some ridiculous reason, Growl was loyal to his cruel father.

"A monster like me," he murmured.

"Like father, like son?"

Growl shrugged. I could tell that he was done with our conversation, but I was way too agitated to let the topic drop so quickly. "Maybe you shouldn't take your father's horrible nature as an excuse to be a monster yourself. Maybe you should strive to be better."

He let out a low breath, which might have been a laugh, I wasn't sure.

"I'm not joking."

He rose to his feet. "I'm not a monster because of my father. I'm a monster because I chose to be."

I doubted that was the truth. He'd been a young boy when he'd experienced horrors even grown men could hardly imagine. "It's never too late to change and to make up for your mistakes."

Growl shook his head. "You're naïve if you think that's an option. I won't change. I don't want to. My life is good as it is."

"You're working for the man who killed your mother. I don't believe you can live with that."

"I have for a very long time."

"If I were you, I'd want to get revenge."

Growl smiled darkly. "But you aren't me. And you don't know me."

He turned around and left the room. A second later I heard the back door open and close.

He was right. I didn't know him. Yet. But today he'd handed me a few pieces of the puzzle that was him—and I was determined to get the remaining pieces as well.

chapter 15

—CARA—

I decided not to push Growl further regarding Falcone and what happened. I had a feeling that he would close up completely if I tried again too soon. At least he didn't seem angry enough about my questions to stop sleeping with me.

When we lay next to each other in my bed after Growl had driven me to three orgasms, my mind was racing for a way to make him stay with me. He usually left directly after we were done, giving me no chance to get to know him better. We didn't even touch afterward. Or hadn't so far, at least.

Now Growl's arm was lightly brushing mine. It wasn't by accident. Perhaps deep down he longed for closeness beyond sex?

His eyes were half closed and his breathing was already slowing. His muscled chest glistened with sweat. "What happened to my father after you took me to your house?" I asked.

Growl opened his eyes. "He was dead."

"I know," I whispered harshly. "That's not what I meant. Where is his body? What did you do with it?"

Growl turned his head toward me, frowning. "What does it matter? He's gone."

"People bury their dead for a reason. Because they need a place to feel connected to them, a place where they can go to say goodbye or talk to what remains of the people they love. It's what humans do."

Growl didn't seem to understand. "Maybe. I can't see how that helps."

"You don't have to understand," I said quietly. "Just accept it. I really need to know where my father's body is. I need to say goodbye to him to find peace."

"He was buried outside the city borders."

"Buried? So he wasn't dumped somewhere, or worse?"

"I wasn't there when they buried him. But it's what they told me."

"Do you know where it is? Can you take me?"

Growl let out a sigh. He sat up like I'd expected and swung his legs out of bed, turning his back to me. That, too, was covered with tattoos, thorns and roses, skulls and snakes, and intricate black letters that read "Pain," nothing else. There were more scars on his back, shoulders and neck.

"You have to move on."

I stifled my frustration. He simply couldn't understand. So many human emotions and habits were foreign to him. I pushed into a sitting position and scooted closer. I hoped it was a good sign that he hadn't gotten up yet. Perhaps something in him wanted to stay with me?

My fingertips grazed the strange round scars that littered his back and upper arms. They didn't look like gunshot wounds, more like someone had burned Growl. After a moment of hesitation, I asked quietly, "What are those?"

Growl peered over his shoulder, amber eyes softer. "Cigarette burns."

My fingers froze. He sounded so detached, as if we weren't talking about his body. "Who did this to you?"

"Perhaps I asked someone to do it to me," he said.

"Why would anyone ask for pain?"

"I like pain. Learned to like it over time."

"You like it?" I repeated, dropping my hand from his skin. Did he ask someone to burn him? Was he that messed up? The idea didn't sit well with me. Someone who did this to themselves would probably do much worse to others. Though the fact that surprised me was ridiculous. I knew what Growl was. More monster than man.

A corner of his mouth twitched in an almost smile. That small gesture managed to change his entire face, making him seem more approachable, less dangerous. But the usual hard line returned to his lips too quickly. "Not getting burned. I didn't ask for those scars," he said roughly. "When I was a kid, I wasn't into pain yet."

My eyes trailed over the many burn marks, counting almost a dozen. "Someone did this to you when you were a kid?" I paused, unsure about the next question. "Your mother?" That would at least explain why Growl didn't want to avenge her.

Growl shook his head. "She wasn't the best mother. She worked as a whore. Her addiction and job didn't really help with raising a kid, but she never beat me or hurt me physically."

I licked my lips. This was dangerous territory I was treading. My curiosity made me eager for more, but at the same time I was equally scared of the horrors I'd hear and what they would make me feel. With every piece of Growl's past and his character that I uncovered, it became more difficult to not feel compassion, and more. "Then who did?" I asked despite my worries.

"After my mother died and I was released from the hospital, Falcone gave me to one of his henchmen, Bud, who was responsible for one of the brothels. He was a pimp, really, and didn't want a kid around. But he couldn't give me away if he wanted to get in Falcone's good graces, and so he kept me. But he was a sadistic bastard and when he grew tired of beating the shit out of his whores, he liked to torture me."

"Why didn't Falcone stop him?" I shook my head. "I don't know why I'm even asking. The guy almost killed you. It's not like he's a decent human being, or anything close to that."

"He didn't kill me, though he could have. And he never actually touched me. He let one of his men cut my throat. And Bud always made sure that he beat and burnt me where nobody could see it."

"So you think Falcone didn't know what was going on?"

"The whores knew and they liked me. They could have told him about it."

"But he didn't do anything," I concluded.

Growl shrugged. "The beatings made me stronger. After a while, you don't experience pain like other people do. It becomes familiar, almost like a friend. You stop fearing it, and even like it."

That explained the tattoo on his back.

I moved so I could see his face and was stunned by the almost serene expression there. I hoped it was a perfect mask because if he was really this calm about the whole thing, there was little hope for him. When his eyes met mine, I saw a flicker, a crack in the flawless mask he'd built over time, and almost exhaled in relief. I put my chin down on his shoulder, bringing my face closer to his. "There are other things that make people strong, not just pain. It's horrible what happened to you. Someone should have protected you. All the people who stood by while you were tortured, they should rot in hell."

"You shouldn't care," Growl murmured.

"I know." I didn't say more. Did I really care? The man in front of me today didn't deserve my pity or help. He wasn't the helpless boy from long ago anymore. And yet part of me felt for him. I couldn't help it.

For several heartbeats we stared at each other, and unspoken words seemed to hang in the air between us. I was so close to breaking down Growl's walls, so close to gaining his trust.

"Bud's dead now. Got what he deserved," Growl said eventually.

It took me a moment to free myself from the strange connection I'd felt before. "Did you kill him?"

It was scary how easily the words left my lips, and how little impact they had on my conscience.

"When I was ten," Growl said with a hint of pride in his deep voice. Perhaps that should have made me uneasy—and maybe it would have, even though Bud had deserved to die, if the idea of getting deadly revenge on Falcone hadn't dominated my thoughts in the last couple of weeks.

"He'd beaten the shit out of a whore, but that didn't really do anything for him. Falcone hadn't given him the second brothel Bud wanted, and he needed to let off steam. When he came into my room, I knew he was out for blood. And I let him take it. He kicked me and beat me, and I let him but then I decided it was enough, and I fought back. I always had a Swiss knife in my pocket, and when he paused to light a cigarette and turned away from me, I slashed his hamstring in one clean cut."

My eyes grew wide.

"He screamed like a pig in the slaughterhouse. Didn't lose his balance like I'd hoped. Tried to kick me again, so I stabbed him in the upper thigh. Sliced his artery by chance. He bled out quickly. And I watched. I was still watching with the knife in my hand when one of the whores found me and ran away screaming. And I still stood there when Falcone arrived some time later. I was covered in blood from head to toe. Had stabbed the dead bastard a few more times to release some steam."

The images flashed up in my mind and with the blood came more pictures, images of my father and how he'd died. But I couldn't allow myself to dwell on that memory. It wouldn't help me, nor my mother or sister. "What did Falcone do? You killed one of his men. Shouldn't he have killed you?"

"No, he decided it was time to take me under his wings and show me what else I was capable of."

"To kill and maim and torture," I said quietly.

Growl's eyes were almost resigned. "That's all I can do. If there was ever more in me, it didn't survive."

He'd said similar words before. And I started to realize that he might be right.

"So Falcone taught you how to kill? When did you become his assassin?"

Growl thought about it for a moment. "I killed the second man a few months after I killed Bud. Falcone had told me the name of the guy who'd cut my throat and where I could find him."

"So he wanted you to kill the guy?"

"He didn't say it, but I went and killed him. Falcone told me that this was his gift to me and that I was never going to kill without his explicit permission again, and I never did."

"So you got revenge on the man who burned you and the man who cut your throat, but not the man who is the reason why these things happened?"

Growl was silent.

"He is the reason why you have this." I reached out to touch the scar on his throat, curious how it would feel, but Growl's hand shot out and his fingers curled around my wrist.

"Don't," he said quietly, warningly. His eyes were haunted as they fixed on me.

I wound out of his grip and put my hand back into my lap. "Why? It's not like I haven't touched your other scars." *And every inch of your body.*

"Don't," he repeated in a voice that made me shiver. "Nobody is allowed."

More questions lingered on the tip of my tongue, but Growl didn't give me a chance to voice any of them. He untangled himself from the blankets and got to his feet. "You should sleep." He walked out without looking back. Sighing, I lay back down. I didn't bother putting my nightgown back on. I was exhausted. Always exhausted. Worry kept me awake too many nights. I strained my ears, listening for Growl, and as usual I heard the creak of the back door and a few barks of the dogs before they fell silent again. Growl was a creature of habit. Maybe that was why the dogs were loyal to him. He gave them a hint of normalcy.

I shook my head in the darkness. Normalcy. My life had always been a good cry away from normal, but now?

Growl was more detached in the days that followed. I'd thought we'd finally made a true connection during our last conversation, but now he was pulling away again. He didn't want me close. And I wasn't sure how to change that. If he didn't trust me, how could I suggest that he help my mother and sister? What if he told Falcone everything? Then it would all be over. And yet part of me was sure he wouldn't tell Falcone about a single word we'd exchanged. Growl kept things to himself. He was that kind of guy.

He didn't even come to my bed at night anymore. He was really trying to stay away from me. Was he worried I'd get too close? Was that even a possibility with him?

"Falcone agreed to let you visit your mother," Growl said out of the blue while we were having coffee in silence one morning.

I almost dropped my cup. "Really? Why? Why now?"

"Apparently your mother is depressed and Falcone thinks that's why the negotiations with New York are going badly. I told him it would be good for your mother to see you were all right, so she'd have something to fight for."

I set the cup down on the counter and bridged the distance between us. I wrapped my arms around his middle and hugged him tightly, my cheeks pressed up against his chest. He tensed, then relaxed. We'd slept with each other several times, but this was the first time we actually hugged. I realized he never kissed or touched me if it wasn't meant to lead to sex.

"Thanks," I said, then pulled away and took a few steps back.

He was watching me with an odd expression. Was there longing in his eyes? God, why did he have to be so difficult to read?

"I will take you to her now on my way to work," Growl said.

I couldn't wait to see my sister again, but at the same time I was terrified of facing her after what I'd done in the last few weeks. I'd been sleeping with Growl, and not because he'd forced me, not even only because I hoped to gain his trust. I enjoyed it. There was no denying it. If my mother knew, she'd never look at me again.

Pulling up in front of my old home felt strange. It didn't feel like home anymore. Falcone and his men had ruined the place for me. My memory of the house I'd grown up in would forever be tainted with the blood and death of my father.

The windows hadn't been cleaned since I'd left. Water stains and dust covered them.

"I thought you'd be happy," Growl said as he led me to the front door.

I'd thought I'd be happy too, but I felt guilty and miserable and scared. I forced a smile, worried Growl might decide it was better not to let me visit my mother, if it made me sad. That was the last thing I wanted, even if setting foot into my old home made my stomach turn. "I am happy, just nervous."

Growl looked doubtful but he rang the bell anyway. It took a long time until finally one of our old bodyguards, Daryl, opened the door. So he was guarding my mother? Had he always been Falcone's spy? Probably. There was no loyalty in this world. Even my father had betrayed his boss for whatever reasons. Not that I didn't understand him.

The bodyguard stepped back, an expression of caution on his face as he watched Growl. I felt a sick satisfaction at his discomfort. *I* wasn't scared of Growl anymore.

Daryl gave me a nod, but I ignored him and quickly walked past him into the lobby. It was quiet in the house. Such a vast difference from the last time I'd been here.

"Cara?" came Mother's meek voice from the living room. I rushed off toward my mother and found her sitting at the living-room table, which was set for lunch. I hesitated in the middle of the room. My mother had lost weight. Her cheeks were sunken in, her cheekbones protruding. She wore no makeup. She always had. And her dress was crinkled as if she couldn't be bothered ironing it. Mother would have never worn a dress that hadn't been ironed. She'd changed. *I had changed.* It was ridiculous to think that my mother or sister wouldn't. God, Talia. How was she doing?

My mother rose from the chair and opened her arms. I didn't hesitate. I flew into her arms. It felt good to embrace her, to smell her comforting scent, even if she hadn't put on her usual perfume. Mother buried her face in my hair and took a deep breath. I closed my eyes, allowing myself a few moments of peace.

"I need to leave now."

Growl's voice sliced through the quiet. My mother and I stepped apart.

Mother glared at Growl with disgust and fear.

I nodded. "Okay."

"I will pick you up in two to three hours." There was a hint of warning in his voice. I didn't say anything. I wanted him gone, worried that Mother might notice something strange between us. I almost sighed in relief when he'd left.

Daryl was still in the room, though.

"Can you give my daughter and me some privacy?" Mother asked politely. She looked controlled now.

Daryl hesitated, but eventually he gave a terse nod. "I'm outside the door. Remember there are cameras."

Mother tilted her head, looking dignified, but the moment he closed the door, she grabbed the edge of the table and sank down on the chair. I pulled a chair up beside Mother and grabbed her hand.

She searched my face, then checked my arms as if she was looking for bruises. "I'd thought I wouldn't see you again. I was sure that monster would kill you."

"Growl?" I said. "He didn't hurt me."

Mother shook her head. "Don't lie to me. I know this world. I know the rules. I know more than I've let on in the past because I wanted to protect you and your sister." She let out a sad laugh. "I failed."

"You didn't fail. What could you have done? They were armed. We had no chance against them."

Mother touched my cheek, looking hopeless. "I wish I were stronger. I know I should ask what has happened to you, but I'm not sure I can bear the truth. You are so much stronger than I am, Cara. That you are here, looking healthy and unbroken…I can't fathom how that is even possible."

I smiled shakily. "I'm really fine, Mother. Please don't worry about me."

Mother closed her eyes and shook her head. "I don't know how you can even talk to me after what I did."

"What did you do?"

"I'm working for Falcone, helping him. After he gave you to that monster, I shouldn't help him, no matter what he threatens me with. If your father knew, he'd be disappointed. He wouldn't even look at me now."

"Father is the reason why this happened. He is the reason we went through hell. It was his punishment that we had to bear. If he were alive, he wouldn't have any right to judge you. He would have to apologize to us for being so selfish, and not thinking about the consequences!" It burst out of me. So far I hadn't allowed myself to be angry, but now I realized I was. I was furious because Father should have known better. It was his job to protect us, and *he'd failed*.

Mother watched me with widened eyes, uncomprehending. "Don't talk about your father like that. He was the best husband I could have imagined and an even better father. He deserves nothing but our respect."

That was a lie. Father hadn't been the worst father, but he had been a far cry from a good one. He'd been too busy with his work, and often too impatient to spend time with his two chatty daughters. I'd loved him, and I missed him. I wished he were still alive, and I'd forgiven him for what he'd done because he surely couldn't have fathomed where it would lead.

"I don't want to fight," I said quietly, squeezing Mother's hand. "I know you're grieving, but eventually you'll realize that Father did this to us."

Mother stared. She didn't protest again, but I could tell that she wasn't ready to admit Father's faults yet. His death was still too raw.

I decided to change the topic. "I know what you're doing, that you're talking to New York on Falcone's behalf."

"How?" Mother whispered.

"Growl told me. But that's not important. Are you making progress?"

Mother shook her head. "I haven't even talked to Luca Vitiello yet. It's difficult to get through to him. New York doesn't want anything to do with us." Mother touched her forehead. "I can't fail. If I do, Falcone will hurt your sister. I don't know what to do."

"Keep trying. There has to be a way to get through to Luca Vitiello. I'm sure."

Mother nodded. "Perhaps. I sent his wife a letter. I hear she's kind. She might be our last chance."

"Don't give up. We'll figure something out," I said firmly, trying to convey with my eyes that I was working on a plan.

Mother's brows drew together, but she didn't ask what I meant. She was a clever woman. We had to be careful what we said aloud.

She pointed at the sandwiches piled up on the étagère. "I made them myself. Something to keep myself busy. And I miss cooking for all of you."

I grabbed a salmon sandwich and took a bite, then smiled. "It's delicious."

Mother leaned back in her chair and watched me eat another sandwich. I swallowed the last bite, then asked, "I've been wondering, why did you even leave New York and your family? You were part of the leading family, after all. You could have led a great life there."

New York might be the enemy, but there was no way they could be worse than the Camorra.

Mother looked tired. "I was. But my brother was the Capo, and he was as bad as Falcone. Of course, back then I didn't know how cruelly Falcone ruled in Las Vegas, or perhaps I would have stayed in New York." Then she smiled sadly and shook her head. "Though I was head over heels in love with your father and would have followed him anywhere."

I touched her hand. "How did you two even meet if Father was one of Falcone's men? New York and Las Vegas hated each other back then too, didn't they?"

Mother nodded. "Oh yes, they did. But Falcone had only just been made boss, and his father still had some say in the city. And the old man wanted to try to make peace with New York, so they sent your father because he always knew how to be diplomatic. Falcone would have ruined everything if he'd tried to do the negotiations himself."

"But they didn't make a peace treaty, did they?"

"No. Salvatore and Falcone were too alike. They both wanted to have the last say, so nothing came of your father's visit in New York."

"You two fell in love."

"Yes, yes. In the three weeks that he was in town, he completely captured my heart. I begged my parents to let me marry him, but of course they refused, and Salvatore was furious that I'd even suggested such a horrible thing. He chose someone else for me, but I wanted nobody but Brando, and so your father took me home with him, and told Salvatore that he'd done it as revenge for insulting Falcone. I'm not sure if Falcone believed the story, but he was happy to taunt Salvatore like that, and so your father and I married two days after we'd left New York. The party was the story in every newspaper in Las Vegas and beyond. Peace was out of the question after that. Falcone got exactly what he wanted, and so did your father and I. It seemed like the perfect solution at the time."

"Do you think the head of the Famiglia, that Luca Vitiello, would allow us to stay in New York?" I asked in a bare whisper.

Mother touched my cheek. "I don't know. I only saw him and his brother once when they were small boys."

"You visited them? But I thought that was forbidden?"

"Oh, it was. But Salvatore's wife and I really liked each other. I always felt sorry for her because she had to marry my sadistic brother. And once, when I was pregnant with you, I was in Aspen at the same time as Salvatore's wife. She was there with the kids and so we met in secret. We'd been talking on the phone regularly, but that was the first time we met since I'd run off. It was wonderful.

And the boys were real cuties, though it was unmistakable that my brother was their father. They were too controlled and serious for boys that young. Especially Luca gave me the chills sometimes."

"Perhaps he will remember you and help us. It's our best chance."

"It is," she agreed, then her expression turned almost frightened. "Do you know where they took your father's body? I can't bear the thought that Falcone gave him to his dogs as food. It breaks my heart. He doesn't deserve that."

I patted her arm. "Growl told me that someone buried Father in the desert. They didn't feed him to the dogs."

Mother's shoulders sagged in relief.

But suddenly I wondered if Growl had told me the truth. There was no way I could know. I had to trust his word.

Time passed too fast with my mother and I reminiscing about old times, family vacations, wondrous memories that would never take place again.

When we heard Growl's car pull up in the driveway, Mother pulled me against her body and whispered in my ear, "You are such a good girl. I don't know how I deserve you. Be strong, sweetheart. Don't let that monster break you."

"I won't," I promised automatically. She watched me with love and pity, and I had to look away. If she knew, what I'd done and what I was doing...

I could never tell her.

chapter 16

—CARA—

I barely glanced Growl's way as we headed back to his house. He shot me a questioning look. "What's wrong?"

"Nothing," I said harshly, then bit my lip. I didn't know what to do. I needed Growl to be on my side, and my body wanted him, but I was going against everything my mother had taught me by sleeping with him.

Growl's hands on the steering wheel tightened, the tendons in his forearms flexing, but he didn't push the matter. I usually initiated our conversations, so it didn't come as a surprise that he accepted the tense silence between us.

I focused on the window, on the flashy neon signs advertising casinos and hotels. My mind was whirring with what I'd learned today about my mother's family, about *my* family. I needed Growl if I wanted any chance to help my mother and sister, if I wanted any chance to escape from Las Vegas and find shelter in New York, but I wasn't sure how to do it. Growl would never help me if it meant losing me, or his position as Enforcer of the Camorra. He was proud of his job. The only way he'd support me was if I promised to stay with him, and asked him only to help my sister and mother, but even that seemed unlikely.

I lay awake that night, staring up at the ceiling, when the door to my room creaked open. I knew why Growl was here, what he wanted, but I was so conflicted.

He prowled toward the bed, his tall frame backlit by the light from the corridor. He scanned my face and I only stared up at him, at his hard angles. He wasn't wearing a shirt, and my eyes traced the lines of his muscles, the way the light accentuated his six-pack. I wanted this man. Seeing him always made my body tingle, no matter how torn I was. My gaze lowered to the bulge in Growl's pants. God, why did I have to want him?

Something on my face must have showed my thoughts; Growl put one knee on the bed, which groaned under his weight. His breathing was low, controlled, but faster than usual. Aroused. He'd always been the more active participant in our sexual life, but I always reacted in some way. I could see frustration and confusion in his eyes, then he crawled toward me and hovered over my body. His warm smell enveloped me. I put my hands against his chest, torn between pushing him away and pulling him closer. My fingertips brushed over scars and his soft chest hair, over hard muscle.

Growl made the decision for me. He grabbed my hands in one of his and pressed them into the mattress above my head. Then he lowered his head to my breasts and sucked one nipple into his mouth through the silky fabric of my nightgown. I pressed my lips together, trying to keep a moan in, but that seemed to spur Growl on. He sucked harder as his free hand ran down my body between my legs. He shoved them apart, released my nipple and crawled down until his head hovered toward my panties. I knew I'd be putty in his hands if I let him pleasure me with his mouth. I struggled against his grip but his other hand came down on my hip, holding me fast. When his face was mere inches from my center, he drew in a deep breath. Heat rose into my cheeks like it always did when he did something like that. But despite my embarrassment, my body flooded with need for his touch, for his mouth.

Growl licked over my panties, and I stilled as my core tightened and my body began to tingle. I struggled even harder but Growl ignored me completely. He nudged my panties to the side with his nose and licked over my bare flesh.

He slid his tongue up and down, firm licks, over and over again. Wetness pooled between my legs. I hated my body for it, for always surrendering to him.

He dipped his tongue into my opening and let out a deep rumble. I squeezed my eyes shut, fighting my body's reaction, trying to hold in a moan. I wouldn't give him that satisfaction. But he didn't stop. He seemed to enjoy every moment of it. Every time he hummed, a stupid part of me was turned on. I still couldn't believe he liked how I tasted down there, but he obviously did.

He moved his tongue higher and licked over my clit. My hips bucked, but this time it wasn't in an attempt to get away. Growl kept a steady rhythm. I had no chance to resist him. My body was always eager for his touch. He must have felt my surrender because he let go of my hip and brought his hand down between my legs. He used his thumb and forefinger to part me, allowing his tongue even better access. I couldn't keep a loud moan from escaping.

Wrong, my head screamed. But I gave up resistance.

Again my hands found Growl's head, but then he curled his tongue in a way that made me cry out from the sensation.

Growl knew he had won. I could practically feel his smugness. His mouth closed over my center, plunging his tongue even deeper into me, and my fingers dug into his scalp as I pushed his head to where I needed him. My body started shaking, and Growl's tongue pressed even harder against my clit. My last resistance crumbled as a shockwave rolled over me, rendering me helpless and stunned

I wasn't sure how long I stayed like that. Growl dipped his tongue lower and my muscles clenched around him. I couldn't move, could hardly breathe, my heart pounding in my chest as I stared into the darkness. Shadows danced in the distant streetlights streaming through the window. Growl pressed another lingering kiss between my legs, then got to his knees.

He leaned over me and kissed my lips. I could taste myself on him, could smell myself. I sucked in a breath. "This is wrong," I said quietly. Was this betrayal? Being intimate like that with the enemy, with someone like Growl, with a monster—that was wrong on every level I could imagine. He had helped take my father down. He was part of why Father was dead now. And yet, here I was, sharing a bed with him and enjoying it.

"Stop overthinking every fucking thing," he murmured.

"You can't understand," I said harshly. For him, sin and guilt and shame weren't words that mattered.

"Perhaps," he admitted. "But I understand your body." He pressed two fingers against my wet center, swirled them around and brought them to his lips, licking them. "And your body likes it."

"You're disgusting," I said. I tried to turn away, to get away, but it was close to impossible with his body hovering above me. "Maybe my body reacts to you, but I will never feel anything but hatred for you, you monster." I closed my lips with a snap, unable to believe what I'd said. How could I tell him something like that if I wanted his help?

"I'm a monster, you got that right. Have always been, will always be. I'm good at being a monster. Few people ever find something they're good at, something they were meant to be," he said simply. He didn't sound angry, only resigned.

"That's crazy. Nobody's meant to be a killer. Nobody's meant to be like you. You want to be like that. You said you like blood and pain and death, and you pretending to have been born a monster is your excuse to justify the horrors you've committed."

"You're right. There's nothing better than the rush of the kill. It's exhilarating. It's you against them. It's all or nothing. Nothing in this world makes a person feel more alive than that. I like it. And I don't give a fuck about justifying anything to anyone. I'd do everything again. I regret nothing."

I swallowed. "I don't get it. How does anyone become like that? It can't all be because of that scar on your throat."

He got off the bed. "I have many scars, and they all made me the man I am today."

I searched his face for a hint of the humanness I'd seen before, but he looked so *other* in that moment. "That doesn't mean it can't be different. You act so strong and unbeatable, but you let your past and your supposed fate dictate your life. Why don't you fight for a better future?"

"For me there's no future."

"But there could be," I whispered.

Growl searched my face again. There was longing. He wanted more out of this life, even if he couldn't admit it to himself yet. "I didn't come to talk," he growled. He slid down his pants, and returned to the bed. His strong body covered mine as he moved between my legs. His tip slid over my wet entrance, and then he thrust into me in one swift move, filing me completely with his length. He groaned. I wrapped my legs around his hips as he began pounding into me. His mouth found mine, tongue plunging in, and he angled his thrusts higher, toward a spot that made my toes curl. I moaned against him. He slipped a hand between us, fingers reaching for my breast, thumb and forefinger pinching and twisting my nipple. Pain and pleasure mixed deliciously. I cried out, close to release. He sped up, our bodies slapping against each other. I scratched my nails down his back and he tensed with his release, taking me with him over the edge.

My cries were swallowed by his forceful kiss. His movements slowed but he kept kissing me. When he finally drew back, I was flushed and breathless. My legs dropped from his waist, heavy and limp. He pushed himself off me, leaving me no choice but to lower my arms from his back. He picked up his pants off the ground before he left without another word. The soft click of the door made me wince. I stared into the darkness. I could still feel him inside of me, was still throbbing with the remnants of my orgasm, but my chest felt empty.

I was too agitated to sleep and so I got up eventually. For some reason I needed to be close to Growl now.

It was silent inside the house when I stepped into the corridor. My slow breath felt like an intruder of the quiet. I headed toward Growl's bedroom, but the door was open and he wasn't inside.

Where was he? I crept through the darkness when my eyes registered a dim light spilling into the house from the backyard. I tried to move soundlessly as I approached the terrace door. Growl sat at the small shabby table. A half-burnt-down candle on a saucer hardly broke through the night but managed to cast eerie shadows across his face. The dogs were stretched out at his feet as usual. They didn't react. Either they hadn't noticed me, which didn't really qualify them as guard dogs, or they'd deemed me too uninteresting for a reaction. Growl looked lonely. In the short time I knew him I'd learned to read his expressions better, but I still didn't understand him.

He sought out my closeness, was trying to treat me right, even though he'd never learned how. Had anyone ever treated him right? Except for his mother, perhaps. I considered returning to my bedroom, but something kept me rooted to the spot.

"I know you're there," Growl said quietly.

I walked outside hesitantly. The cold bit at my skin, especially where

Growl's mouth had wetted my nightgown. He looked tired. "You should be sleeping," he said.

"You too."

"I can't," he admitted.

"Me neither."

We looked at each other. "Can I stay?"

Growl nodded. I took a step toward the free chair, then changed my mind and headed for Growl. His brows crinkled as he watched me. I crawled on his lap and put my head down on his shoulder. He smelled of sex, of us. He let out a low breath but didn't do anything else.

He was warm and strong. I drew in his scent that lingered beneath the sex. It didn't take long before my eyes felt heavy. When I was almost asleep, I felt Growl's fingers glide over my hair. Up and down. And then I drifted off.

I was back in my bed when I woke the next morning, and Growl was back to being his usual distant self when I entered the kitchen and grabbed the cup of coffee waiting for me.

"I will show you where they buried your father," Growl said without warning.

I froze. My throat tightened with emotions and most of my anger drained out of me. "You will?" My voice was shaky.

Growl nodded, eyes almost kind. "You should get the chance to say goodbye. If it'll make things easier."

I wasn't sure if that was true, if it would make things easier, but I was grateful anyway. His acts of kindness still surprised me. I wasn't sure what to make of the man in front of me. "Did you get the chance to say goodbye to your mother?"

Growl's expression became even more guarded. "I saw her die, and that's when I said goodbye. After that, they cut my throat, and I had to fight for my life."

I flushed. Of course. He'd been a small boy who'd suffered horribly. It was hard to imagine Growl as anything but the powerful and cruel man in front of me. That he had once been an innocent boy was easy to forget.

I changed the subject. "When will you show me?"

"As soon as you're done with your coffee." He emptied his own cup and set it back down on the counter. I took two long swallows that burned my tongue and throat, then nodded. "I'm ready."

We drove for a long time until the flashy lights and crowded streets of Las Vegas lay far behind us. The landscape got rougher, and fewer and fewer signs of civilization were visible. Rocks rose up beside the street, glowing red and orange in the afternoon sun. The Valley of Fire. I'd only driven through it once before, and that had been in the evening when the power of the colors had been dimmed by the impending darkness.

Despite having lived in Las Vegas all my life, I'd seldom explored its surroundings. My family had never been the kind to do road trips. Our vacations had been to Aspen, Mexico or the Bahamas. My chest tightened sharply at the memories of our last ski trip to Aspen in February. Even Father had allowed himself enough free time to ski with us, and in the evening we'd all gathered in front of the roaring fire in our ski lodge.

Suddenly, I couldn't appreciate the sparse landscape anymore. This road trip was one of goodbye. I'd never spend a vacation with my whole family again, never see my father struggle to keep the fire burning in the fireplace, letting out curses while Mother reprimanded him for it. I wasn't even sure if I'd ever see my sister again, and if something happened to her, neither Mother nor I would be able to live with it.

I had to force myself to keep breathing, despite the tightness of my throat. Growl peered at me but I ignored him. I didn't want to talk to him. My emotions were a whirlwind I could hardly understand. I doubted he'd be able to, and I worried that he'd try to talk me out of visiting my father's grave after all.

Eventually he pulled the car off the asphalted street and drove along a dirt road. Our wheels swirled up red dust that settled in a thick layer on the windows. Growl tried to get the dust off with the windshield wipers, but in vain. The vibration of the car as we drove over bumps and smaller rocks made me feel sick, and I closed my eyes. I was no longer sure if this was a good idea, but now it was too late to turn back without having to explain myself to Growl. I didn't want to appear weak.

The car came to a halt and I looked outside. We were in the middle of nowhere. There wasn't even a dirt road anymore. There was absolutely nothing.

"It's here," Growl said as he pointed at a place beyond the windshield. He looked at me as if he was waiting for some kind of response, but there were no words in me at the moment. I nodded merely to show him I'd understood. He opened the door and got out. I took a deep breath and pressed my flat palm against my stomach, hoping to calm myself. No chance.

I got out of the car and the dry air clogged my throat. Desert. No green. No sign of beauty or life. How could anything survive out here? My eyes searched the horizon for any sign of civilization, but we were the only people around.

"Come. I don't want to stand around all day."

He stalked off, not even checking if I was following. Of course he didn't have to be worried that I'd run away. There was nowhere to run out here. I'd die of dehydration before I found another person. I realized then that he had been less cautious in general around me recently. He'd begun to trust me.

As I followed Growl through the sand, another thought suddenly struck me. What if Growl had grown tired of me and decided to dispose of me out in the desert? Perhaps I'd asked too many question, gotten too close for comfort? I wouldn't survive long out here if he abandoned me. He didn't even need to kill me—the desert would.

I shook my head. My imagination was running wild. Growl had no reason to get rid of me. He enjoyed my company, even if he tried to hide the fact.

Growl led me to a spot surrounded by a few dried bushes. There was no hint of a grave. "He's there." He pointed at the dusty ground.

I crouched beside the spot and laid my palm flat against the sand. My eyes prickled but I didn't cry. "I really thought you fed him to the dogs."

Growl frowned. "That's not how you should treat the dead."

I let out a laugh. "Really? You don't mind killing and hurting people, but you care about their corpses."

"Death was their punishment. There's no sense in defiling their bodies."

"I know Falcone's done it before. Father told Mother about it, and she even asked me about it when I visited her. I even heard rumors that he fed bodies to his fight dogs, and made the families watch."

Growl shrugged. "I don't always agree with what Falcone does."

That was at least something, I supposed, even if it was obvious that he didn't really care. "Have you ever seen him do something like that?"

Growl nodded. "Once. But the family didn't have to watch. Falcone knows I don't care for useless violence, so he usually doesn't ask me to stay to watch."

I lowered my eyes back to the ground. It was hard to imagine that my father was below me. Father had known the risks of his job, had earned a lot of money with it, and had probably been responsible for several people's demise, but he hadn't deserved this. I wished he were here, so I could have one last long talk with him. I couldn't remember when we'd had our last conversation. Too long ago. "When you came to our house, did you think you were supposed to kill my father?" I wasn't sure why it mattered. I knew Growl was a killer and that he wouldn't have hesitated pulling the trigger.

"Falcone hadn't told us who was going to kill your father."

"But you knew that he wanted him dead?" I raised my eyes to meet his.

He gave me a confused look. He wasn't sure why I was asking those questions. "Your father betrayed Falcone. Death is the punishment for that."

I sighed and rose to my feet, dusting off my pants that were covered in a fine layer of red sand.

"Do you ever go to your mother's grave?" I asked.

"No," he said. There was no emotion in his voice. "It's just her body down there. And I don't even remember her much. I prefer not to stay in the past."

That was probably a necessity considering the many dark aspects of his life. "And yet to some degree you do."

More confusion filled Growl's face. "What do you mean?"

"You let the past determine who you are now, and you're bound to a man who made you who you are today. There's so much past in your life."

Growl considered that. He really looked as if my words were getting through to him.

I risked the next step. "Don't you want revenge? Have you never dreamed of killing him? Of hurting him for what he's done to you? You could end it all. Free yourself of your past once and for all."

Growl shook his head. "I told you, what he's done to me made me who I am. I would not be here without him. I would not be here *with you* without him. He gave me you and that's more than I ever hoped for."

For a moment I could not breathe, could not move, could do nothing but stare and try to come to terms with what Growl had just said. How could so few words mean so much to me? How could something that man, that monster said, mean anything at all? It seemed impossible, even now.

He took a step closer and brushed a strand of hair from my face before he took my hand in his. It wasn't a romantic gesture, more like he needed to convince himself of something, needed to make it tangible to comprehend. "But him giving you to me wasn't kindness," he said. "Nothing like that. It was cruel and degrading. He wanted to punish you, and he knew I was the kind of punishment that would break you." He turned my hand over, revealing my pale wrist and forearm. "Just look at your skin. Unblemished. Clean. Perfect. And look at me." He released me and held out his arms, covered in tattoos and scars, tanned and muscled. His life showed on his body.

I didn't know what to say. Self-loathing seeped from every pore of his body, and I wasn't sure how to handle it. I wasn't perfect as he made me out to be.

"Falcone hoped I'd do to you what he did to me. Turn you into something gruesome. Break you apart," Growl rasped, eyes fierce and wild.

I grabbed his hand firmly. "You didn't break me," I said stubbornly. But I wasn't sure it was true. I wasn't the person I used to be. Some part of me had been broken, not through violence by his hands and yet, I had changed all the same.

"Stop hating yourself," I said angrily. "You aren't helpless. You are perhaps the only person who can do something against Falcone. If you feel so bad about why Falcone gave me to you, then help me. You always say that you are lost, that you can't redeem yourself. But that's not true. You could make up for your sins by helping me and my family."

Growl curled his fingers over my hand. "By exacting revenge," he said curiously.

I hesitated. "Yes." Was I being a hypocrite for suggesting something like that? "Falcone deserves death. We'll never be free with him around. Not just because he can tell us what to do but because he controls our past, he shaped it, shaped us irrevocably."

"You can't ask that of me." Growl backed away, dropping my hand. "Don't ask me again. I can't help you. I won't."

My heart sank. For a moment, he'd actually considered saying yes. I'd seen it in his face. Should I keep trying even though he told me not to? Or should I accept what obviously couldn't be changed and hope everything would turn out okay for my mother and sister anyway?

I couldn't say any more.

chapter 17

—CARA—

Growl pulled away from me in the days after our visit to the grave. I let him. I wasn't sure what to do.

He hadn't even visited me in my bedroom and I was starting to miss it, miss him.

Lying awake in my bed, I listened for every sound outside. Growl had left without an explanation after dark again, and I was terrified in this creepy neighborhood all by myself at night.

Eventually, when every creak made me jump, I got out of bed. I crept out of the room and paused in the dark corridor, listening for the sound of claws on the floor, but there was nothing. Perhaps Growl had let the dogs sleep in his bedroom. I headed toward it, but behind the door I didn't hear a sound. I tiptoed into the living room. It was dark in there as well. Only the dim moonlight streaming through the windows allowed my eyes to make out anything at all. Outside I could hear the occasional shouting or a siren in the distance, sounds that seemed to fill all the nights in this area. I wasn't sure why Growl chose to live here. How could he bear it? Or maybe the hopelessness and brutality that filled so many of the houses in the street were something familiar to him, something he could grasp.

A movement in the corner made me tense. Then my eyes made out Coco's head, and beside her that of Bandit. The dogs were watching me but they didn't stir from their sleeping spots. I didn't want to return to my bedroom. I was so tired of feeling alone all the time, of being alone with my thoughts and fears and worries. I walked to the sofa and sank down. Coco rose from her blanket and trotted toward me. I wasn't exactly scared of the dogs anymore, but sometimes they still made me nervous, especially Bandit. I couldn't read their movements very well, since my family had never had pets. But right now Coco didn't seem in a bad mood. She stopped next to my legs and put her big head down on my knee, peering up at me expectantly. I raised my hand carefully, not wanting to startle her, and held it in front of her nose, so she could sniff it like Growl had showed me in the beginning.

Coco didn't sniff me, though; instead she licked my hand. Her tongue was warm and rough but not disgusting at all. Although the idea of all the places that tongue had been before wasn't comforting, the dog's warm breath on my skin and that obvious sign of tenderness brought tears to my eyes. I gently ran my hand over her soft ears and head, and she let out a deep breath. I couldn't help but smile. I stretched out on the sofa and patted the spot beside me. Coco didn't hesitate. She jumped up and lay down beside me, her muscled body pressed up against me. I stroked the length of her back, relishing in the feeling of her warm body beside me. The sound of claws on wood made me raise my head, in time to see Bandit leap off the ground and land on the sofa at my feet where he curled up, his back pressed against the curve of my knees. I knew I'd be safe with them, and the scary noises from outside stopped bothering me.

With their bodies warming me, sleep quickly fell over me.

I wasn't sure what woke me but when I opened my eyes, the sun had only just risen outside. Coco and Bandit were still snuggled up to me; that was probably the reason why I wasn't cold, even though I didn't have a blanket.

I had slept without nightmares, something that hadn't happened in a while. Coco lifted her head to look at something behind me. I glanced over my shoulder and found Growl leaning in the doorframe, watching me, and the dogs. "They usually don't warm up to people easily. They must really like you for them to sleep at your side like that."

I sat up, which wasn't easy as Coco and Bandit were pressed up so closely to me. Both dogs gave me what I could only call reproachful looks because I disturbed their sleep, but finally my bare feet hit the ground and I was sitting upright. "Maybe they were lonely."

"Why would they be? They aren't alone. They have each other and I don't leave them alone very often."

"Just because someone isn't alone doesn't mean they aren't lonely," I said quietly.

Growl searched my face. "Are you lonely?" The intensity of his gaze made me want to hide. Instead I lowered my eyes to Coco and scratched her behind the ears. I heard Growl come up behind me. His hand brushed my shoulder, then throat.

"Sometimes," I admitted. "This house isn't a place where it's easy to feel at home."

His fingertips traced my collarbone and the touch raised goose bumps on my skin. He didn't say anything; neither did I. Slowly his hand slid under my nightgown until his fingertips brushed my nipple. I shivered at the tingle that shot through my body.

His hand cupped my breast and squeezed lightly. A small moan slid out of my mouth. Growl made a movement with his other hand and both dogs jumped off the sofa. Growl's other hand joined his first and cupped my other breast. He twirled my nipples between his fingertips lightly, gently, and I trembled under the soft ministrations. He tugged a bit harder and pain mixed with lust. My legs parted as the pressure and heat between them became close to unbearable. I wanted him to touch me there, wanted him to elevate my need. This was the extent of closeness he allowed, and I had to accept it.

He leaned down, caging me in between his muscled arms, and let one hand glide down over my stomach and through my trimmed curls. I shivered again and parted my legs a bit wider. After days without his touch, my body was practically thirsting for it. His fingers brushed over my clit as they slid lower.

Growl plunged a finger into my tight center, making me cry out. He twisted my nipple again and I moaned loudly. My head fell back and landed on his shoulder, my gaze finding his. His lips were parted as he breathed heavily. I was already so wet, and as Growl tugged my nipple in rhythm with his finger pushing into me, I almost came apart. I fought my orgasm. I didn't want to give him the satisfaction of making me come within a minute of him starting to touch me. I didn't want this to be over, didn't want him to pull back again.

His breath was hot against my throat as he licked the spot over my pulse point, then drew the skin into his mouth and suckled. I bit down on my lower lip, hoping the pain would calm me. He released my skin, then let his nose brush my throat up to the spot behind my ear. He let go of my breast and a low sound of protest pressed out between my lips. Growl purred deeply, and the sound made me tremble in delight. His palm cupped my cheek and he angled my face toward his, then crushed his lips against mine. His tongue conquered my mouth. He tasted of fresh coffee and his mouth was unbelievably hot; everything about him was.

He dropped his hand from my face and returned it to my breast, continuing his attentions. My nipple felt almost raw from his twisting but it was too thrilling, too good to ask him to stop. A second finger joined the first. I exhaled, getting used to the fullness again, but Growl didn't give me much time. He established a fast, hard rhythm. He claimed my mouth and breasts and pussy, my whole body. My legs began shaking as the pressure built higher and higher, and then I exploded. Waves of lust spread through my body from my core. I arched off the sofa, and cried into Growl's mouth. He pushed his fingers even harder into me and gave a final tug of my breast. I sagged against him, completely spent and breathless.

Growl pulled his hand away and a sense of cold overcame me at the lack of his touch as he straightened beside the sofa. He unzipped his pants and let them slide down his legs. His erect cock sprang free, already glistening. He cupped the back of my head and I let him guide me toward his cock, parting my lips as his tip brushed them. Growl held me in place as he fucked my mouth slowly. I knew he liked it like that, but suddenly the desire to have more control overcame me and I pushed backwards. The grip on the back of my head tightened briefly but then he released me, confusion flashing across his face before it was replaced by a neutral expression. The moment he dropped his hand from my head, leaving me free, I leaned forward and took him into my mouth again. Surprise filled his eyes, then pure desire. I swirled my tongue around his tip, then pulled back again to run my tongue from his base up to his tip. I curled my fingers around his length and moved my hand up and down slowly, trying to figure out what to do. Growl watched me as I licked over his balls. They tightened and a new drop appeared at the tip of his cock, emboldening me even further. One of my hands cupped his hard ass. The muscles flexed under my palm. The feeling of his strength gave me a thrill. How could his power intimidate me in every other situation, but turn me on the moment we had sex?

I shut off my brain. I didn't want to think, only feel. Sex was the only time when I experienced something akin to freedom and happiness. Maybe it was wrong, but I was determined to cling to anything that would help me through the near future. I pumped his length fast and worked the tip between my lips. Soon Growl started to thrust slightly, driving himself deeper into my mouth. I let him and then he tensed, letting out a guttural sound. I tried to swallow everything, but a few drops ran down my chin. I quickly wiped them off. Growl hoisted me to my feet and claimed my mouth for another kiss. I kissed him back, wanting him to taste himself like I did. When he pulled back, we were both panting and sweating.

Growl let go of my shoulders and took another step back, building the wall between us again just like that. "Let's have breakfast. I'm starving." His voice was even deeper than usual. His eyes held mine for a couple of seconds more. He wanted to say something, it was clear on his face, but then he turned around and headed for the kitchen. I wasn't even sure what I was hoping for exactly. Sometimes I wasn't sure what I wanted. In the beginning everything had been about making Growl trust me so I could use him for my purposes, but now there was more.

I shouldn't wait for something that was never going to happen. And what was even more important: I shouldn't long for something that was so wrong. I couldn't allow myself to forget why I was here, even if pretending made life easier. But I was a prisoner. Growl practically owned me, and even if he decided to let me go, which I doubted he'd ever do, no one in our world would touch me after I'd been with Growl, much less marry me. I was stained. Not fit for a good match anymore. I could never return to society. Las Vegas was dead for me. I leaned back against the sofa. A wave of loneliness was about to claw its way out of my chest again.

I caught Coco watching me. She looked perplexed "I don't understand any of this either," I whispered. She tilted her head to the side. A small smile tugged at my lips at her confusion.

I pushed to my feet. I wasn't going to drown in self-pity. It wasn't like I needed or wanted Growl's affection or closeness. Sex was a means to an end. It helped me feel better and it helped me understand Growl better. If I wanted a chance at manipulating him into letting me go and helping my family, I'd have to use any tricks I had.

—GROWL—

My dogs didn't like humans. Even I had to fight a long time for them to trust me. But Cara, they seemed to love her. If dogs were even capable of that kind of emotion. I was certain that the majority of humans weren't either. They liked the idea of love, but never reached that level.

Love. A silly notion. And dangerous. Horrible things had been done in the name of love. Or the idea of it.

I didn't think I'd ever felt anything like it. At least I couldn't remember. Perhaps I'd loved my mother when I'd been a small kid. I'd gotten a scar for it.

Love.

It wasn't something I could comprehend.

Cara. That woman.

I felt something. But I didn't know what it was. I'd never felt like this before.

She made me want to treat her right. She made me want to be better. She made me want so many things I shouldn't desire

She was dangerous to me, to the life I'd built, to the person I'd become.

She wanted me to go against Falcone, against everything I'd worked so hard to achieve. That was why she let me touch her and why she sometimes smiled at me, why she talked to me and accepted my closeness. There could be no other explanation.

I knew that, and still I was like a moth drawn to her light. The only light that had ever penetrated the darkness that was me and my life.

chapter 18

—CARA—

"There's something you should know." Growl leaned against the kitchen counter as he so often did. He wasn't tense but his gaze worried me. Something told me I wouldn't like what he had to say.

"Okay," I said slowly. "What is it?" So many horrible things had happened in the last few weeks, there wasn't much left that could devastate me—and then fear struck me. "Is it about my mother or sister? Has Falcone decided he doesn't need them anymore?"

Growl frowned as if he couldn't imagine how I could have drawn that conclusion. Perhaps worry for others was something entirely foreign to him.

"No," he growled. "It's about your fiancé."

"I doubt he is still my fiancé," I muttered. Who would want me after everything that had happened? I was a pariah in our society.

Growl's frown deepened. "He's not. You're right."

His gaze was starting to unsettle me, which was surprising considering that in the beginning everything about him had unsettled me. Apparently now I needed an additional reason to feel uncomfortable in his presence. "Good," I said firmly. "I wouldn't want to marry him anyway."

Doubt crossed Growl's face. "Why?" he rumbled. There was something in his voice I couldn't quite place.

I huffed. "Why? Do you really need to ask?"

Growl remained silent, that same stoic expression on his face.

"He betrayed my father to better his own position. He betrayed my family. He betrayed me. I don't want a man like that: a man who is selfish, who doesn't care whom he hurts to reach his goals. I don't want a man I can't trust. He's a pig, and I wish I could spit in his face."

"You will get your chance," Growl said.

I paused. "What do you mean?"

Growl ignored my question. "What I need to tell you is that Cosimo and your friend are going to marry."

I wasn't sure I'd heard correctly. "My friend?"

"That Anastasia girl. Falcone told me last night. They announced their engagement yesterday."

I couldn't move. If this was a nightmare, I wanted to wake now. "Are you sure?"

Growl nodded. "Cosimo has a position of power now. He needs a wife and an heir."

I laughed bitterly. "Didn't take him long to find a new woman to marry." I hated how the news made me feel. Despite my hate for Cosimo, I felt crushed. Not because I wanted to marry him, but because this made my life as it was now even more of a reality. There was no going back. Change was irrevocable. And Anastasia, how could she do this? I'd always known that Anastasia could be vicious and selfish, but we'd been friends since we could walk. We'd experienced so many things together. Didn't that mean anything? How could my friend betray me this way? Had Anastasia known about everything? Had she already known at Falcone's party? Perhaps that explained why she'd looked so pissed when I had danced with Cosimo.

No, it couldn't be.

I didn't want to believe that my friend wouldn't have warned me. It seemed cruel. Crueler than what Anastasia was capable of. She liked to trash talk and destroy people's reputations, but this was a different matter altogether.

Maybe Anastasia was a victim. Maybe her parents and Falcone had forced her to marry my former fiancé now that I wasn't eligible anymore. After all, Anastasia was the same age as me and from a good family. I wanted to believe that, but the look Cosimo and Anastasia had exchanged at the party flashed in my mind. There had been something like familiarity between them. Or was I reading too much into it now that I knew of their engagement? I wasn't in the right state of mind to think clearly, so I pushed the image away. I wasn't able to bear the idea of my friend's horrible betrayal. Not as long as I didn't know all the facts. There was no sense in driving myself insane going over all the possibilities.

Growl was still watching me. I wasn't sure how long I'd been lost in my thoughts, and I hoped my face hadn't given away too much of my inner turmoil. "This doesn't concern me anymore," I said. "It's not like I'm still part of their circle."

"Why would you say that?"

Was he serious? "Oh come on. You must realize what's going on in our society. Even if you don't care about any of it. There are rules. And I was as good as exiled."

"Because you're with me." Was there hurt in his voice? His constant growl made it even harder to hear the nuances of his emotions.

I pursed my lips. Had I offended him? "With you?" I asked curiously. "You make it sound like we're a couple when I'm only your gift."

Growl nodded. "You were. But now that you're mine, you have the same status that I have."

"That's not true," I said, frustrated at his lack of understanding. Did he really think that any part of the life I'd had before could survive? I had made the best of my fate, but that didn't mean I'd have chosen it.

Growl looked as frustrated as I felt, but I didn't care. I didn't have the energy to explain anything to him. Sometimes his inability to grasp human relationships drove me insane.

"Maybe you aren't as special as you were before," Growl said, the word *special* like a curse from his lips. "But you are part of this world."

I glared at the counter. "I don't want to be part of this world anymore."

"That's not up to you. We're invited to Cosimo's and your friend's engagement party," Growl said.

My breath hitched and my eyes flew up to look at Growl. "You can't be serious."

He stared. He obviously wasn't joking.

"I'm not going," I said, my voice shaking. Coco trotted toward me and rested her head on my knee. I put my palm atop her soft head, but it didn't manage to calm me. Even Bandit had come from the living room to watch me with curious eyes.

"Yes, you are. Falcone wants us there, so we will be there."

"I don't care what he wants. I hate him. And he only wants to humiliate me anyway. Everyone knows that Cosimo was my fiancé and that Anastasia is... *was* my friend. They will all laugh at me."

I could only imagine the humiliation I would be subjected to. I didn't think I could stand it.

"Nobody will laugh at you when I'm at your side," he said in a low voice. His expression was deadly, a threat but not to me.

I paused. "Why do you even care?"

"You're mine, and I won't let anyone talk shit about something that belongs to me."

Of course. It was an ego thing. He didn't care about me. He only wanted to make sure people showed him the necessary respect, and that included respecting his belongings. I wanted to scream in frustration but I bit it back. This party was my chance to ask my friends for help. We'd known each other practically all our lives. Now that Growl had made it clear that he wouldn't help me against Falcone, they were probably my last chance.

I'd dreaded this day since Growl had told me two days ago, but I promised myself to hold my head high. I was stronger than I used to be. I would get through this party. I no longer needed my friends' approval, or anyone's for that matter.

Growl stood in the living room, tugging at his white dress-shirt collar with one hand while a tie dangled from the other.

It was obvious how uncomfortable he felt dressed up like that. It wasn't who he was. Putting him in a suit was like putting a tiger in a cage. At Falcone's party he'd hid his discomfort behind a mask of indifference, but now in a moment where he thought himself alone, his defenses were down. It wasn't the first time I'd seen a glimpse of something human outside of our nights together. It was disconcerting because I didn't want to see him as anything but a monster. It made things easier. I didn't want to risk actually hoping for something that was absolutely unrealistic.

Growl put his tie around his neck and then fumbled for a minute with both ends until he made a sound of frustration and threw the tie on the ground. That was probably why he hadn't worn a tie at the last party. A small smile tugged at my lips, and I stepped forward. "Do you need help?"

Growl's eyes darted toward me, looking caught. Then they slowly slid down the length of me. Only moments before I'd felt bad because the dress wasn't new, because everyone would know I'd worn it before, but now, with the way Growl was looking at me, that suddenly didn't matter anymore.

I quickly looked away, scared of the way his expression mattered to me, and pointed at the tie on the ground.

"Can you fasten a tie?" he asked with a hint of surprise.

"Of course," I said as I walked toward him. His eyes followed my every move. I often had trouble reading his expressions, but now there was no need for guessing: lust and appreciation. It sent a thrill through my body.

"You look like a lady," he rasped.

—GROWL—

Her movements were pure grace. There was nothing mundane, nothing cheap about Cara. She was a girl born to be a princess, and now she'd been degraded to a mere servant. Maybe Falcone had wanted to take everything from her, but this, her upbringing, her beauty and grace, that he couldn't take. Perhaps he'd hoped I would break her so irrevocably that she'd become someone else, that she'd lose that part of herself. But I wouldn't do that.

I was a monster. Would always be. But I could appreciate something precious, something as valuable as Cara, and I would never destroy it. I wasn't good, or even decent—there was nothing gray about me. I was all black, but I was trying to be good to her. Never as good as she deserved, but as good as I was capable of. It wasn't enough—I realized it every day. I would never be enough.

She picked up the tie and stepped close to me, her sweet, flowery scent filling my nose and making me want to bury my face in her long brown hair.

Her long, elegant fingers nimbly tied the knot. Fingers meant to hold breakable glasses of champagne and be decorated by only the finest jewelry.

She smoothed down the tie once she was done. There was no hesitation or fumbling. She was made to be the wife of a man who wore suits every day. I sometimes caught myself wondering if she'd imagined being Cosimo's wife, tying the knot of his tie in the morning and greeting him with a kiss when he returned in the evening. She admired her work, then peered up at me with her blue eyes. "Done."

I'd never felt less worthy than in that moment. The dress she wore was perfection on her, as if it had been made for her. She was made for cocktail parties and elegant soirees. I was made for dingy pubs and dark-alley clubs.

Our paths would have never crossed if it weren't for Falcone's vengefulness. Cara's suffering had led to the most precious thing in my life, and still I couldn't regret it. I was selfish. I was glad I'd been given the chance to have someone like her.

I peered down at my watch. "We need to leave."

Cara tapped a finger against the glass of my watch. "I wouldn't have pegged you as the Rolex-wearing kind," she said curiously.

"I'm not. The watch belonged to Falcone, and he gave it to me as a gift for a job well done."

Cara's expression became stone, eyes flashing. "Like me." A bitter smile tugged at her perfect red lips. "But I'm not as valuable as that piece around your wrist."

"You are worth more than anything I've ever owned or will ever own."

—CARA—

He meant it as a compliment, but the words stung nonetheless. Being compared to a watch, even if you won in the end, wasn't something I enjoyed. I knew he couldn't grasp the effect his comparison had on me. He was trying to be kind to me, and that was still a surprise to me every day.

There was a moment of silence before Growl cleared his throat, a rough and deep sound. "We shouldn't be late."

I nodded. I didn't care if we were late. Everything in me screamed at the mere idea of going to that party, but I had to keep my calm if I wanted to get through the evening without making a complete embarrassment out of myself.

Growl headed toward the door and unlocked it. Bandit and Coco accompanied us to the threshold and watched us close the door with accusing eyes.

I let my gaze wander over the neighborhood. An elderly black couple sat on their porch two houses down. I'd never seen them before, and they looked too decent for this area. Perhaps they'd lived here all their lives, and only in the last few years everything had become run-down. Their heads turned our way as Growl and I strode toward his car. We must have seemed like an apparition, dressed in our finest evening wear. People around here usually had no occasions to get dressed up at all. Growl nodded at them and they nodded in turn, but then quickly turned their heads away.

To my surprise Growl opened the door of his car for me and I climbed in, careful not to jam the hem of my dress in the door.

I gathered my hands in my lap and started rubbing them against each other when Growl pulled out of the driveway. My fingers were icy despite the mild weather. When rubbing didn't help, I raised them to my face and blew warm air into my palms. Growl turned his eyes away from the street to look at me. "What are you doing?"

"Nothing," I said quickly.

Growl grabbed one of my hands, startling me. "You're cold," he said, surprised.

"It's been like that all day. Probably nerves." The moment the words left my mouth, I regretted them. I hadn't wanted to admit that much to Growl.

"Nerves?" I was glad when he finally had no choice but to return his attention to the street. "Nobody will hurt you."

I laughed humorlessly. Not physically, perhaps. "That's not what I'm worried about. I just don't want to see Cosimo and the others."

"Why?"

I often forgot how little Growl understood human nature. He reminded me of someone who'd grown up around animals and now had to figure out how human interactions worked.

"Because it reminds me of everything I've lost," I admitted eventually.

Growl scowled at the street. "Did you love him?" His lips twisted at the word, as if it left a bitter taste in his mouth. "Did you love Cosimo?"

There was a hint of something hard and dark in his voice. And this time I caught the hidden emotion behind his coldness. Vulnerability and hurt. I shook my head. Love? I knew nothing of love. "No. I never wanted to marry him. I barely knew him. My parents chose him for me." My father. But saying his name aloud was too much tonight. I couldn't arrive at that horrid party teary-eyed. I wouldn't give any of them that satisfaction.

"Then why are you sad that you lost him and that he's going to marry that girl?"

Was I sad? Not about having lost Cosimo. I couldn't care less about him now, after everything. I *was* sad though. But sadness was only a small part of the emotions I felt. With every passing second, another, a darker emotion, grew stronger in me. Hate. And the bone-deep desire for revenge. "I'm not sad, not about losing him. If I'd only lost him..." I laughed. "God, that would be splendid. But I lost everything."

Growl's body tensed beside me, but I didn't stop.

"And sad? No," I said quietly. "I'm angry. I want them to suffer. I want them to regret the day they decided to kill my father and destroy my family. Cosimo, Falcone and everyone else who was involved in this."

Growl nodded, as if that was an emotion he could comprehend. He wasn't even offended that my list possibly included him as well. He had been part of the attack on my family, even if he wasn't the head of the operation, merely Falcone's brutal hand.

"Don't say anything like that at the party," Growl warned.

"I'm not stupid. I won't say anything like that." But I remembered the last time I'd seen Falcone and how I'd challenged him. My hatred for him had only grown since then. Stopping myself from trying to scratch his eyes out, or better yet cut his throat with an oyster knife, would be hard.

"I know you're not stupid. But stupidity's got nothing to do with it. Emotions follow their own rules."

How would you know? I wanted to ask but kept the words to myself. As ridiculous as it may sound, Growl was perhaps my only ally at that party tonight. I wasn't sure what to expect from Trish and Anastasia, though I hoped we'd still be friends and they'd help me.

Cosimo's house was smaller than Falcone's but he, too, had a fountain in his driveway, although it was also smaller than Falcone's. When Growl and I entered the house, every pair of eyes zoomed in on us. Conversation died down, only to pick up a moment later, but this time behind held-up hands and with stolen glances in my direction. Everyone was talking about me. Heat rose up into my head, but I forced myself to stand tall and appear relaxed despite the urge to flee. Growl put his palm against my lower back and the gesture actually managed to relax me, but people quickly noticed the touch and I could almost hear their nasty words. I took a small breath and let Growl push me further into the room. Small tables with appetizers were spread out in the large living and dining area. I supposed Cosimo had chosen the same caterer as Falcone. He seemed very keen on imitating his boss in every possible way.

And though everything seemed like a cheap copy of Falcone's party, I caught myself wanting to be the hostess. This was supposed to be my engagement party. The happiest day of my life, at least for outward appearances. And now...

My eyes registered Anastasia and Cosimo at the end of the room, near a huge golden champagne cooler. Anastasia wore a new floor-length silver gown that made her look like a princess, and beside her stood Cosimo in a dark suit, one arm wrapped around his fiancée's waist. Bile rose up in my throat and the smile plastered on my face turned painful. I needed something to drink. Something strong. Growl seemed to read my mind because a moment later, a glass with red wine appeared in front of my face. The other women drank champagne or white wine, so I was surprised by his choice.

"Red is supposed to calm people down. Maybe it will work for you too."

I could have kissed him then. I'd have never expected something as thoughtful from a man like him, but my moment of peace was short-lived as we made our way toward Falcone. He acted like he was the host of this evening, making grand gestures with his arms and laughing the loudest while the people gathered around him tried to act like he was actually saying something funny.

I took a big gulp of wine, praying it would calm me quickly before I did something that would prevent me from ever getting the chance to see my mother and sister again. I couldn't lose it tonight. There would be time for revenge one day, but not at this party.

Growl's grip on my back tightened when we stopped in front of Falcone, as if he was trying to warn me.

"Nice party, Boss," Growl commented.

Falcone smiled broadly. "Not my party, sadly. Cosimo did a good job. He's trying to impress his little lady." Finally, his cold eyes settled right on me, boring into my own eyes, triumphant and taunting. My fingers tightened on my glass but I forced my face to remain calm. I doubted I was successful. Practically every inch of me was burning with hatred, with the need to make this man in front of me suffer.

"I hope you are as happy for your friend and Cosimo as everyone else," he said falsely.

Say something. Say something. But all I could think was if it was possible to smash the glass and cut Falcone's throat with one of the shards before any of the men around us would come to his aid.

Growl would probably be the first to save his boss.

"I'm happy," I forced myself to say, but the words sounded fake even to my own ears. Falcone sneered, then he turned back to Growl. "I'm surprised you managed to tear yourself out of bed. But even you, my bull, need a pause now and then, eh?" Falcone clapped Growl's shoulder in a gesture meant for buddies. "I hope you're still satisfied with your gift. Otherwise there's another sister for you to try, if you ever grow tired of this one."

"Talia? Where is she?" I blurted before I could control myself. The triumphant expression on Falcone's face conveyed that he'd gotten what he wanted. He knew exactly where to push my buttons. He wouldn't give me the answers I yearned for.

Growl squeezed my side in warning again, but it was too late. I pressed my lips together and had to fight back tears. Falcone was a worse monster than Growl.

"I won't grow tired of Cara," Growl said.

Falcone's smile turned lewd as his gaze traveled the length of me. "That good, is she? Maybe I should have kept her for myself then." He laughed.

Growl didn't say anything. His face was stone, and his grip on my waist painful. I glared at Falcone, hoping he could see the promise in my eyes. *You will die.*

His smile only widened, but my resolve was set. I wouldn't stop until that man was lying dead at my feet. I hated blood and death, but I would watch every second while the life drained out of his body and relish it.

Growl seemed to sense the growing danger. "We need to go to the happy couple now."

"Yes, you should," Falcone said, but his eyes never left me.

I shuddered when we had walked a few steps away from him.

"You need to be more careful," Growl murmured.

I glanced up at him. His gaze was set straight ahead, expression stony. People watched him with fear and revulsion, but he didn't care. The only man who could control Growl was Falcone, and that scared me senseless. "Don't give me to him."

Growl frowned down at me. "What are you talking about?"

"To Falcone. Don't give me to him," I whispered.

Realization flashed across Growl's face, then determination. "Never. You are mine. He won't take you away from me."

"Are you sure? He's your boss. He could tell you to give me to him." It was a surprising twist of fate that I preferred being Growl's possession, but anything was better than belonging to Falcone.

"You are mine," Growl repeated, and then he stopped and I noticed we'd arrived at the end of a line of people who were waiting to congratulate Cosimo and Anastasia.

chapter 19

—CARA—

I exhaled slowly. I needed to get a grip. I'd nearly lost it in front of Falcone. At least in front of my treacherous asshole of an ex-fiancé, I wanted to keep my cool. He didn't need to know how broken I was. Anastasia was busy not looking my way, but even she must have realized that I'd arrived at the party. Everyone had fallen silent at our arrival, after all, and Anastasia had always had ears and eyes for gossip. But her ignoring me gave me the chance to sort through my thoughts and calm myself. I sipped at my red wine. The alcohol was starting to relax me. It wasn't surprising that so many people in our circles were alcoholics. This life could often only be tolerated drunk.

Cosimo's eyes briefly came to a stop on me, and I froze with the glass against my lips. Slowly I lowered it, but then Cosimo looked away. His face had been emotionless. There hadn't even been pity, or anything really. He truly couldn't care less about me. I wasn't sure why that came as a surprise. After all, he'd acted no different when he and Falcone had come to my family's house to ruin our lives.

There was only one couple in front of us now, and my palms became sweaty with nerves. This was perhaps my only chance to talk to Anastasia and find out the truth. Growl leaned down, his warm lips brushing my ear, and I couldn't stop myself from remembering how his lips had felt on other parts of my body. I shivered.

"Remember to stay calm," he rumbled into my ear, then straightened, and suddenly we stood right in front of Anastasia and Cosimo. It was our turn to congratulate the happy couple. Only the thought left me feeling nauseated, but I put on a brave face and smiled. Anastasia looked unsure and her smile was more than just a little forced. I wasn't sure what to make of it. She made no move to hug me or step closer. When Cosimo and Growl shook hands and engaged in fake-friendly conversation, I used my chance and pulled Anastasia tightly against me, trying to ignore the way her body tensed at our closeness. Was she worried I'd attack her? Or was she actually disgusted by being so close to me now that I was less? I banished the thought before it could distract me from my plan. I brought my mouth close to her ear. "Please, Anastasia, help me. We can help each other run away."

Anastasia gripped my upper arms, nails digging into my skin, and pushed me a few inches away before she leaned just close enough so nobody would hear her words. "I don't want to run away," she whispered, then added loudly, "I couldn't be happier." She gave her best Grace Kelly smile into the round of gathered guests, looking like this was the crowning moment of her life.

I stared, unable to comprehend what was going on. Was Anastasia putting up a show? Was she worried about someone overhearing?

But when I stepped back to allow the next people in line to congratulate Anastasia and Cosimo, I took a closer look at Anastasia. She wasn't putting up an Academy Award-worthy performance. There weren't the telltale signs of lines around her eyes when she was forcing a smile. This was real. Growl started to lead me away, but I kept glancing back at my former friend and my former fiancé. They looked happy. Nobody had forced Anastasia. She really wanted to marry him.

Nobody could help falling in love, right? If Anastasia had told me, I would have tried to convince my father not to arrange the match. I would have wanted Anastasia to be happy, and I'd never even cared about my fiancé.

How could Anastasia have let this happen? How long had this been going on? But even now, I didn't want to believe that she had known before the party. Maybe she had found out afterward, when it was too late. I allowed myself one last glance at Anastasia before I turned away. She didn't want anything to do with me tonight, and I suspected that wasn't just because other people were around. She had a perfect future ahead of her, the one she'd always wanted. She wouldn't risk it for me.

I emptied my glass and put it on a tray a server was carrying. Suddenly I felt tired, and not just from alcohol. This evening was like a nightmare I would never wake up from.

Growl stopped in a corner of the room and leaned against the wall. I glanced up at him. He seemed to be done with this party too.

"Can't we just leave?" I asked.

Growl shook his head. "Do you really want to show them how much this is bothering you? Show them your strength. Don't cower."

"I'm not cowering," I hissed, then sighed. "But I feel drained. I'm not strong. I don't care if they think I'm weak." It wasn't true and I'd later regret my lack of control, but right now I wanted to escape.

"Never show those people weakness," Growl said in a low voice, leaning down until we were very close. "You are stronger than you think. No woman has ever given me such a hard time like you do every day. If you can act strong around me, you can be strong around those weaklings. They are nothing."

I blinked up at his amber eyes. For the first time I actually considered grabbing his face and kissing him. I wanted to do it in front of everyone. And that, too, scared me. I nodded instead. "You are right." I lowered my eyes, unable to stand his closeness any longer. I caught a few people watching us with open mouths. Apparently they were waiting eagerly for a scene between Growl and me. They'd probably be horribly disappointed if this evening didn't end with me being beaten to a bloody mess by Growl.

I glared at them and they actually looked away.

"That look is good. Show them who you are."

"If I only knew," I whispered. Across the room I suddenly spotted Trish, and relief flooded me. Trish had always been the kinder of my two best friends. Growl followed my gaze. "Go ahead and talk to her. She's your friend, right?"

"How do you know?"

"I saw you at Falcone's party together."

"Okay," I said distractedly, already thinking of how best to go about talking to Trish. I couldn't risk scaring her away.

"And don't do anything stupid," Growl said when I was already a few steps away.

"I won't."

I hurried past people who openly stared and pointed at me, who whispered my name like a curse and even laughed at me, but I ignored them.

All that mattered was talking to Trish and finding out as much as I could.

Trish spotted me when I was still a good distance away and for a moment I was sure she'd turn around and run, but she squared her shoulders and waited for me. I was grateful for that small act of bravery on her part, especially considering the many eyes that followed my every move. When I arrived in front of her, neither of us did anything for a few heartbeats. Then Trish awkwardly patted my arm and I stiffened under the forced gesture. Any hope I'd had left for my friendship with Trish vanished then too.

I cleared my throat. But I wasn't sure what to say. I'd made so many plans. They seemed silly now. My eyes darted toward Cosimo and Anastasia again.

Trish followed my gaze and nodded. "I'm sorry, Cara. You know Anastasia always gets what she wants."

Her words struck me as strange, but I put on a brave smile, remembering Growl's words. "You can't help who you fall in love with."

Trish huffed. "Love. Anastasia only loves herself, you know that." For the first time, Trish voiced criticism against Anastasia, and I realized I'd underestimated her. I'd never pegged her as particularly clever, and she'd always played the stupid blonde, but her attentive eyes now made me comprehend how wrong I'd been. She'd probably seen through Anastasia a long time ago.

"What do you mean?" I asked quietly.

"She wanted him because of his position. He's a good catch, and after the thing with your father, an even better catch. That's all."

My stomach tightened. "Did she know before it happened?" I couldn't even say the words.

Trish shrugged. "Probably. She called me the same evening and told me about it."

"But you didn't know..." My voice died away. I wasn't sure how much more I could take.

Trish lightly touched my arm. "No. I didn't. And I'm sorry for everything." Her eyes darted around at the people watching us, and her expression became more guarded.

I knew what was going to happen. Trish depended on the approval of others like I had before everything had been taken from me. And she, more than I, had always been Anastasia's sidekick. That wouldn't change. She couldn't let it change. Trish wouldn't risk her reputation by spending time with me in the future. And the worst part was, I couldn't say I wouldn't have done the same if our positions had been reversed.

I took a step back, forcing a smile. "I know we can't see each other anymore," I said firmly. "Just one last thing: do you know anything about my sister?"

Trish shook her head. "Anastasia probably does. Ask her." I could tell she was eager to end this conversation, and I made it easy for her. I turned and started walking away, but I didn't know where to go. Wherever I looked, I saw people who wanted nothing to do with me. Not all of them appeared as if they thought my family and I had gotten what we deserved, but nobody looked like they were going to help me, or even talk to me. I'd never felt more alone in my life, and this time there wasn't even a mobile in my purse. And even if there were, there was no one I could have called. My desperate gaze settled on Growl, who was no longer talking to the group of men. Instead he was standing by himself, a glass of red wine in his hand, gaze glued to me.

I hesitated for a moment. But he was the only person I could go to. I glanced around again, toward the doors and windows, then stared down at my feet and laughed bitterly. When I raised my eyes, Growl was still watching me. I knew he'd never taken his eyes off me. There was no way I could escape, not without help, and even though it hurt to admit, I knew no one at this party who cared enough about me to risk it. Trish twirled around the small dance floor with a young man I didn't know, and Anastasia was smiling up a storm at Cosimo's side. Everyone was drinking and laughing and living their lives. But I didn't miss the glances they kept throwing my way. In some I caught pity and sympathy, but as soon as those few noticed me looking at them, they quickly averted their eyes as if they were worried my bad luck would rub off on them, or perhaps that they'd feel compelled to help me.

But there were also the others, those who watched me with curiosity, desperate to fulfill their craving for sensation. They would probably have approached me to get an update on the gossip regarding Growl if they didn't have to risk their reputation to do so.

I squared my shoulders and headed toward Growl. When I stopped by his side, he held out the glass of red wine for me. I raised my eyebrows. "Are you trying to make me drunk?"

"You look like you need it," he said.

I snorted. "I don't think wine's enough."

Growl didn't laugh or smile, only mustered me with his keen amber eyes. He was still holding the glass out and I finally took it.

"Isn't that yours?" I asked but took a large sip before he could reply.

He didn't seem to mind. "I don't drink."

"You don't? They all do." I nodded in the general direction of the other guests.

Growl didn't take his eyes off me. "Alcohol makes people careless. It brings out the worst in them."

"You kill for a living. I don't think it gets much worse."

Growl nodded. "Perhaps. But I won't let alcohol dull my senses."

I emptied the rest of the wine. "That's exactly why I drink."

"Don't. It was wrong to give you the wine. It doesn't make things better. It only makes you believe that it does."

I was starting to feel shaky and dizzy. "Maybe that's enough. If things can't get better, than at least I can pretend they will."

Growl sighed. "I will tell Falcone and Cosimo that we're leaving. You will stay where you are while I'm gone."

I leaned against the wall. I didn't feel like going anywhere. The room was spinning and I was starting to feel hot. With another look at me, Growl headed off to where Cosimo was talking to Falcone. The crowd parted for him with fear and sick fascination, and he towered over them, strong and tall and proud, despite their whispers.

I wished I could be like that, but deep down I still cared what people said. It hurt to see them judging and pitying me. I closed my eyes against their scrutiny and soon lost all sense of time.

A touch on my shoulder roused me from my stupor. My eyelids felt heavy as I opened them. Growl scowled down at me, and I shied back from the anger on his face. "Never close your eyes around your enemies. You won't survive like that."

I smiled tiredly. "As if you ever take your eyes off me. Nobody can hurt me when you're around. If someone ends up killing me, then it's probably you."

Growl didn't deny it. He wrapped his fingers around my upper arm and steered me toward the door. I followed him in a trance-like state. When we got outside, the fresh air helped me regain my senses and I gulped down the oxygen eagerly.

But I still wasn't in the best state of mind, and it took me a while to notice a man leaning against a car and smoking a cigarette. I didn't know him, but Growl seemed to recognize him from the way his fingers on my arm tightened in warning.

"Nice catch," the man called.

Growl ignored him and tried to pull me past him, but the man pushed away from the car, threw the cigarette down on the ground and smashed it with his shoe. He smirked. "How do you fit your big cock into that small lady mouth of hers?" He sounded drunk, and I swore to myself never to drink as much as tonight again.

Growl suddenly tore away from me and I stumbled but caught my balance in the last second, bracing myself against another car. I whirled around upon hearing a muffled scream. Growl had grabbed the man by the neck and thrown him down on the ground. He kicked him in the ribs twice before he leaned down and punched him in the face. The man moaned and blood spewed out of his nose and mouth. "Don't," Growl rasped in a voice that sent cold chills down my back. "Don't ever talk like that again, or I'll gut you and strangle you with your fucking bowels."

The man coughed.

"Understood?" Growl asked, shaking the man roughly.

"Yeah," gasped the man in a blood-soaked voice.

Growl wiped his hands on the man's suit before he straightened up and sent one of the bellboys a warning look. Then he returned to me with a calm expression. No sign of his previous fury was visible.

"Why did you do that?" I asked as he led me toward his car, which was parked on the side of the road near the entrance gates.

Growl helped me into the passenger's seat. "Because you're mine and I won't let anyone talk shit about you."

"In the house, at the party, they were all talking about me."

Growl looked back toward the brightly lit house, and for a moment I worried he'd storm back inside and beat up a few more guests, but then his gaze settled on me. "They were clever enough not to say anything when I could hear them, and most only feel sorry for you. They say bad things about me, not you."

The way he stood there, with a few droplets of blood on his white shirt and cold determination on his striking face, he looked like my avenging angel. Who could be better to seek revenge than Growl? He knew how to hurt people, how to destroy them. Could I convince him to help my sister and mother? Even if he never let me go, perhaps he'd at least help them get away from Las Vegas and start anew. He was conflicted, I could tell. Could I make him go against Falcone after all? His amber eyes bored into mine, and a flicker of hope rose in me. I wouldn't give up. *He* was my only chance.

—GROWL—

I had been suspicious from the start. Why would Falcone invite us? Now I knew. It was to humiliate Cara, and by doing so, me. I had never cared about what people said, what Falcone said. I'd lived my life, tried to survive, never wanted or needed much.

Falcone's only purpose tonight had been to humiliate Cara. My blood boiled at the memory. I didn't let anyone humiliate something that was mine, especially Cara.

For some reason that girl meant something to me. I'd never cared for anyone, except for my dogs and perhaps myself, but with Cara, I wasn't sure what was happening to me. I didn't want to care about her. I knew she didn't want me. What she was doing was a tactic, a way for her to survive what had been meant as a horrible punishment.

I didn't know what was going on in her mind. Perhaps she didn't hate me as much as I suspected. Sometimes she looked as if she didn't loathe being around me that much. She enjoyed my touch and sex and my kisses, that was obvious. That was something I could understand, but beyond that, she remained a mystery to me.

And it didn't matter either way. She was mine and I would protect her. Even against Falcone. That man had been ruining my life for far too long. I'd never found the motivation to go against him despite everything Falcone had done to me.

I wasn't even sure why. I would kill anyone who tried to kill me. I wouldn't even hesitate. But Falcone? I couldn't identify what had been keeping me from revenge all these years. Falcone was my father, but I didn't think that was why. I didn't feel anything when I said or thought the word "father." It was an empty word for me. And yet my father was still alive. Had I been hoping deep down that Falcone would see me as his son? I couldn't answer that question. And now

I didn't have to anymore. It was irrelevant why I hadn't taken revenge on the man yet.

Something had changed. And the reason for it was Cara. In some way, Falcone had set everything in motion. By giving Cara to me, he'd signed his own death warrant, because I wanted to help Cara get revenge. I wanted nothing more. Falcone always called me his killing machine. Falcone had created the monster, and now it would come to kill its creator.

Perhaps she'd stop hating me if I did this. I couldn't hope for more than that. I knew nobody could ever truly come to care for me, and I'd accepted that.

chapter 20

—CARA—

Growl had been very quiet since we'd returned from the party yesterday. I couldn't tell if he was still thinking about helping me.

Growl flicked his thumb over my clit, tearing me from my thoughts. He pushed a finger into me. "I want your full attention," he rumbled, pushing into me again.

I nodded quickly, and banished any worry from my mind. This was my reprieve.

Suddenly Growl pulled his hand away. Confusion rushed through me. "What's wrong?" I asked.

"Touch yourself," he ordered, sitting back on his haunches.

I flushed with embarrassment. The last time I'd done that had ended in mortification. "It's not right," I said.

Growl barked out a laugh. "I don't give a fuck about right as long as it feels good. We've done so many things that are not right. Don't tell me this is worse."

I stared at him, arms at my side. "I can't do that with you watching."

"But you've touched yourself before?"

I hesitated. "Yes," I admitted reluctantly. Again shame washed over me like so many months ago. I wasn't sure why it still bothered me so much. After all, Growl was right. I'd done a lot of worse things with him.

"And it felt good, right?"

I shrugged half-heartedly. "It was okay."

Growl raised an eyebrow. He gripped my wrist and pushed my hand between my legs. I jumped at the feeling of my fingers brushing my center. I tried to jerk away, but Growl was holding me tight. "Stop trying to do what's right and do what feels good for you. You're fucking overthinking everything again."

I glared at him. "Don't tell me what I like and what I don't. Maybe I don't enjoy touching myself."

Growl just looked at me. He covered my forefinger with his and guided mine between my folds. My fingertip brushed my clit, then glided through my wetness. I shuddered at the sensation. Growl kept sliding our fingers back and forth in a slow rhythm. His eyes bored into mine, and it took everything I had not to close my eyes to hide from his gaze. He guided my finger lower until I nudged my opening. My eyes grew wide. I'd never done that. I knew how much I liked it when Growl did it, though. I hesitated, but Growl didn't let my insecurity get the better of me. He used his finger to push my finger into me. I gasped in surprise and lust as both our fingers filled me. The feeling was incredible, and the hunger in Growl's amber eyes only added to my own desire. This felt so wrong but so unbelievably good. Growl established a slow rhythm, sliding our fingers in and out of me. It was incredible how wet and soft I felt.

"How does it feel?" Growl rasped.

I shook my head, unwilling to give him a reply. I couldn't admit aloud that this felt good. It was bad enough that I was enjoying it so much. Growl halted our fingers, his gaze becoming challenging. "How. Does. It. Feel?"

I bucked my hips, trying to keep the sensation, but Growl stopped me with his arm.

"Good," I said angrily. "It feels good."

A smirk crossed Growl's face, then it was gone, but he finally started moving again. He pushed our fingers harder into me, and I grew closer to my orgasm, but something was still missing.

"Touch your clit," Growl said.

This time I didn't hesitate. My other hand came down, and I pressed two fingers down on my clit. I moaned, but quickly clamped my lips together, embarrassed by the sound when Growl was watching me so closely. As if he could tell that I had trouble letting myself fall over the edge while he was watching, his gaze travelled down my body and he watched how our hands and fingers moved in sync to drive me closer to release. And then when it finally crashed down on me, everything fell out of focus and I let it all out, even when Growl turned his eyes back to me. I couldn't hold back, didn't want to.

I hadn't even caught my breath when Growl pushed to his feet and started undressing. I didn't think I'd ever get used to the sight of him naked. His tattoo, his scars, his muscles, all of him screamed danger, screamed stay away, and yet every cell in my body seemed to crave his closeness. His cock was already standing to attention, and it intensified the prickling between my legs again. I knew what was coming now and I couldn't wait. For a moment he stood in the middle of the room, admiring me. But I, too, couldn't get enough of letting my eyes roam over his body. Would this ever stop?

When my eyes returned to his face, his expression almost made me moan. He staggered toward me and climbed on the bed. I waited for him to position himself on top of me and fuck me. But he surprised me by lying flat on his back. Confusion drew my brows together but before I could ask what he was doing, he gripped my hips and lifted me on top of him, so I was straddling his hips. His tip pressed against my opening, and a thrill shot through my body at the sensation. Growl's hands on my waist tightened after a moment. Uncertainty flooded me. I wasn't exactly sure how to do this, but I didn't want to admit it aloud. Gathering my courage, I steadied myself against Growl's rock-hard chest. Focusing on his muscles and not the intensity of his eyes, I slowly lowered myself on his cock. A long moan escaped my lips at the feel of his length sliding into me deeper than ever before. I exhaled slowly when he was all the way in and I sat comfortably on top of him. I'd never felt this full before. It was incredible.

Growl moved his hips upwards a few inches and my eyes flew up to his. There was strain in his face. I smiled and his eyes flashed. Digging my nails into his chest the way he liked it, I lifted myself slowly, letting his cock glide out of me. I focused on tensing my inner muscles to make it even more intense for Growl, wanting to drive him to the brink of insanity. He gave my butt a light clap, making my eyes go wide, and a surprised gasp, followed by a laugh slipped out of my mouth.

There was something close to playfulness in his expression. I started moving faster. My butt cheeks accidentally brushed his balls and he exhaled sharply. I faltered, unsure if that was a good sign, but one look at his face erased all of my worries. He liked it. A lot.

I twisted my hips, making sure to press my butt against his balls every time I lowered myself. Growl's breath grew faster, and the low growls I adored came from deep in his throat again. My own body tightened in anticipation of an orgasm, and when I leaned forward slightly, my clit brushed his pubic bone and I came apart. My fingers dug even deeper into his skin and I moved faster, pushing my own orgasm to new heights. And then Growl's body shuddered and I felt him release into me, teasing my tender inner walls even more. I cried out, throwing my head back. "Oh God," I said.

When my heartbeat slowed, I opened my eyes and peered down at the man beneath me. He was watching me with surprise.

"What?" I said self-consciously.

Growl ran his finger over my breast, then slowly down my stomach until it came to rest over my clit. I shuddered, still too sensitive for his touch.

"This was the first time you were loud."

My already hot face heated even more. "Loud?" I glanced toward the curtain-covered window, worried about the neighbors. Had they heard anything?

"Don't worry about them. They don't care if that bastard from across the street beats his wife to a bloody pulp. They won't give a shit about you screaming your head off because you're getting off."

I stared at him. His dirty language still got me sometimes. But he was right. I'd lost count of the times I'd heard the woman from across the street scream, and nothing had ever happened.

—GROWL—

Watching her touch herself was the hottest thing I had ever seen. God, I'd told other women to do the same thing for me, but it had always looked false and wrong. But with Cara, she'd really let loose. She trusted me in bed. It was more than I deserved for sure.

I'd wanted many things in life. I'd wanted to possess, to destroy, to subdue. I'd never wanted to be kind to someone, or be with someone beyond the simple act of fucking. I'd fucked many women; none of them had meant anything to me. I didn't despise women. I didn't like them less than men. I just didn't like humans in general. They were backstabbing, disloyal creatures. That's why I preferred the company of my dogs. They wouldn't wait for me to fall asleep before killing me. If one of my pits wanted to kill me, he'd take my face off in the middle of the day. I liked it better that way.

Cara was sprawled on the bed beside me, her chest rising and falling rapidly, her peaked nipples even pinker than usual against her white skin. A few trickles of sweat trailed down her stomach, and I had to stop myself from licking them off her skin. I needed to talk to her, not distract myself with another round of sex. Though the sight of her naked, finally without shame, made it hard to contain myself.

Cara turned her head, raising her eyebrows. "There's a funny look on your face. Did I do something wrong?" Two pink spots appeared on her cheekbones, and I leaned forward and kissed her forehead. I didn't know why. I'd never done it. Never even thought about doing it. The forehead wasn't a very interesting place for a kiss. Cara was turning me upside down, that was for sure. "You did nothing wrong."

Surprise filled her pretty face. Even she didn't understand why I'd done it, and she was usually good at deciphering emotions and human actions.

She put a hand on my chest. A small gesture that didn't make sense either. Perhaps not everything had to make sense. "Are you all right?"

"I will help you," I said firmly.

She blinked. "Help me?" Her hand against my skin began to tremble. "You mean with Falcone?"

I nodded. There was no turning back now. I'd made my decision and nothing would stop me. I'd die if necessary. She would be worth it. "I will help you get revenge."

—CARA—

I couldn't believe it. I'd hoped for it of course, dreamed about it. But it had seemed unlikely, impossible. Growl was Falcone's man, his most feared assassin. How could I have changed that?

"So let me get this straight," I said slowly, wanting to make sure that I wasn't getting things wrong. "You want to help me get revenge, even though you never tried to get revenge for what Falcone did to you and your mother? Why? I don't get it. You didn't even like my father."

My mind was screaming at me to stop asking questions, but I needed to know. I was starting to accept that for some reason, part of me felt something for the man in front of me. And I needed to know if he did too.

"It's not because of your father. I don't care that he's dead." The words barely stung anymore. I'd gotten used to Growl's harsh words. He was honest—that was something I appreciated.

I propped myself up on my elbow and searched his face for answers. "Then why?" My voice was a bare whisper.

Growl's amber eyes traced my face. "Falcone's gone too far. You didn't deserve what he did to you."

"What do you mean?" I asked carefully, not sure what he was getting at.

"You were innocent. He punished you for something your father did. That's not right."

"And he punished you when you were a little boy for something your mother might have done, punished you for doing absolutely nothing. That should have been enough to make you want to kill him."

"I always wanted to kill him."

"Then why didn't you?"

"When I was a small boy, I would have killed him, but back then I didn't have the skills. And later when I had them, I felt obligated to him, for giving me the skills, for showing me what I could do. Without him, I wouldn't be what I am today."

"A monster? A killer? You could have become so much more, if he hadn't killed your mother and destroyed your childhood. He broke you." I winced the moment the last words left my mouth.

Growl's face flashed with bitterness. "I was the son of a whore who worked for Falcone. I would have become one of his men anyway, but without his cruelty, without what he'd done to me, I'd have never become ruthless enough to become his best hit man."

"So you're helping me because Falcone treated me wrong? He's treated many people worse than me."

Growl nodded. He ran a finger down my arm, then back up again. "He did. I did. But I want to help you be happy. I want you to get out of this miserable city and life. I never wanted that for me, but you, for you I want everything."

"Thank you," I said quietly. I couldn't say more. This was overwhelming.

I cleared my throat. Emotions had never been part of the plan, or even a possibility in the beginning. I needed to focus now.

"What are we going to do with my sister? We don't even know where she is."

Growl pulled his hand away from my arm. I felt bad, but I knew I had no reason to. I had never chosen this.

"I will find out," Growl promised.

"I thought Falcone wasn't sharing that piece of information with you."

"So far he hasn't. But now that things are going worse with New York, I think he might soon have reason to tell me where your sister is."

I sucked in a breath. "Because he thinks you will hurt her."

"But I won't."

"I know," I said without hesitation, and I did. How could things have come this far? I was falling for him, and I wasn't sure how to stop myself from feeling that way. But I had to. There was no future for Growl and me.

He had been a monster all his life. Even if I told him he could redeem himself by helping me, I'd never really believed it, had I? How could I be with someone like that? How could I explain that to my mother and sister? How could I explain it to myself?

chapter 21

—CARA—

The screaming from the neighbors grew louder. It was early in the morning. The sun had barely risen yet, but I'd been lying awake for hours. Not just because of the fighting in the neighbor's house, but also because of Growl agreeing to help me.

I scrambled out of bed and peered out the window toward the house across the street. This time the couple had taken their fight outside. They were facing each other on their front lawn. A small boy stood in the doorway, perhaps two years old, watching how his parents screamed at each other.

The man raised his hand and hit the woman so hard that she stumbled and fell to the ground, but that didn't stop him. He leaned over her and hit her again. The boy started crying, his face contorted with terror.

"Growl," I called, then louder. "Growl!"

My door flung open, and he stepped in, looking alert. He was wearing only boxers. "What's wrong?"

"The guy is beating his girlfriend up again."

Growl gave his "so-what" look. "He's doing it almost every day and she doesn't leave him. It's not our problem."

Another scream drew my eyes back to the couple. The woman was trying to crawl away from her boyfriend but he grabbed her by the hair and twisted her around, hitting her again.

"Help her," I said firmly. "Please. Or I will do it." I turned and headed out of my room, then continued to the front door, ripping it open. I knew it would be near impossible for me to stop the man because he was tall and big.

Growl was close behind me. "You need to learn to mind your own business."

"Why? So I can become as ruthless as you and Falcone? No, thanks!" I hissed as I stormed down the sidewalk.

Before I could reach the street Growl grabbed me by the arm, jerking me to a stop. I whirled on him. The howling of the young boy carried over to us and tore at my heart. Nobody else was helping, though many faces appeared in windows, watching what was going on. "This boy has to watch his father beat up his mother. You should know what it does to a child to watch that kind of horrors. Do you really want that boy to share the same fate as you?"

Growl's eyes flashed with uncertainty, then his gaze fell on the scene across the street. Resolve and fury took over his face. Relief flooded me. I knew that expression.

Growl crossed the street without looking left or right, and not caring that he was only dressed in boxers. I followed after him. The guy hadn't noticed us yet and was insulting his girlfriend and alternately kicking and hitting her. Growl was like a bull as he rammed the man with his shoulder. The guy let out a cry and tumbled to the ground. He looked like he wanted to punch whoever had attacked him, but when he raised his head and realized it was Growl, he shied back.

I crouched beside the woman who was still sitting on the ground, pressing her hand over her mouth. Blood was dripping down her chin. "You're okay now," I murmured as I touched her shoulder. Her unfocused eyes settled on me. She didn't say anything. I could smell alcohol on her breath. Her son came running toward us and hugged her around the neck. "Mom…Mommy."

She ignored him, eyes only for Growl who was hitting and shaking her boyfriend, and saying something we couldn't overhear.

"Don't let him kill my Dave," she said almost pleadingly.

I stared. After everything, she was worried about her abusive boyfriend?

"You should go to a women's shelter with your son."

The woman shook her head. "Dave isn't a bad guy. Don't let him hurt my Dave."

I stood. Growl shoved the man toward his car. "Fuck off," he growled, sounding as menacing as he looked. The man got into his car and drove off.

"You should really leave as long as he's gone," I told the woman. But her eyes followed the car with despair and longing, and I knew she wouldn't leave. I ruffled the boy's hair, and the gesture brought a smile to his face. That poor child.

I helped the woman and the boy inside their house, ignoring her constant questions about her boyfriend. Inside the house was crowded with empty beer bottles. It stank of smoke and alcohol, and then I decided that I needed to save the boy at least. I lifted him into my arms and carried him out again. The woman didn't stop me. She was fumbling with her mobile, trying to call her abusive boyfriend.

Growl gave me a look but didn't comment as I came out with the young boy. We walked across the street, and only when we entered Growl's house did he say, "You can't keep him."

"I won't. We have to call child services. We have to do something."

"You can't save them all."

"But I can save him, and that's enough," I said firmly. The boy was looking at Bandit and Coco curiously.

Growl glanced between me and the small boy, and nodded. "I know someone I can call. They will find a good place for him." The boy reached out and touched one of Growl's tattoos in fascination. Growl's expression softened a tad, and then he headed off toward the phone as if he was scared of his own reaction. There was hope for him after all.

An hour later, two women came and picked the boy up. That evening I heard his parents screaming at each other again, but they didn't come to ask for him.

When I lay next to Growl after sex that night, I whispered, "You did the right thing today."

He had. Perhaps I was wrong; perhaps he could make up for his sins by doing good.

Growl turned to me. "Maybe But that woman is still with the asshole. Some people know nothing but misery. It's something reliable. Change scares them more than their shitty life."

I traced the inked thorns over his forearm. "Like you."

Growl narrowed his eyes. "I'm changing my life for you by going against Falcone."

"I know, and I'm grateful for that. But you're doing it for me. It's like you still don't think you deserve anything good," I said. "You live in this place, even though you don't have to. I can't imagine Falcone is paying you that badly. You are like that woman—scared of change."

He sat up. "Living in this house isn't like being beaten up by someone." He hesitated. "Is it that bad for you?"

I sighed. "This place makes me miserable."

"You mean I make you miserable."

"No," I said, and I wasn't sure if it was the truth or still part of my plan to make him trust me. "This place. The people are hopeless and ignorant, and there's no beauty here, only desolation."

Growl looked around the room. "Beauty is fleeting."

"And desolation and despair aren't?" I sat up as well, and leaned my chin on his shoulder, breathing in his musky scent. I didn't want him to leave, but I could tell that he was already growing restless.

"It's familiar. It's reliable," Growl murmured. "I always liked that." And I had messed things up for him, changed up his routine. A creature of habit, indeed. And yet, he was giving it up for me.

For a while there was silence, then he slowly withdrew, and I had no choice but to let go of him. He perched on the edge of the bed as if part of him wanted to stay, but then he got up. "Sleep tight."

"I would sleep better if you stayed," I said.

Growl hesitated, shoulders tensing, breathing deeply, but then he strode out without a word. Every time I thought we were getting somewhere, he did something to remind me that we couldn't. Perhaps at some point my heart would accept it too.

We drove toward the Las Vegas strip with its skyscrapers. Everything was bright and the people were enjoying themselves. This was a far cry from the neighborhood where Growl lived. We stopped in front of a tall, sleek skyscraper with bellboys in front of the sliding doors. Growl got out before the man could open his door, so he helped me out of the car instead. It felt strange to be surrounded by this luxury again. I almost felt like I didn't belong, as if the last couple of weeks had changed me so much already that I couldn't possibly fit into the world I'd been part of all my life. It was a scary thought.

Growl led me inside the building with a hand on my back. It was a possessive gesture, and at the same time I thought he was trying to show me something else. Or was I trying to see things Growl wasn't capable of? The receptionist gave us a too-bright smile as we headed for the elevators.

We got out at the very top of the skyscraper and stepped into a massive penthouse. Everything was white and glass and gold. "What is this?" I asked. It was furnished with black and gray furniture. Everything was sleek and perfect.

"My apartment," Growl said simply.

I froze on my way toward the floor-to-ceiling windows. "This is yours?" This apartment looked completely unused. And in the six weeks that I'd been with him, he'd never mentioned it to me. I startled. Had it really been six weeks? God. And at the same time, six weeks seemed way too short a time span for everything that had happened.

Six weeks. Without my sister. She was fine, Growl had assured me. And my mother—I hadn't seen her in so long.

"I got it a few years back," Growl said, tearing me from my thoughts. "Falcone gave it to me as payment for a job well done, but I don't use it."

"If you have this," I motioned around myself, "then why are you living in that awful house? This place doesn't look like you've ever set foot in it. There's nothing that belongs to you."

Growl gave me a strange look. "Because this isn't who I am. The furniture was there when I got it and I never changed anything," he said in his usual low rumble. "This is too…" His eyes searched the room. "Too noble for someone like me. It's just not me."

I stopped at the window and let my gaze wander over the Las Vegas strip stretching out below us. In the distance I could see the endless red desert. I preferred to live in a house, had always loved my old home and the garden, but anything was better than the shack Growl called home. "For someone like you?" I repeated his words.

Growl approached me slowly and followed my gaze. "And Coco and Bandit wouldn't feel comfortable so high up. They'd miss their garden. Around here there's nowhere I could walk them."

I gave him a look, but he avoided my eyes. There was something strangely vulnerable and out of place in Growl. Why did he feel so uncomfortable in a luxurious apartment? "It's not like the area where we live is great for dog walks."

Growl gave me a strange smile. "Bandit and Coco are used to places like that. They know how to handle drunkards and junkies, whores and the homeless. The people around here with their fake smiles—that's something they can't handle. People like that sent them into dog fights."

"You know, there are places where normal, decent people live. You compare one extreme with the other."

"Normal," Growl said quietly, testing the word. "I've never had normal." He turned to me. "Can you imagine me among normal, decent people?"

I didn't say anything. Growl with his scary tattoos and scarred throat always drew attention to himself, and that was only his intimidating appearance.

He must have read my thoughts. He nodded. "Normal people wouldn't want me in their neighborhood—they'd be scared of me. And the people around here, they don't want me either because they, too, fear me."

"Everyone fears you," I said matter-of-factly. "Even the criminals and junkies in your area. If you want to live where no one fears you, you'll have to move into the wilderness." It was meant as a joke, to lighten up the mood, but Growl nodded thoughtfully.

"Animals don't fear me, only humans do. I'm a man-made monster, maybe that's why." He took in our surroundings again. "Monsters aren't meant for a palace like this."

He thought he didn't deserve to live in a nice place. Maybe along the way he'd started to believe what everyone said, that he was below everyone else, that he wasn't worth anything. For some reason I felt for him, even though I told myself he didn't deserve my compassion.

"You belong here," Growl said quietly. "A princess in her tower."

My lips parted in surprise. It wasn't the first time he'd said something like that, but it caught me by surprise every time.

"So why are we here?" I asked him.

"You hate the house," he said simply.

"And?"

"We can live here for a while. It'll make you feel better until I figure out the best day to go through with our plan."

I was stunned into silence. Growl was really considering moving into this place because he wanted to see me happy. "Are you sure?" I wanted nothing more than to live here, in this bright place, away from the misery.

He nodded, but I could detect a hint of uncertainty.

"What about Bandit and Coco? You said it yourself, they need a yard. Will they get used to this?"

Growl brushed a strand of hair from my shoulder. "I'm away on business most of the time. I can take them with me. I'm often out in nature where they can run. And I won't sell the house, so we can return there if we don't want to stay here."

I doubted that I'd ever want to return to Growl's house. It wasn't even because it was small and in a bad neighborhood. The place was filled with too much desolation; it seemed burnt into the walls and floors. There was no escaping it.

"I'd love to live here," I admitted eventually. And I really would.

"We might not be living here for very long though. After we're done with Falcone, we have to leave Las Vegas."

I knew that, and after everything that had happened to me here, I wasn't sad to leave my hometown. I wanted a new start. *With Growl?* a sharp voice inquired in my head. And part of me wanted to say yes.

"I know, but even a few weeks or just days are good. I love seeing the horizon," I said. I peered up at him. There was a soft edge to his expression, and I couldn't help it. I'd never wanted him more than in that moment. I wasn't sure if this was still part of the plan, if my actions toward Growl were only intended to get him on my side, to reach my goal of revenge and safety for my family. I stood on my tiptoes, grabbed him by the neck and pulled him down to me for a deep kiss. He immediately responded. I pressed up against him and he grabbed my butt with one hand, squeezing. I started pulling at his clothes, and soon we were both naked, our hands roaming over every inch of uncovered skin. My body was aflame with need. Growl lifted me up and pressed my back against the window. I let out a surprised laugh. "Here?" I asked. He nudged my entrance with his length.

"It's a nice view," Growl said dryly.

I kissed him hard, and he pushed into me at the same time, making me gasp into his mouth. My back rubbed over the window as Growl pounded into me. Our eyes stayed locked on each other, and I got to see past the darkness, past the anger and violence, to the part of him he'd thought was dead. And then we both came at the same time. Growl sank to his knees with me still wrapped around him. We both panted. My eyes sought out the Strip as I rested my chin on his shoulder, admiring the neighboring skyscrapers, the blue sky. "Is this reflecting coating?"

Growl shook his head. "I don't think so."

I leaned my forehead against the glass. "So someone could have watched us?"

"Do you care?"

"No," I said. And it was true. A few weeks ago, this would have been impossible, but so much had happened since then that the idea of someone seeing me having sex wasn't something that could ruin my day. Far from it.

chapter 22

—CARA—

"Why do you always leave after we sleep with each other?" I tried to sound merely curious, but a hint of vulnerability slipped through.

"I can't sleep with someone else in bed," he said. "I never even thought I could share a house..." He glanced around our new surroundings. "...or apartment with anyone."

"Why?" I doubted he was worried that I'd kill him.

"I just can't. I prefer being alone, *preferred* being alone."

"Not anymore?" I asked hopefully.

"I don't sleep very well. And if someone was in bed with me, it would be worse," Growl said instead of answering my question.

"Maybe you need to get used to it. Maybe it takes time. You've been alone for a long time."

"Forever," he murmured. "I've been alone forever. Even when my mother was still alive, she worked a lot, especially at night. And after she was killed and I lived with Bud, I was glad to be alone. Being alone meant no pain. That was good."

My heart clenched for him. So much horror in his past. I didn't know if I, if anything could ever compete with that, ever win against the shadows of his past.

"Humans aren't meant to be alone. We need companionship It's in our nature. We need to be touched. We need to talk to someone. To have someone to trust. Otherwise we become..."

"Like me," Growl rasped. "I'm better off alone. I'm meant to be alone."

I stared at his tattoos, the ridges of his scars, his hard eyes. "Perhaps you're right."

Even if I didn't want to accept it, Growl might be one of the people who couldn't be with others for long.

He pushed up again, and this time I didn't try to stop him. My eyes followed the line of muscles from his broad shoulders down to his firm butt. My cheeks didn't heat anymore, but the fire in the pit of my stomach ignited once more at the sight. I'd never felt anything like it before. I'd had crushes, had felt butterflies, but this was something else, something stronger and darker. I desired him, perhaps even...loved him. I couldn't be sure. Not now, not when my life was in upheaval and my choices weren't my own. Could love be born out of captivity? Wasn't it something that could only thrive in freedom?

Growl didn't turn again as he strode toward the door and left. The fire in my belly died as if someone had killed it with water. I pulled the blankets up to my chin. I'd never known that loneliness came with a sensation like icy dew covering my skin. Cold. I felt cold.

I felt tender between my legs from Growl, but the rest of me was nothing. This ache between my legs was all that reminded me of him. Soon, if...when our plan was successful and we were all safe, what would happen to me? To Growl and me? He struggled with emotions. Most of the time I wasn't sure if he could even understand them. Perhaps for him they were what letters were to people with dyslexia. But couldn't those people learn to live with their limitation, and learn to read and write despite it? So why couldn't Growl learn emotions? He had already come a long way from when we first met. Perhaps emotions were foreign to him, like passion had been to me, but it didn't always have to be like that. Growl had taught me passion, had given me no choice but to surrender myself to it. Was I foolish to hope I could teach him emotions as he'd taught me desire?

Perhaps you have already, a meek voice whispered in my head. Perhaps. And perhaps it wasn't enough.

My eyes were drawn to the skyline of Las Vegas. He'd moved to this place for me. For whatever reason, he'd turned his life upside down for me. The next few weeks would tell. If our plan to get revenge went wrong, nothing mattered anymore. Least of all my emotions. Soon everything would be decided.

—GROWL—

"Falcone won't tell me where your sister is, and I think he's growing suspicious of my interest. Negotiations with New York don't seem to be going very well, which could mean that Falcone won't need your mother's help much longer, and then he'll end it. We can't wait for that to happen," I said a few days later as I came back to the apartment after doing Falcone's biding as I had all these years. Coco and Bandit welcomed me, wagging their tails wildly. I patted their heads but kept my eyes on Cara, who rose from the sofa where she had been reading.

She must have realized that if Falcone didn't need her mother's help anymore, he'd probably get rid of her, and Talia.

She wrapped her arms around her chest, blinking hard. "But what can we do if we don't even know where my sister is? We can't get revenge as long as she's not safe."

"I will get the information out of Falcone, don't worry. We'll kidnap him and I'll make him talk. Once I know where your sister is, I will kill Falcone, and we'll come to New York with your sister." Falcone was a sadistic fucker, but he would yield under pain. They all did.

Cara took a few hesitant steps closer. "What about me and my mother?"

"You will leave right after I have Falcone in my hands. I don't want you in town when I'm dealing with Falcone. We'll all meet up in New York."

She shook her head. "I won't leave without my sister. What if something goes wrong and we can't free her? I want to be there to make sure everything is okay."

"You can't help. You'll only be a liability because I'll have to keep an eye on you, too, and won't be able to fight as freely as I usually would."

"Do you think there will be fighting?"

I laughed humorlessly. There would be a bloodbath. "Falcone is never without bodyguards, and I suppose your sister will be guarded as well. I will have to kill anyone who gets in my way. We can't let anyone survive. They might give something away. We can't risk that."

"So we'll drive to Falcone's house and kidnap him?"

"He usually meets with me once a week to give me new jobs. That's the best day to attack. He will expect me, so he won't grow suspicious. I'll take him to a safe place, get the information we need and kill him. Then I'll get your sister."

She frowned deeply. "I told you I won't drive ahead. I will stay as long as it takes for all of us to be safe and Falcone to be dead."

I didn't say anything. I didn't understand her. Why would she want to risk her life?

"And I need to talk to my mother. She needs to know what we've planned," Cara said.

I shook my head. "No. She might give something away by accident. She doesn't need to know." I paused. "Cara, I really want you to drive ahead with your mother. You shouldn't be in Las Vegas a minute longer than necessary." I wanted to know she was safe, or as safe as she could ever be in this messed-up world.

"No!" she cried out. "I want to be there. I want revenge more than you do. Shouldn't I be there when it happens?"

I bridged the remaining distance between us and touched her cheek, not even sure why I always yearned to touch her face. "Are you sure you want that? It'll change you, believe me. Having blood on your hands changes everything."

Her eyes were glassy as she looked up at me. "My life changed when Falcone killed my father; seeing Falcone die for his sin will only make things better."

I considered her words. Could I keep her safe? I could. *I would*. I nodded. "Okay. But when things get dangerous, you'll have to listen to my commands. If I tell you to run, you'll run, and you won't hesitate or argue. Understood?"

"Understood." She moved closer to me, her pliable body pressed up against mine, and put her hand against my chest. "I can't believe you're really doing this."

I couldn't believe it either, but I had never been more sure about something in my life. I wanted, I *needed* to help the woman in front of me. "I promised. I will do this for you, and perhaps then you can forgive me."

"Forgive you?" she whispered as if she'd never heard the word, and of course it was fucking ridiculous of me to think she could ever forgive me for what I'd done, for having kept her like a possession. I silenced her with a kiss, fucking scared of her next words, not wanting to hear them, and led her into the bedroom.

—CARA—

Growl's eyes were closed. He wasn't asleep though. Not that I knew how he looked when he was actually asleep, since he never let me be anywhere close when he was that vulnerable. Whenever he got this close to sleep, he'd send me away or he'd leave if he was in my bedroom.

I scooted to the edge of the bed and untangled myself from the blankets. I'd stayed for far too long already. My eyes were growing heavy. I didn't want to be woken and sent away by Growl later. It was easier this way, when leaving seemed like my choice and not a result of his incapability or unwillingness to share a bed with me, his incapability of giving me more closeness than was absolutely necessary. It was ridiculous how this small semblance of choice made me feel better.

My feet hit the cold floor and a familiar shiver raced down my spine. This time I didn't allow myself to perch on the edge of the bed. I stood. I hadn't moved a single step when a strong hand wrapped around my wrist. "Stay," came the rough command.

I froze, my gaze darting toward Growl. He was still sprawled out on the bed, his eyes still closed. Nothing in his demeanor had changed, and if it weren't for his hand holding on to me tightly, I'd have convinced myself that I'd imagined the word.

I didn't dwell on why he'd changed his mind. I slipped back under the covers, and only when I lay beside him did Growl let go of my wrist.

"Why?" I asked softly. He stayed on his back, didn't reach for me, and I didn't try to snuggle up to him. It would have been too much. This, inviting me to stay the night, was already a huge step for him.

"Don't ask," he rumbled.

Growl extinguished the lights and darkness fell over us. I hardly dared to breathe, much less move, acutely aware that Growl was probably listening to my every sound. Was I intruding? Was he already regretting that one word?

I pushed the thoughts away, and then when I least expected it, Growl put his hand against my back. A light touch, but enough. Another step in the right direction. With the sound of his unchanging breathing in the background and the feel of his palm lightly resting on my back, I slowly drifted off to sleep.

chapter 23

—CARA—

That night I was woken twice by nightmares. Not my own, though. Growl was writhing and panting in his sleep. I hadn't dared waking him. I had a feeling he wouldn't like that I knew of his troubles.

It was strange seeing him distressed, his face twisted with agony. I'd never considered that something could bother him so much. Perhaps he was even more human than I thought.

He wasn't in bed when I woke, but I found him in the kitchen leaning against the counter with a cup of coffee as usual. Even now that we had a kitchen table in the penthouse, he still preferred to stand, as if he needed to be prepared to run at any moment. And for a moment, I allowed myself to regard him: how out of place he looked in the sleek, expensive kitchen, how out of place he obviously felt.

Coco and Bandit were sitting by his side, staring up at him with adoring eyes.

"Morning," I said.

Growl filled a cup and handed it to me. I smiled and briefly touched his forearm in thanks. He didn't move away, and his gaze gave me pause. I drank my coffee, giving him the time he needed to say what he wanted.

"I have a request," Growl said quietly.

"Okay." What could I possibly do for him?

He peered down at Coco and Bandit. "Will you take care of my dogs in case anything happens to me?"

I frowned. "Nothing will happen to you. We'll all go to New York together."

"You should be looking forward to the prospect of my death," he rasped. "I'm sure you've wished for it often."

I should hope for it, and in the beginning I had. I had even tried to kill him myself, after all. Soon we'd risk our lives. Perhaps this was the last time we'd be together. It was strange to think about it. Even stranger that I was sad about it. I scanned his face. I was no longer scared of him, and I no longer wished for him to die—far from it.

I reached out very slowly and traced the scar around his neck. Growl stilled but he didn't stop me. Surprise washed over me. It felt like a miracle that he let me do this, and deep down I was suddenly afraid; afraid of my emotions and what the future held for me.

"You won't die. You're the strongest person I know," I whispered. I stepped very close to him and locked eyes with his.

"I'm not." His amber eyes sucked me in. So many horrors lay beyond them, and yet I didn't hate him, not anymore.

How could I have let this happen?

"What's happening to us?" I asked quietly.

Growl frowned.

"What am I to you?"

"You are mine," he said simply. *His.*

His possession? His gift? Only that, or more?

It didn't matter. Once I was in New York, there was no future for us. I wouldn't stay with Growl. I couldn't, couldn't do this to Mother and my sister. They wouldn't understand, and how could they, when even I didn't know how it had happened.

—GROWL—

"I will take care of your dogs if that's what you want," Cara said.

I wanted many things, things I'd never wanted before. Most of all I wanted to tell her that I didn't want to lose her, and that for the first time in my life I was scared to die because I wanted to have more time with her. Yet at the same time I was scared not to die, because then I'd see her leave me the moment we were in New York.

"Coco and Bandit love you," I told her, and it wasn't all I wanted to say, but I couldn't speak the rest.

She searched my eyes, but I wasn't sure what she was looking for. Even now I hardly understood the workings of her brain. She was a mystery to me, would probably always be, but it didn't matter. Somehow, she'd done what no one else had ever accomplished She'd bound me to her, and I would always be loyal to her.

I'd been loyal to Falcone too, but it had been a different kind of loyalty. I would have died for Falcone, because I had never before cared if I lived or died. But now, now I wanted to live, and yet I'd gladly give my life for Cara, so she could be happy.

"And I love them," Cara said softly.

The word "love" from Cara's lips did something to me, something I could not understand.

—CARA—

The next morning Growl woke me before sunrise. He had been gone all night and I'd been sick with worry because he hadn't warned me that he'd be gone so long.

"We have to act today," Growl said as he hovered over me.

I rubbed my eyes and sat up slowly. "What..." I stopped myself, realizing what he meant. I sat up. "Why? Did something happen?"

"Falcone is tired of negotiating with New York. I doubt he'll have use for your mother much longer."

I pushed out of bed. "Are we ready?"

We couldn't fail.

"Ready enough," Growl rasped. "We have to risk it. We can't wait. I found someone who will help us. I can't take care of everything on my own."

"Can we trust him?"

Growl shook his head. "I don't trust anyone. But he's on Falcone's hit list, and I offered him a chance to escape. It also helps that Falcone killed his brothers and he's out for revenge like we are. I was supposed to kill him."

"Okay," I said uncertainly.

"And I know him from when we were kids. His mother was one of Bud's whores. He and I occasionally spent time together in the brothel."

"You were friends?"

"No. I had no friends. He was scared of me even back then, but we often hid from Bud together, so we were allies."

"Okay, if you think he won't betray us, I believe you."

Growl reached out as if to touch my cheek but dropped his arm. Disappointment filled me, but I had no time to dwell on it. "You need to get dressed. Grab a few things for the drive to New York. I want to leave in fifteen minutes."

I put on comfortable clothes and stuffed a toothbrush and my remaining clothes into a backpack before I rushed out of my room. Growl waited in front of the door. Bandit and Coco were nowhere in sight. "I put them in the car," he said, as if he'd seen the question in my eyes.

I nodded, drawing in a shuddering breath. I wanted to say something but my mouth was too dry. Instead I stood on my tiptoes and gave Growl a lingering kiss. His eyes softened, but mostly they looked melancholic.

"Let's go," he murmured.

In the car a strange sense of wistfulness overcame me. Not because I would miss Las Vegas, but because I'd miss whatever odd connection Growl and I had developed. I wasn't sure what the future would bring, but I knew Growl and I couldn't be together. It wouldn't work. It was wrong.

I risked a glance at the man beside me. Almost two months ago, we'd been in a car together as well, and back then my life had seemed over. I'd hated him, feared him, wanted him dead. He'd been nothing but a monster in my eyes. His gruesome tattoos didn't repel me anymore, and neither did his scar, which I now knew was only one of many. I understood him better now.

He wasn't a monster. He was monstrous in parts, had no choice but to turn that way to survive the horrors of his past. But there was a human side to him as well. It had shone through more and more in the time we spent together. Perhaps eventually it would triumph over his monstrous side, but I knew I couldn't travel his path to humanness with him. I had to think of my mother and sister.

The hope of being reunited with both of them gave me strength. I didn't want to consider that I could lose everything.

"I didn't tell anyone that we'd be going to your mother today. First, I thought about pretending you wanted to visit her, but after Falcone's words yesterday, that would have only caused suspicion. He might have worried that you would warn your mother of his plans to stop the negotiations."

"You're probably right," I said. "Where will we meet the guy who's helping us?"

"Mino will be at a meeting point in a deserted factory."

"So he won't help you fight Falcone's bodyguards?" What was his purpose then?

"I prefer to fight alone."

Suddenly it struck me that Mino was only meant as a driver, but that only made sense if Growl didn't expect to be able to drive us himself.

I had no time to think about it because we parked in front of my old home.

Growl didn't hesitate. Everything had to go very fast. He practically sprang out of the car and ran toward the house. He rang the bell, and after a moment a man I didn't know opened the door. Growl grabbed his head and twisted violently like I'd seen him do two months ago. The man dropped to the ground, and then Growl disappeared inside the house. My hand reached for the door. It was hard to stay in the car and wait. What if something went wrong and I wasn't there to help?

What could I possibly do though? If one of Mother's guards managed to overpower Growl, then that person would definitely have no trouble with me.

The seconds were trickling by and my palms were becoming sweaty. Then, finally, Growl stormed out of the house, dragging Mother after him. I let out a sigh of relief.

Mother was struggling against him, obviously convinced he meant her harm. I opened the door and that's when she spotted me. Confusion crossed her face but she stopped fighting Growl, not that she'd been getting anywhere with her struggle anyway. I knew the power behind his grip.

Growl opened the back door and pushed Mother inside, then threw the door closed again. The dogs began barking in the back. Growl sat behind the steering wheel mere seconds later, and we drove off again.

Mother sat up from where she'd been sprawled out on the backseat, then noticed Coco and Bandit behind her. She gasped and shied away.

"They're harmless," I assured her.

She gave me a questioning look. Her eyes darted between me and Growl, obviously unsure if she should speak in front of him. "Everything's going to be okay," I tried to calm her. "Growl is helping us run away from Las Vegas."

Mother's eyes widened. "But what about Talia?"

"We'll get her first and then we'll drive to New York."

Mother shook her head. "I didn't succeed. Luca wants nothing to do with the Camorra. He won't help us."

"You aren't part of the Camorra," Growl interrupted. "You are family. He will take you in."

I stared at him. "But you are. Doesn't Luca know?"

"He knows. I've done too much in Falcone's name."

I didn't understand. Would Luca take him in anyway? Or perhaps Growl had no intention of joining us in New York, and that was why Mino was supposed to drive us.

I noticed Mother's scrutiny and averted my eyes from Growl. She couldn't find out about my feelings.

"What about Falcone?" Mother asked.

"There's no time to explain," Growl said impatiently. His body was tight with tension.

He stopped the car behind a pickup parking on the side of the street. "This is Mino's car. I want you to get in there, and I'll take care of Falcone."

I glared at him. "I thought he would be waiting in the abandoned factory for us after we were done with Falcone."

"I don't want you around when I'm dealing with him. You'll only be in the

214

way, and there's not enough room for Falcone if you and your mother are there."

A burly man got out of the pickup and waited.

"I won't leave," I said firmly.

Growl pressed his lips together. He was getting angry, but I didn't care. I wanted to be part of this. "All right," he muttered. "But your mother will leave."

He got out and flung open the back door. Mother gave me a frightened look. "What are you doing, Cara? This is madness." She didn't get further. Growl pulled her toward the pickup and put her in the backseat, then he was back behind the steering wheel and we drove away. I peered over my shoulder at the pickup that pulled away from the roadside and went off in the other direction.

"Your mother is safe. Mino needs our help. He and his family can only hope for safety if New York grants them protection, and the only way that will happen is if your mother puts in a good word for him. He has no choice but to make our plan work."

That information calmed me. If you could trust in one thing, it was that people wanted to save their own hide and protect their family.

The gate to Falcone's mansion appeared in the distance. "There is a blanket in the back. Crouch in the legroom and cover yourself with it. I don't want them to see you."

I grabbed the blanket and did as he'd asked, trying to be as still as possible. A few minutes later, the car stopped and I heard the window slide down, then a male voice.

"Morning. Mr. Falcone is awaiting you."

After a brief moment of panic, I reminded myself that Growl had mentioned he was supposed to meet Falcone to discuss another job. At least, that way nobody would grow suspicious. I heard the muffled shot and a body hitting asphalt. My heart pounded in my ears when the car was set in motion again.

chapter 24

—CARA—

"Stay here. I will probably take a bit longer to disable Falcone's guards," Growl said as he pulled the blanket off me. He held a gun out to me. "Do you know how to use it?"

My eyes widened and I shook my head. He quickly explained the basics to me, then he got out, and I wished he would have given me a kiss in case he didn't return.

Don't even think about it. If Growl died, all of us would.

Growl opened the trunk and the dogs jumped out. I stayed crouched in the legroom but peeked out of the window. Coco and Bandit followed after Growl as he headed for the door. Someone opened it and Growl shoved a knife into the soft spot below his chin, then Growl went out of my sight.

It took an endless ten minutes until finally Growl appeared in the doorway. Blood was trickling down his forehead and his shirt was ripped. My heart skipped a beat at the sight, until Growl stepped out, holding Falcone by the collar. One trouser leg was torn as if Coco or Bandit had bitten Falcone there. I smiled to myself despite my tension. I left my hiding place and slipped into the passenger seat, making room for Falcone in the back.

The trunk was still open, so Coco and Bandit jumped in without needing to be told. Coco's maw was covered in blood. Bandit's fur was too dark to tell what kind of liquid was wetting it, but I assumed it was also blood.

Growl thrust Falcone into the backseat. The man's hands were tied together with tape, and so was his mouth. He glared when he spotted me in the car.

Growl got into his seat and started the car. We needed to get away from the house as quickly as possible. Nobody tried to stop us as we left the premises.

"Is everything okay?" I asked, scanning the cut on Growl's head. It didn't look very deep, but blood was running down his face and getting in his left eye.

He wiped it off impatiently. "I killed them all before they could ring an alarm."

Falcone made a muffled sound. He looked pissed, but there was also a hint of fear that gave me a sick satisfaction.

I smiled grimly at him before turning back to Growl. "What about his wife and children?"

"His sons are in boarding school in England, and his wife is in Aspen."

Good. At least that blood didn't have to be spilled. I didn't like Falcone's wife much, but she probably had suffered enough in her marriage. She didn't deserve death.

Falcone tried to say something again. Growl parked on the side of the road and turned in his seat. He shoved the sleeve of Falcone's shirt up, and pressed the knife into the skin a few inches below the crook of the elbow.

"What are you doing?" I asked.

"He implanted a GPS tracker into his body so we could find him if he was ever kidnapped," Growl said.

Falcone gasped in pain as Growl dug the small device out of his flesh with the sharp tip of his knife. The blood-covered tracker fell onto the backseat. Growl opened the window and threw the tracking device out.

Then he pulled off the tape over Falcone's mouth before we continued our journey.

"Are you sure it's a good idea to let him talk?" I asked.

Falcone panted in the backseat, the skin around his mouth red, and glared at us. "What did that whore do to wrap you around her fingers? I'd have thought you were immune to manipulation."

"You manipulated me all my life," Growl rasped.

"Did she tell you that? She must have sucked your brains out."

"Be careful," Growl warned.

Falcone tried to push himself into a sitting position but with his tied hands it wasn't easy. Eventually he gave up, which was probably for the best considering that Bandit had stuck his head over the backseat and was only too eager for another taste of the man "Is she worth losing everything? You could have become my successor. You still can if you kill that bitch now."

I laughed. And Growl, too, smiled bitterly. "As if your men would have ever accepted me as their boss. I know what everyone says about me, even you. A bastard can never amount to anything but a henchman. I'm not stupid. I know what's been going on behind my back. And you have legitimate heirs—you don't need me."

"This life is all you know, all you have. If you risk it for her, you'll be left with nothing. She isn't worth it, believe me."

Growl's eyes slanted over to me briefly. "Yes, she is. She's worth more than you and I. She'll be worth losing everything for."

My heart swelled with love, and at the same time my stomach tightened. This wasn't meant to happen. Falling in love with a man like Growl was the worst thing I could do, but it was too late now. I couldn't deny my emotions for the man next to me.

"I should have killed you when you were a useless boy. You are worthless. The son of a cock-sucking whore. If you don't work for me, what will you do? There's nothing you can do. You are a monster. You've always been. I knew it when I first saw you, when you were a screaming ugly baby."

Growl pulled into a deserted parking lot. The store had been closed for a long time from the looks of it. He jumped out of the car and dragged Falcone out of the backseat, then pushed him to the ground. Falcone cackled.

I got out of the car as well.

Growl grabbed Falcone by the throat. "You've done enough damage. I won't listen to you anymore. You will die today."

"My men will kill you. You can't stop them all. They're probably already looking for me."

I froze. How?

Growl narrowed his eyes. "You're lying."

Falcone's smile widened. "I have a second tracker somewhere in my body. After the thing with her traitorous father, I decided I needed additional safety measures. Someone will wonder why I'm leaving my house, and then they'll find me." Falcone fixed me with a terrifying look. "Your little sister will suffer badly."

I released a harsh breath.

"It'll be a while for your men to notice you aren't in the house. They have no reason to check your tracker," Growl said, but he didn't sound sure.

"We have to find Talia," I begged.

Falcone smirked. "I won't tell you."

Growl smiled grimly. "Oh, you will." He turned to me. "You should return to the car. This will get ugly."

"No. I want to watch."

Growl hesitated, but then he took out his knife and knelt beside Falcone.

"I'd love to do this slowly," he murmured in a voice that reminded me why I'd been scared of him at the beginning. Why I should still be scared of him. "But we're out of time." He silenced Falcone with tape again, grabbed Falcone's tied hands and pushed the tip of the knife beneath one of his fingernails.

My eyes grew wide when I realized what he was going to do, and then Falcone's muffled scream sounded and blood was spilling over Growl's knife. I retched and turned away, my chest heaving in an attempt to stop myself from throwing up.

Another muffled cry. I began shaking, and slowly raised my hands and covered my ears. I'd wanted this, had wanted Falcone to suffer, but I couldn't watch. I couldn't bear seeing Growl as the monster I didn't want him to be. Falcone deserved this. He was the reason why Growl was capable of such atrocities in the first place. Now he got a taste of his own medicine.

A hand on my shoulder made me gasp, and I whirled around to find Growl watching me with haunted eyes. "We need to go. I know where your sister is. It's not far from here." I peeked behind him to where Falcone was lying on the asphalt, clutching his bleeding hand against his chest and crying. When he noticed my scrutiny, he scowled. He would kill me if he got the chance. "That was quick," I said, relieved.

Growl scanned my face then nodded. "He's not used to pain anymore. It makes things easier."

I wondered how often Growl had done this before, but I knew I'd never ask him.

"I couldn't watch," I whispered.

"That's good. You are a good person."

"I'm not," I said. "If I were a good person, I wouldn't want him to suffer and die, but I do. I'm only too weak to watch."

Growl touched my cheek. "It's better, believe me."

"Will you kill him now?"

"No. We might still need him as a shield. And we should hurry." He dropped his hand and loaded Falcone back in the car, not caring that he got blood all over the seats. Growl's shirt was already covered with it. But before he got in the car, he changed into a fresh shirt.

After a short drive, we arrived in front of a small house. "This is where your sister is kept," Growl said. "I'm not sure what to expect."

"That's why I should stay in the car," I finished for him.

Grown nodded. "I will be back soon." He pulled Falcone out and began to drag him toward the house, but Falcone struggled. He managed to free himself. I quickly got out of the car.

In that moment, another car pulled up. Cosimo was behind the steering wheel. He opened the door of his car.

Falcone stumbled a few steps away from Growl. I was about to call a warning, but Growl grabbed Falcone and cut his throat. Bile rose in my throat as blood spilled out. But this time I couldn't look away. "Now you know how it feels," Growl rasped.

Falcone dropped to the ground in a puddle of his own blood. My eyes flew back to Cosimo. He watched with wide eyes, then his gaze moved from Falcone to Growl and he got back into his car and began backing off. "Growl," I called.

Growl cursed, but didn't stop Cosimo from escaping. "I can't shoot him. It's too loud. Stay here." With those words, he ran toward the house, gun drawn. I picked up the gun Growl had given me and crawled on the backseat, shuddering at all the blood there, but I wanted to be at Talia's side.

I counted the seconds until suddenly Talia came running my way. "Here!" I screamed and her terrified eyes focused on me. She fled toward me and flung herself into the car. I clutched her against me, thankful to have her back.

Shots rang out. Growl limped toward the car and half fell into the seat.

He pressed his lips together as he started the car. "Get down," he ordered, and only a second after Talia and I had crouched in the backseat, a bullet tore through the window. Talia screamed, and I hugged her more tightly. "It's okay. Everything will be okay."

chapter 25

—CARA—

Two cars followed us but eventually we managed to shake them off. Growl steered the car toward the vacant factory that he and Mino had chosen as their meeting spot. When we arrived, the pickup was already waiting and Mino was smoking a cigarette. I didn't see Mother anywhere.

Talia raised her head when we came to a stop, her face tearstained and frightened. "What's happening?"

"We're leaving," I told her, stroking her hair. She didn't ask more questions. I could tell she was in shock. We left the car and Growl opened the trunk so Bandit and Coco could jump out. I had to support Talia. She was shaking too hard to walk on her own, but Growl, too, had trouble. His limp had gotten worse. He noticed my gaze and gave a shrug, as if it was nothing. I didn't believe him. I knew he had to be in a lot of pain.

"What took you so long?" Mino asked, then noticed Growl's limp as well. "Have you been followed?" Worry filled his face.

"Probably. Let's hurry," Growl said. The words had barely left his mouth when a car turned the corner and barreled our way. "Take the dogs and the girls, I'll stop them!"

"What?" I cried out, but Growl was already pulling his gun and shooting at the car, which jerked to a stop. Four men got out, and a second car shot around the neighboring building. Growl quickly aimed at its wheels and one of them exploded. The car spun around itself, then halted.

"Quick now!" Mino screamed, pulling at me.

"Cara," Talia whimpered. Her eyes were pleading with me, and that made me move. Mino and I carried her toward the pickup. Mother was in the back, and when Mino opened the locks I realized why she hadn't been getting out to help us. He'd locked her in. Probably for good reason. Talia got in the backseat with Mother, but I wanted to go back to Growl. I never got the chance.

Mino grabbed me and shoved me into the backseat with them, then shut the door. He got behind the steering wheel and activated the locks so I couldn't get out.

"What are you doing?" I screamed as I watched Growl fighting several men. He was crouching behind his car and shooting at them. But how long would he be able to keep them away?

"Let me out!"

Mino ignored me. He hit the gas and the car lurched into motion.

—GROWL—

I allowed myself a moment to watch the car drive away, watch Cara leave. I'd probably never see her again, and that was for the best. She would be happier without me in her life.

I shoved a knife into my next attacker before I fired two shots at the car to my left. I would fight and I would die today, but not in vain. For once the blood spilling would serve a good cause.

And if I died, I'd die with the memory of Cara's sweet taste, the feel of her perfect skin, and the image of her pretty face branded into my brain. I'd close my eyes with a good memory, no matter what awaited me after.

—CARA—

I banged my fists against the window, ignoring the dull pain zipping through my arms from the force of my motion. "Let me out," I screamed again, even louder. Not that Mino hadn't heard me the first time. We were barely two feet away from each other. Instead of listening to my request, he drove even faster.

I thrust my arms up and braced myself against the glass. Growl was surrounded by Falcone's men. Even a fighter like him couldn't possibly stand a chance against so many opponents.

I cried out. "Please, we have to help him."

Mino shook his head. "I have strict orders to take you away from here."

"But the man who gave the orders will be dead soon if we don't help him!"

"Even so. A promise to a dead man isn't worth less."

I sank back against the seat. We were too far away. I couldn't see Growl anymore. He'd survived so much. He couldn't die, not like this. Not so soon.

"Cara?" came Mother's soft voice, and I realized I'd completely forgotten about her and Talia. I turned to them. Confusion flickered on Mother's face, but also a bitter realization. I'd given myself away, but I couldn't bring myself to care.

My eyes found Talia. She was staring down at her hands, which lay limply in her lap.

I took her hand but she didn't react. "We'll be safe soon."

I didn't know what she'd gone through in the two months since I'd last seen her. She had lost weight but seemed physically unharmed, but that meant nothing.

Mother wrapped an arm around my sister but kept her eyes on me. "Why did that man help us?"

"I suppose he felt guilty for what he did and wanted to redeem himself," I said.

Mother pursed her lips. "That man doesn't know what guilt is. He's a monster. He's been Falcone's cruelest assassin for so many years—no one could do that without turning into something less than human."

I couldn't deny it. Growl had been cruel. He was a murderer. He'd done too many horrible things to count. There was no way I could explain my emotions to Mother, because I couldn't explain them myself.

"I heard the stories," Mino said. "How Falcone gave you to *him* as a gift. It was meant as punishment for your family for your father's betrayal."

He was watching me through the rearview mirror, a curious expression on his sun-weathered face. I didn't react to his words. It wasn't meant as a question.

Mother had paled at the mention of Father, but she remained silent.

"What I don't get is why you are crying over him. Shouldn't you be relieved to be rid of him? He was a monster," Mino continued.

I raised my fingers to my cheeks, feeling the wetness. "He was," I agreed.

I wasn't delusional. I'd witnessed Growl's darkness, his irredeemable side, and yet I'd come to love him. Maybe because I knew of the other Growl, the person he kept hidden beneath many layers of brutality. That tender and vulnerable side, that caring and loving side. That had won me over. I knew the man in front of me wouldn't believe me if I told him about that Growl. And it was probably for the best. Growl had always done his best to keep that side of him hidden, to protect himself. I wouldn't destroy the image he'd worked so hard on, even if I hated the mask he'd created for himself. But now that he was gone, it was too late anyway.

My heart clenched into a tight fist.

"Maybe you should see someone, a shrink. I heard about this shit. Stockholm Syndrome."

Anger surged through me. I hated that he wanted to put a label like that on my feelings. Mother touched my arm and I could tell that she agreed with him.

Perhaps they were right. I didn't know. Didn't know if my feelings for Growl would have survived in freedom, I'd never get the chance to find out.

We drove for two days and only stopped for toilet breaks. Talia didn't speak at all the first day. On the second, she finally told us that she was okay. That she hadn't been hurt. That the wife of her guard had taken care of her as well as she could.

I was so relieved, even though another hurdle still lay ahead of us. Convincing the head of the New York Famiglia to help us and take us in. Mother had called him from an old pay phone at a rest stop and told him we'd be coming. He hadn't made any promises.

He probably thought we were spies.

It was hard to be scared of the future. I felt numb. Too much had happened. The man I loved was dead. He'd died for me. I wasn't exactly sure what I believed, only that there had to be something after this life. I hoped Growl's acts of kindness would be seen as a step to redemption and grant him access to a better place in the afterlife. He'd suffered so much while he was alive, and even though some of it was his own fault, I wanted happiness for him now that he was dead.

We entered New York in the afternoon.

"What happens if they don't allow us to stay?" Talia whispered.

"Either they think we're spies and kill us, or they'll send us away and Falcone's men will kill us," Mino said tightly. I could have hit him for that statement, even though it was probably true.

Coco yowled behind me. I turned around and scratched her behind the ear. She tilted her head to give me better access. Bandit wedged his head under my arm, begging for attention as well. I started tickling him beneath his chin the way he loved, and he closed his eyes in obvious enjoyment. These powerful animals that had scared me so horribly in the beginning had somehow sneaked their way into my heart. Just as their master had. Both shared a frightful exterior and the potential for destruction, but beneath that, there was something tender and vulnerable, something that made you want to take care of them and love them.

Now Coco and Bandit were all that was left of Growl. I'd take care of them for as long as I could, would try to protect them from harm. I owed it to Growl. My eyes began burning as they had so often in the last two days, but I blinked the tears away. I couldn't cry anymore. It seemed to drain me of all my energy, and I needed it for the meeting with the New York Famiglia.

Only a couple of months ago my life had been in shambles, or so it had seemed. I'd thought I wouldn't survive, but I'd been stronger than I'd thought possible. I was strong. If anything, my time with Growl had taught me that. I'd figure out a way to convince Luca that we weren't the enemy.

The car finally came to a stop in an industrial area that gave me little reason for hope. It was a place where you took someone you wanted out of the way. My eyes flitted to Mino. "Where are we?" I asked, my voice hoarse but firm.

"That's the address Vitiello gave your mother," Mino said. He glanced out of the window worriedly. He seemed to share my concern.

Two black cars were parked a good distance away from us.

"Perhaps we should get out so they can see that we aren't dangerous," I suggested.

"They could shoot us," Mino said.

"I know. But we don't have a choice."

I opened the door and got out. I moved slowly and held my arms away from my body, so they could see I wasn't armed. Usually Made Men weren't overly concerned about women being a danger to them, but I didn't want to risk anything. The dogs barked in protest.

My heart pounded against my ribcage as I took a few steps away from the car. After a moment of hesitation, Mother and Talia followed my example and joined me. We didn't move, only waited.

Mino stayed in the car. I gave him a look, but he appeared determined to wait. As a man he was in more danger of being shot on the spot. Even among mobsters, women were usually spared.

A huge man got out of one of the cars. He was tall and muscled like Growl, but his hair was black and he had no visible tattoos, and yet for a maddening moment I'd thought it was him, risen from the dead by some miracle.

"Luca," breathed Mother beside me. A second and third man stepped up to Luca's side a moment later. How could we know life here would be better than in Las Vegas?

I didn't know these people, had only heard stories, few of them flattering. Mother had left New York because her brother had been cruel, and now his son Luca would decide our fate. Was he better than his father, better than Falcone, or had we exchanged one evil for another?

After a short discussion, Luca and the second man began walking toward us. The third stayed back, but there were probably more in the cars. I was surprised that Luca was risking that much. Falcone would have stayed behind and let his men do the dirty work. I wasn't sure if it was a good sign that Luca had decided to meet us personally.

They stopped a good distance away.

"Your driver needs to get out," Luca said. He and the other man were holding guns.

I faced Mino and motioned for him to get out. His eyes darted to Luca but he remained firmly seated.

"If he doesn't get out soon, I'll get him out myself and he won't like that," the other guy said. He had dark brown hair, slightly longer than Luca's, and I realized they shared the same features. So that had to be his brother Matteo, if I remembered correctly.

Mino must have heard him because he finally climbed out of the car, holding his hands up over his head. Another man I hadn't noticed before ran around the car and grabbed him, twisting his arms behind his back. Mino cried out in pain, but fell silent when he was hit with the hilt of a gun. He toppled over, unconscious.

Talia began crying silently beside me. I took her hand. Mother was already holding the other. Luca scrutinized my sister, then me and Mother. I was too tired and too empty to be scared of them. The fear would come later. If there was a later.

For all I knew they'd see us as the enemy, and kill us. At least I'd be reunited with Growl then, but something in me rebelled against that idea. I missed Growl, missed him more than I'd thought possible. But there were too many reasons why I needed to live, why I wanted to live. My sister and mother were just two of them.

I summoned my courage and said, "I'm Cara. I'm your cousin."

"We know exactly who you are," Matteo said sharply.

That didn't sound as if they were happy to see us.

chapter 26

—CARA—

They didn't let us talk but they took us with them to what seemed to be some kind of dance club, which was deserted as we arrived. Nobody said anything to us as we were led into a room in the back.

"Close the door, Romero," Luca said to the third man. He did so without hesitation, then stood in front of it, his attentive eyes keeping watch over us.

"Where's our driver?" I asked. They'd put him in another car and I hadn't seen him again.

"We need to have a more intense conversation with him to figure out what his motives are," Matteo said with a smirk.

A shiver ran down my back. "Will you torture us as well?" I muttered.

Matteo laughed. "Oh, a cheeky one."

Luca sighed. "You have a cheeky wife already. Don't grate on my nerves by bickering with our cousin too."

Surprise widened my eyes.

Matteo shrugged and sat on the edge of the desk.

"What about the dogs—where did you take them? Please don't hurt them."

"Someone will take care of them," Luca said. What did he mean by that? His face didn't give anything away. It was hard, emotionless.

"We need your help, Luca," Mother said pleadingly. "We are family."

"You left your family to go to Las Vegas. You married a member of the Camorra."

"That's betrayal if you ask me," Matteo said with a twisted smile. "And from what we hear, your family likes betrayal. Your husband already paid with his life for it."

Mother faltered.

"We never betrayed anyone," I said firmly. "And Mother only left New York because she loved my father and because her brother was a monster."

"Well, we hear that you know how to handle monsters, right?" Matteo said, his dark eyes challenging. "And you're talking about our father, don't forget that."

I swallowed. Insulting Salvatore Vitiello in front of his sons was probably not my best idea, but I'd spoken the truth. Everyone in our circles knew what kind of man Salvatore Vitiello had been.

"I knew your father, my brother, well enough to know that you can't miss him very much," Mother said firmly.

Luca shrugged. "He wasn't a good man. But neither am I."

Mother shook her head. "I don't believe you are like him. I saw your beautiful wife in the newspaper."

Luca's expression changed. Mentioning his wife had been a mistake. Protectiveness washed away the blankness. "We won't discuss her." His voice allowed no argument.

The door to the room was pushed open. Romero peered behind it, then turned around with an apologetic expression.

A beautiful blonde woman stepped in. "It's enough," she said. Her voice was quiet and calm, but it held obvious power over Luca.

She was light. That was all I could think of when I stared at her. Her pale skin, golden hair, blue eyes. Light. Pure light, and so beautiful, it almost hurt looking at her.

Her welcoming smile hit me, and the knot in my stomach loosened. Perhaps there was hope after all. She strode toward me. It was hard to miss the disapproval on her husband's face or the way his body tightened in anticipation. As if he worried I'd attack her. That was the last thing on my mind when she could mean our door to safety.

"I'm Aria," she said, holding out her hand to me. I took it with a grateful smile.

"I'm Cara, and this is my sister Talia." I nodded toward Talia, who looked completely frozen up with fear.

Aria patted my sister's shoulder with a compassionate smile. "You don't have to be afraid. Nobody will hurt you in any way, I promise."

"Aria," Luca said in a strained voice.

She greeted my mother before finally she faced her husband. "They are family. And they went through a lot, don't you see? We must help them."

"We don't even know why they are here," Matteo said snidely.

Aria walked up to her husband and looked up at him as she put a hand on his arm. "They are innocent women. They need our protection. Do you really believe they're here to do us harm?"

"No," Luca said with a sigh. "I don't." He looked at us and I had to force myself to hold his gaze. "You can stay. I hope you don't make me regret it."

❖

They took us to a house in the Hamptons after some convincing arguments from Aria. I liked her already, even though I didn't know her. I wondered how she could hold on to her compassion being married to the Capo of the Famiglia. Men who held that kind of position were usually eager to break everyone around them, only because they could.

We were put into the guest wing of the large building, probably for safety measures but I didn't care. We were one step closer to a better future. When Aria showed us to our rooms, I said, "Thank you for everything."

She smiled. "You're welcome."

"I have one more request. Can you please make sure they don't hurt my dogs?"

"Of course," she said without hesitation. "I'll make sure they're safe."

I wondered how she'd managed to make a man like Luca, a Capo, listen to her advice. I didn't know him, but I knew what it took to rule in our world.

Talia crept into my room that night and snuggled up to me. "I was so scared, but now everything is going to be okay, right?" she whispered.

"Yes. We'll start anew." An image of Growl popped into my head, but I tried to keep the sadness locked in. Soon these emotions would have to fade. I had my life ahead of me, and I had to make the best of it.

"Did you really love him?"

I held my breath, wondering what to tell her, then I chose the truth. "I did. I still do," I admitted. I didn't want to lie to Talia.

"I don't understand it." Her warm breath fanned over my throat as she rested her head on my shoulder.

"Me neither. I didn't want it to happen."

"You can't change how you feel. It's okay," Talia said softly, hugging me tighter.

"Mother has been avoiding me. I think she can't forgive me because of

Growl."

"She lost Father. She needs time."

I hoped Talia was right. But even if not, there was nothing I could do against my feelings, much less to change the past.

Aria kept her promise. The next day Coco and Bandit arrived at the mansion. Luca refused to let them run around in the house though. I had to keep them on a leash outside of my room. Aria joined me as I showed them the garden. Both Coco and Bandit seemed to like her presence.

Luca trailed after us like a shadow. He still made me nervous, especially since he was holding a gun. "They were used in dog fights. You should be careful. Most of them are nasty beasts. If they act up, I'll put them down."

Aria sent him a glower but he ignored it.

"They are good. Better than most people," I said sharply.

"That's not difficult. Most people are assholes," Matteo said with a shrug, as he headed in our direction. "As long as those beasts are here, I won't allow Gianna to come visit."

"As if you could tell Gianna what to do," Aria teased, then turned to me. "Don't listen to them," she said apologetically. She crouched before Coco and Bandit. I knelt beside her and patted Coco's head. After a brief moment of hesitation, Aria did the same.

"Aria," Luca said in warning, pointing his gun straight at Coco's head.

"See," she said with a glance over her shoulder toward her husband. "They're harmless."

"They might act harmless now, but they've lived through a lot. Sometimes they lose control. I don't want them near you."

Aria sighed then whispered to me. "Keep them on the leash until he's calmed down."

I nodded. I had absolutely no intention of going against Luca's orders.

I led the dogs into my room, unleashed them and stretched out on the bed. The animals inspected the room but didn't take their eyes off me. I had the feeling that they were looking for Growl. They probably missed him too. Eventually I patted the empty half of the bed. "Come on up."

Coco lifted her head, ears perked up.

I patted the bed more firmly and repeated my invitation. Coco was the first to trot toward the bed and join me with a hesitant jump. When I didn't chide her, she curled up and pressed against my side. Bandit didn't need another invitation. Soon he was snuggled up against Coco and me. I scratched them behind the ears, enjoying the feeling of their soft fur.

With their warm bodies giving me the comfort I needed so much, I relaxed against the pillows and extinguished the lights. I hadn't slept well last night, I'd dreamed about Growl's death, imagining one horrible ending after the other. I wished I knew exactly what had happened to him. The truth, no matter how hard, was always better than not knowing.

chapter 27

—CARA—

A couple of weeks later, my family and I were starting to settle in, and Talia was almost back to her usual self. She didn't talk about what happened to her, and eventually I stopped asking. She wanted to move on. We all did.

We would be leaving the Hamptons in a couple of days to live in an apartment in New York—an apartment Luca owned. It didn't sit well with me that he would take care of everything, but we didn't have money and none of us had ever worked. Not that we would ever be allowed to do so. We were women, and family of the Capo. The Famiglia money would provide for us as long as we lived.

I returned from my walk with Coco and Bandit on the vast premises of the Vitiello mansion and was on my way into the guest wing when words carried over to me from somewhere else in the house.

I *knew* that voice. Every night I heard it in my dreams, most of them nightmares.

But he was not the cause of my fears, not anymore. So much had changed.

I dropped the leashes and began running toward that voice. I didn't stop until I spotted him in the living room. I skidded to a stop, my heart beating in my throat.

And there he was, dark and tall and bruised. One of his eyes was swollen shut, and several cuts and more bruises littered his skin.

I couldn't move. The dogs didn't share my hesitation. They'd followed me, dragging their leashes behind themselves. They lurched forward, yapping and wagging their tails.

Luca, Romero and Matteo startled and pulled their guns, but Coco and Bandit didn't attack. They squeezed against Growl's legs, yowling and barking, and he reached down to pat their heads but his eyes went to me, piercing me to the very core.

Two weeks since we'd last seen each other. Two weeks of me thinking he had died. Where had he been? Why hadn't he given me a sign that he was alive? I'd mourned his death, had made plans for a future without him, but now that he was here I wondered if we even had a future together. We'd never talked about it.

I had been his, not by choice, and now that I was free I wondered if we could make it work. Did I really want to live with the man who'd as good as owned me? Did he even want me now that I wasn't a mere gift anymore? And what about Growl's future? He'd betrayed the Camorra, broken his oath. That was the ultimate sin in our world. Would the Camorra come after him? And how would the Famiglia deal with someone who'd betrayed his cause? So many questions raced through my head and left me reeling.

I searched his eyes and realized that just for an instant, before Growl could put his shields back up, I saw my own questions reflected in them.

"You are alive," I said simply.

He didn't move closer. "I am hard to kill."

I noticed Aria in the corner, watching us.

Luca broke the tense silence. "Is it done?"

Growl finally tore his gaze away from me. "I killed many of Falcone's closest men. There's a lot of fighting going on in Vegas now. From what I hear Falcone's sons have come to the US. Soon they and Cosimo will be fighting for power. It'll keep them busy for a while."

Luca seemed satisfied with that. Business. This was all about business. Was that why they'd taken Growl in? Because Growl had important information about the Vegas Camorra?

I wanted to run toward Growl but he didn't seem to want that. Confusion filled me. I needed fresh air. I needed to think. I turned around and hurried back outside. I stopped when I reached a bench and sank down on it.

Aria joined me a few moments later. "You love him. Why don't you show him?"

I stiffened. Was it that obvious? "Because he doesn't love me. He can't. This thing between us has no future."

I wasn't naïve enough to believe that Growl would change. If we stayed in New York and if he was allowed to work for Luca, there was only one job that he could do. He'd become one of Luca's assassins. Too much had been broken in Growl when he watched his mother die and when he almost bled to death himself. I wanted to mend him, but I wasn't sure I'd ever be able to recover all the broken pieces. Some of them might be lost forever.

"Why? If you love him there's always a way."

"He's...not good."

Aria laughed softly. "Luca isn't good either, but I love him with all my heart. You just have to allow yourself to love his good parts."

I loved his good parts and I loved his ugly parts, loved him more than I should.

He'd stolen my freedom, my life, and somehow along the way, without me realizing it, he'd also stolen my heart.

"He loves you. I don't know exactly what Luca and Growl talked about when they first met yesterday, but I have a feeling that the only reason Luca trusts Growl is because he realized that Growl loves you. And Luca knows what love can do to a person." She paused. My mind reeled with the knowledge that Growl had waited a day to reveal himself to me. "Your sister mentioned that your mother doesn't approve. But don't let that stop you, if you really love him. My sister Gianna didn't like Luca very much in the beginning either."

I nodded to show her I'd listened, but I couldn't say anything.

—GROWL—

I paced the corridor in front of Cara's room. I wasn't sure why I was waiting for her to show up. What was there left to talk about?

The moment she'd left for New York without me, I'd known it meant the end for us. The realization had been like a punch in the gut, the realization that she wouldn't stay with me, a monster. No one would. She'd seemed to enjoy my company in the end, enjoyed my closeness and my touch, but I didn't fool myself.

Her affection for me had been born out of necessity. She'd had no choice. She couldn't get away from me. She had sought my closeness because she was relieved it wasn't brutality that I showed her. But now everything had changed.

In New York, Cara would be free to do as she pleased. No one was stopping her. I knew enough of Luca to know that the man wouldn't support me in keeping Cara. And though it had taken a while for me to realize it, I didn't want to have Cara as a possession. I wanted her to want to be with me. I knew that meant I'd lose her altogether. She'd live her life without me. She'd find a new guy, a nice guy, someone who hadn't caused her so many nightmares. Maybe

Luca already had a husband in mind for her, a Made Man with good standing and upbringing.

It was difficult for me to understand emotions, and that would never change. But her expression made it clear even to me that she didn't want me. Perhaps she'd pretended to tolerate me for her own sake; because she wanted me to help her revenge her father and kill Falcone. I couldn't really blame her.

I often wished I'd never had her in the first place because it was easier to live without something you'd never had. I hadn't known what I was missing, but now it was difficult to give her up.

I had grown used to Cara's presence. I'd always taken myself for a loner. Had thought I didn't want other people around me. I'd enjoyed living with only my dogs for company. My life had been mine alone. It had been uneventful and driven by habits, but it had been safe. Now that I'd experienced living with someone, living with Cara, I had a hard time imagining being alone again.

I would get by. I always had. I'd work twice as hard, would put all my energy into making Luca trust and value me. I'd make a name for myself here in New York, and eventually I'd forget about Cara and return to the life I'd had before.

Steps sounded and I looked up. The moment Cara turned the corner, I realized I was fooling myself if I believed I could ever forget her.

—CARA—

I froze when I spotted Growl in front of my room. Bandit and Coco lay curled up at his feet as if they'd all been waiting for a while.

I approached him slowly, trying to get a grip on my emotions. Coco wagged her tail when I stopped in front of them.

Growl pushed his hands into his pockets, face blank and his body tense as a bowstring. "There's no reason for you to stay with me. You are free now. Even if I could force you to stay with me, I won't. You are free to choose your own life."

The words I'd been longing to hear from the moment Falcone had given me to Growl suddenly stung. "So what is it you're saying? Would you prefer if I left you?" How could I leave him when we hadn't been a couple in the first place?

"That's the last thing I want," he said fiercely. He pulled his hands out, restless, almost as if he wanted to grab me and shake some sense into me, but he didn't touch me.

"Then what do you want?" I shot back, growing frustrated. Maybe I should have accepted Growl's words and left.

Mother would have preferred that, and it would have been the right choice morally. Yet I stayed.

Growl had monstrous parts, and that wouldn't change. Years of abuse had burned those into him, and if I chose to stay with him, I'd have to live with them. Perhaps in New York, Luca would find better ways to channel Growl's talents into less horrendous tasks, but I wasn't fooling myself into believing that killing wouldn't still be a big part of Growl's life. That was something I'd have to accept. To stay with someone only because one hoped to change that person was an endeavor that had to fail.

Growl's eyes flickered with emotions, too many, and more than I'd ever seen in them. "I want," he began, then stopped and growled. He shook his head and turned his face away so I was left to stare at his profile.

"You once told me I needed to be brave. Who's a coward now?" I challenged.

Growl whirled on me, grabbed me by the shoulders and pressed me against the wall. "I want you. I want you to stay with me because you want to stay. I want you to want me," he rasped.

I exhaled. "I do."

Growl released me. "Do what?"

"Want you. Want to stay with you."

Growl stared. "I...I think." He ran a hand down his face. "I'm no good with words. With emotions. You know that."

"But you could be. Perhaps you just need to try," I said softly.

His eyes filled with resolve. "Not much scares me anymore," he rumbled. "But this, between us, it does. My emotions, they scare me."

"But why?"

"I gave up hoping for something good a long time ago. It made things easier. Nothing could hurt me. Pain was nothing. People's insults meant nothing. I cared about nothing. There was nothing I had to fear. But when I got you, I suddenly realized what kind of life I'd led. How little everything had meant. I like being with you, talking to you, sharing meals with you, walking Coco and Bandit with you, and even sharing a bed with you. I never thought I could like that kind of thing, never thought I might need something like that, but now..." He trailed off, the uncertainty back. "Now I'm fucking scared to lose all that, to lose you. I never knew I needed you, but now I can't imagine being without you. I...I love you, Cara."

I let out a shuddering breath. I'd never expected those words from Growl. Not even close. I touched his heart, feeling its erratic rhythm, then his cheek. "And I love you, Growl."

Aria had been right. I needed to make a choice. And I chose love. Mother would come to accept that. After all, she'd once given up everything to follow love.

"Ryan," he growled. The name sounded wrong coming from his lips, like they weren't used to forming those letters anymore.

"Ryan?"

"That's my real name."

"Oh," I whispered, overwhelmed by the situation. "That's a beautiful name."

He smiled tentatively. It still surprised me how it changed his edgy face. He leaned down and kissed me, then pulled back a few inches.

"I want New York to be a new beginning for me and you, if you want that too. And I want to be known as Ryan in this new life."

"And I want a new beginning with you, Ryan," I said. He wrapped his arms around me and held me tightly.

"I don't deserve you," he murmured against my hair. "But I will."

epilogue

—CARA—

"It's not much," Ryan said quietly as he led me into his apartment. It was in Harlem, near a small park so he could walk Coco and Bandit there when he didn't have time to take them out of the city bounds. He'd had to leave most of his savings behind in Las Vegas, and he'd refused Luca's offer for an advance. He wanted to earn the money he used and I respected that, admired it even. Ryan would have to work his way up in the Famiglia. He had to prove himself to his fellow Made Men. Many people still distrusted him, and that wouldn't change anytime soon. The Camorra was hated in this city.

I followed him inside and squeezed his hand. Coco and Bandit pressed up to me excitedly, yapping and wagging their tails. I patted their heads in passing as Ryan led me through the small corridor into the living room. It wasn't as spacious as the rooms in my family's home, but it wasn't exactly tiny either. The only pieces of furniture were a beige sofa, a coffee table and a TV attached to the wall.

"I think this might need a female touch," I said with a small laugh as I took in the bare walls and lack of decoration in general.

Ryan looked at me strangely. "I thought you could move in with me."

I swallowed. I hadn't expected it. Since he'd come to New York three weeks ago, our relationship had been careful, hesitant. I had moved into an apartment with my mother and Talia, and tried helping them heal, and Ryan had been busy gaining the respect and trust of Luca and the rest of the Famiglia. We had seen each other a few times to walk the dogs together, but except for a few kisses, Ryan hadn't initiated any physical closeness, nor had I.

This was a new start for both of us, and we needed time to find ourselves and find our way back together. "You want us to live together?"

Ryan looked away, amber eyes reflecting his inner turmoil. "I know the rules of our world. I know an honorable woman like you shouldn't live with a man before she's married, and I want to marry you, but I thought…"

"You want us to marry?" I exclaimed. My heart was beating furiously in my chest.

He rubbed his neck then met my gaze. "Yes. I…You weren't supposed to lose your innocence before marriage, and people in the Famiglia might judge you for it. But it was my fault. You had no choice and I want to make things right."

I touched his chest, feeling it heave under my palms. "I don't want us to marry because you feel guilty. If we marry it has to be because we want it."

"I want to marry you," he rasped.

"And I want to marry you," I said quietly. "But I think we should live together for a while, and allow my mother and sister to grow used to the idea. So much has happened, I think we all need more time."

He nodded, then cupped my cheek. "But you will move in with me?"

I looked around. "If you give me free rein over the decorations."

Ryan smiled. The expression still looked unpracticed on his face, but I loved seeing it. "I'll work hard so we can get something bigger soon."

"I don't care about that. I just want us to be happy, and we don't need luxury for that."

"I want to make you happy."

I touched his cheek and stood on my tiptoes, pressing my lips against his. "And I want to make you happy. You deserve happiness as much as I do."

He didn't say anything, but there was still a hint of doubt in his eyes. He thought he didn't deserve to be happy, but I would prove him wrong.

I deepened the kiss then whispered, "I want to be with you."

Ryan's eyes flashed with want but he hesitated, even as his hands lightly brushed my hips. "I thought you might want to wait until we are married before we have sex again."

I laughed then shook my head. "I don't want to wait. I want to make love to you."

He made a low sound in his throat and finally his kisses became more eager. He lifted me up and carried me toward his bedroom, where he laid me down carefully on the bed. He undressed me without hurry, his eyes taking in every inch of me.

"I want to see you too," I said, and watched reverently as he undressed, revealing tattoos and scars and muscles.

"No one's ever looked at me like you do," he growled as he lowered himself on top of me.

"Because they've never really seen you," I said, then moaned as he brought his mouth down on my breast.

I could see how he forced himself to slow down, to touch me lightly, to show me through his touch what he felt, and I enjoyed this softer side of him.

When he finally molded our bodies together and began moving slowly, I leaned forward and gently kissed the scar around his throat. His thrusts faltered briefly, but then he cupped my head and locked gazes with me. I couldn't wait to marry him, to give him the family he never had. For some reason this felt like our first time because we both had come together freely, happily, without reservations—and that's how it was meant to be.

THE END

BORN IN BLOOD MAFIA CHRONICLES

Bound By Honor
Aria & Luca

Bound By Duty
Dante & Valentina

Bound By Hatred
Gianna & Matteo

Bound By Temptation
Liliana & Romero

Bound By Vengeance
Cara & Growl

Bound By Love
Aria & Luca

Read Fabiano's story in the first book of the Camorra Chronicles, a new spin-off series to the Born in Blood Mafia Chronicles:

Twisted Loyalties
Fabiano

Twisted Emotions
Nino

Twisted Pride
Remo

about the author

Cora Reilly is the author of the Born in Blood Mafia Series, the Camorra Chronicles and many other books, most of them featuring dangerously sexy bad boys. Before she found her passion in romance books, she was a traditionally published author of young adult literature.

Cora lives in Germany with a cute but crazy Bearded Collie, as well as the cute but crazy man at her side. When she doesn't spend her days dreaming up sexy books, she plans her next travel adventure or cooks too spicy dishes from all over the world.

Despite her law degree, Cora prefers to talk books to laws any day.

Made in the USA
Coppell, TX
14 January 2022